HEIGHTS AND DEPTHS

BY THE SAME AUTHOR:

DON'T KNOCK THE CORNERS OFF

"She seems to have distanced herself from her subject-matter in a way that even Wordsworth would admire. Caroline Glyn's descriptive gift is quite exceptionally natural and vivid"—*Sunday Times*

"A sparkle and understanding that makes a rare conjunction. Has ... a felicity, a style, and a captivating personal enthusiasm, that make excellent reading. And there is meat under all that mustard"—*The Scotsman*

LOVE AND JOY IN THE MABILLON

"Miss Glyn hits off, with deliciously sly accuracy, the to-and-fro of polygot banter... Charming... Confronted by that most dreaded of writers' hurdles, the second novel, Miss Glyn has sailed over it with every appearance of unruffled ease. How nice that from now on it will be possible to write about her without reference to her great-grand-mother or even her age, and just concentrate on her books"—*Sunday Telegraph*

THE UNICORN GIRL

"Miss Glyn is a born writer if ever there was one... I am not at all surprised to find her striding even further ahead"—*Rivers Scott (Sunday Telegraph)*

"Any child with even dim memories of the depth and wisdom in the human soul, and only too aware of the awkwardness and confusion engendered by entry into the adult world, will be grateful to Miss Glyn for setting down, while she still remembers them, things that are rarely expressed"—*Times Educational Supplement*

"She never puts a foot wrong"—*New Statesman*

HEIGHTS AND DEPTHS

by

CAROLINE GLYN

LONDON
VICTOR GOLLANCZ LTD
1968

575000511

PRINTED IN GREAT BRITAIN BY
NORTHUMBERLAND PRESS LIMITED
GATESHEAD

I

AT A QUARTER-PAST twelve Christine's blind ripped, crashed, cracked and flew across the room, where it pinned itself against Christine's bedhead, lashing her in the face.

It was made of thick black paper. Christine's window had no curtains, for when she reached fourteen and was given a room to herself, it was still wartime. Three years it had survived perfectly intact, for no raid had ever come anywhere near Christine, but this was a blitz of a gale such as surely no Londoner had ever known.

Christine fought her way out from under the blind in a panic, muttering to herself in Welsh, which she still found easier than English. The whole room was in a whirl. All the sky seemed to be forcing its way in. The apple tree, too, seemed to want to do the same. It was shaking and jarring in a way that was untreelike, to say the least, even in such a wind. Christine's window closed on a screw-and-slide system, very ancient. She wrenched and fought with it. The apple tree was trying to come in. It was using the wind to push her back. Indeed the wind seemed to be coming from the tree. Christine twiddled frantically at the silly catch. A great eddying gust burst out of the branches and Christine thought she must be sucked out. She screamed, and something—some voice—answered.

The window had jammed. No, it hadn't. The tree had caught it and was holding on to it, and was shouting at her.

Christine was a sane and sensible girl. She did not believe in ghosts, and thunderstorms had never scared her. Voices out of the wind and trees that tried to push through your window did not form part of Christine's universe. Yet for a paralysing moment she found herself believing that it was the tree indeed which had answered her cry. Or—no—something in the tree. Something all whirlwind and flying cloaks. So strong was the picture in Christine's mind that she wondered if she had in fact awoken. The window had jammed, but that was not how it seemed to Christine. She could not close it because something was coming through it, something impossibly strong. She thought she was desperately pushing back a huge, flapping, angular woman, all claws. Christine felt invaded, overborne. She tried to control herself. Of course there was nothing there but a strong wind and a lot of waving leaves. She had almost succeeded in driving the silly, superstitious image from her mind when a large bony hand did really appear, clutching the window-sill. It was followed by a flapping sleeve, and a huge wild face, which emerged from the branches saying "Damn this wind. Oh, angel girl. Can you let me in?"

Dumbly Christine began to retwiddle the knob the other way to open the window again, and the enormous woman, all flapping scarves and gripping knuckles, climbed in. Christine was stupefied. It was maybe pardonable to imagine things in weather like this, but the sudden apparition live of the very thing she had been imagining left her stunned. She would never have thought herself capable of believing in witches.

With a final triumphant gust the woman blew into the room and said "God!"

Christine stood stupidly, vaguely supposing that witches had the right to swear if they wanted.

"Oh, you are a sweetheart," the woman said. "It's such a glorious night. I completely forgot the time. No, but isn't it wonderful? I only went out for a stroll before supper and look what happened." She strode over to Christine's bedside clock. "Half-past twelve. Oh, my love, I'm so happy. Did you know there's not a single house between here and Penrhyn?"

Christine didn't know, though she quite believed it. It was a quarter of a mile to the bus stop, that was all she knew, and a threepenny ride to Bangor city centre, and that was enough.

"There's magic in those hills," the woman said. "I shouldn't have minded normally, staying out all night I mean, but there are dragons as well as Romans and when you get the two together—well—oh, now, I'm sorry. I forgot I didn't know you. I hope you don't think I'm drunk or anything."

Christine didn't. She knew the nearest pub was the Green Dragon a mile along the road, and since this was a Sunday night that hadn't been in operation for some time now.

The woman sat down on Christine's bed, and suddenly seemed quite human. Not even particularly huge. Her coat spread out all over the bed. She buried her face in her hands and said, "Oh, I'm so tired."

Now this was more what Christine was used to. She knew how to be hospitable if only people didn't come through the window, and the text about entertaining angels was one she reread often. "Yes, weary indeed you look," she said sympathetically. "If you come downstairs it will be warmer."

The woman looked up gratefully and hopefully. "May I?" she said eagerly.

But her very eagerness brought back Christine's fear. After all who, or even what, was this woman, what was she doing, why had she chosen to arrive in such a terrifying way? She looked at the time, half-past midnight. For an instant her superstitious panic returned. Then she looked again at her visitor, and saw her so piteously glad at Christine's offer that her heart melted. She thought again about entertaining angels.

"Well, if you would take your shoes off kindly," Christine said, "and speak softly," for the woman seemed not to have noticed that in Christine's bedroom she didn't need to shout the wind down.

They tiptoed downstairs, Christine wincing at the noise the Englishwoman made at every step. In the kitchen the stove was still warm. Christine put the kettle on, hesitated, thought about angels, and brought out the cake she had made that morning with ration cards saved for a month.

The English witch wolfed at it, but Christine didn't mind somehow. The kitchen had never seemed so cosy. The wind roared round, yet there were none of the usual draughts. She had turned on only the little light over the stove, for fear of waking the family, yet the whole room seemed to glow. The woman sat awkwardly in the rocking-chair as if she didn't know what to do with it, and was caught off balance every time it rocked, yet it didn't feel in the least extraordinary that she should be there. She talked all the time. Christine only understood a third of what she said. She was wearing a very old siren-suit and a long red scarf, and she knocked her tea over twice; her eyes shone, her bones stuck out, and Christine could not imagine how the kitchen had ever been without her.

She was startled suddenly, realizing the woman was praising her and expected an answer.

"You are a most remarkable girl. You let me into your bed-room past midnight, you give me tea, you feed me and look after me, you listen to everything I say" (Christine became embarrassed here) "and you never even ask me who I am."

Christine tried to think of an answer.

"You're right, of course. Names don't matter. I've told you everything about myself that does."

Christine wished she had listened.

"I think you're the kind of girl I was once. So may I ask you a very serious question? Have you ever seen a unicorn?"

Again Christine could only stare.

"You see, I once thought I was followed everywhere by a unicorn, when I was a child your age. He was very symbolic, of course, although I didn't know what of. And since you seem so sensitive and bright I wondered if you had ever had that kind of idea too. I used to fancy the entire universe solid with magical beings. Of course I was very religious then as well. But you know, I don't think I was so wrong. Whenever I go out-doors I feel the whole earth alive, like an electric wire, I expect you know?"

"The earth, alive?"

"Oh, yes! Absolutely buzzing! It's the same as what I used to call magic—still do, come to that. It's the power that makes the world tick, you know. The life-force of the universe. Isn't it exciting to think about? Do they teach you about it at school?"

"But I am not at school."

"Oh, oh I see. In my day such things weren't taught to children. I had to find out for myself. Which I consider I did, with my idea of the unicorn. I realize now he represented the power of the life-force in nature," she said grandly. "Wow! Some power it is too! Listen!"

They listened raptly to the wind for a minute. Then the woman asked abruptly, "How did we get on to this? What was I trying to say to you?"

"I'm sorry, I don't know."

"Oh yes, I remember. I was trying to tell you not to be shy of believing in magic. It's not incompatible with science, at all, as everyone will tell you. Not at all. Words change, but the old things are still there. The life-force isn't going to stop acting just to suit these materialists. Anyway materialism is old hat. All modern scientists accept the life-force theory, don't they? So you see! Don't you be a bit scared of believing in the supernatural!"

She looked glowingly at Christine and then suddenly turned red.

"Oh, my dear, I've been riding my hobby-horse. Oh, I am so sorry." Her embarrassment suddenly made her seem entirely ordinary and unwitchlike. She struggled on awkwardly, "It always comes back to the same thing. I meet a sympathetic soul and immediately I start blurting out my foolish ideas and spoil everything. I don't suppose you even believe in magic, why should you? I'm sorry I ever spoke."

Everything the woman had said was gibberish to Christine, yet now she wanted, badly, to reassure her, to respond somehow to what were obviously her most cherished thoughts. She

A*

leant forward and said earnestly, in answer to the woman's last sentence, "Never I believed in magic, but now I think I do."

The woman stared at her, and then began to laugh. She laughed so loudly and raucously that Christine wanted to make her be quiet, then she looked at the brilliant laughing eyes and started to laugh too. She couldn't help it. The woman rocked to and fro, in paroxysms of joy. Suddenly she jumped up, her face alight with excitement. Christine rose too, and found herself dancing and leaping round her kitchen in the embrace of this strange Englishwoman who had blown in through her window, and who, she was surer than ever now, was a witch.

The woman in fact was a Miss Phyllis Jean Bott and she was supposed to be staying in the boarding-house next door. Christine's family and their neighbours, the couple who ran the boarding-house, had a lot in common. They liked early and regular hours. Thus the boarding-house was locked every night at nine. Each house had the same dark, snug little front room, the same antique Welsh dresser which had been made by the same carpenter in Bangor sometime in Queen Victoria's reign, and a fairly similar back garden. Both the houses were painted white, but one had three rooms more than the other. One had chickens at the end of the garden and the other had an apple tree growing beside it. The reason why one was bigger than the other was that they were built on a sharp slope, but their roofs made a level horizontal line. There were three more similar houses in the terrace. The boarding-house was at the end. It looked out over several miles of uninhabited hill. A hill rose behind the terrace too, which looked down on Bangor. The terrace was supposed to be a village, as it faced a small church and an even smaller post-office. But it was wild; as Phyllis Jean Bott had realized the moment she looked out of the bus, she could not have found anywhere wilder for a holiday. She had seen the word "Rooms" outside the boarding-house. She had rung the bell and leapt off the bus, wasting threepence of her fare. The landlady had been suspicious of her at first, until she paid her night in advance. In fact she had very little money left. She was wearing out her old siren-suit for this tour, and it was perhaps a trifle shabby. But she was happy. She had had incredible luck. First mist, romantic mist, all the way through Cheshire and Denbighshire. Then downpours of pink rain. And then that had blown away in such a glorious stinging October gale that when she had rushed out just for a breath of air before supper, she had felt as if she were flying.

It was nearly three o'clock. Christine had stoked up the stove. She had lost all hope of fitting this encounter into the pattern of social conventions which made up her life. For instance, the woman seemed quite to have forgotten that she still hadn't told Christine her name, or offered an explanation why she had appeared at Christine's window so frantically seeking admittance, and apparently having ridden in on the storm without even a broomstick.

She didn't look particularly frightening any more. Her face had softened a lot since they collapsed back into their chairs, exhausted with laughing and whirling each other round and round. Christine had been giggling nervously and panting, but the woman suddenly sank back into her cushions and looked as if she had never laughed in her life. She sat in the rocking-chair without rocking, and her face grew very still and she stared at the stove with the light reflecting in her eyes. Christine grew embarrassed. She said something about the time, but the woman plainly did not hear. Christine fussed with the kettle and made more tea, using the same tea-leaves, and feeling vaguely that she would do better just to sit still. But when she offered a cup to the woman she took it, and began to sip it mechanically, while her face grew graver and graver. Presently she forgot the tea, and Christine took it out of her hand.

After a while she decided that the woman was listening to the storm.

It was wonderfully still in the kitchen. Christine had never been awake and about before, at this time. She badly wanted to go back to bed, but she couldn't bear to break the atmosphere in the kitchen. She was beginning to share the woman's mood. She drank her own tea and watched the dark angular shape in the chair and the glowing eyes. Yes, she was definitely listening. Was it just to the wind? Christine began to listen too. There were just the ordinary country night noises. More interesting was the intense stillness that seemed to surround the big woman. The stove was beginning to die down, and the reflected glow in her eyes that fascinated Christine was not as good as it had been. The parlour clock next door chimed four, and Christine thought guiltily of her work next morning; then she got up and poked the stove once more. With satisfaction she watched the eyes light up again, but now the woman was less in shadow and Christine saw with astonishment such deep thought in her face that it was plain she was not just listening to the wind. Christine began to grow afraid again.

Suddenly the woman began to speak. This time, instead of shouting, she talked very quickly and evenly in a low voice. She was apparently telling Christine about the Romans in Cheshire, which Christine would have found very dull from anyone, and particularly in English; but odd sudden things like werewolves and prophecies kept coming into the woman's speech, and "woods" and "druids" the whole time. "Of course the trees were alive and did things at that time, those poor Romans just didn't know what they were fighting," she said casually at one point. Christine listened enthralled, understanding scarcely anything, but watching the woman's expression.

"Eagles, eagles," sighed the woman, which was baffling to Christine who had not followed the context. She said, anxious to comfort her, "But I have pigeons." The woman turned her face towards Christine and Christine saw it so lit up with delight and interest that she went on. "Oh, in our house there was always a pigeon-loft. And when I was seven my father gave me a pair of doves, and now I keep them and look after them and we have twelve birds. Pigeons, doves."

"You must love them very much."

"Oh, they're so sweet. Truly I believe they know me and when I go out and a basket of grain with me I carry the doves fly from everywhere to me and sit on my arm."

"You don't clip their wings? You trust them loose?"

"Why, they know me. They know where is their home. One time a bird flew away and he was gone nearly a month, but he came back after that and straight he went to the same house he had lived in before. He was beautiful, too. He always came to sit in my hair. I can tomorrow show you him if you would like."

"I would like very much," the woman said. "How old are you?"

"Seventeen."

"But you smile and talk like a little child!"

Christine knew this, but had never cared, and so was not offended, but would rather not have heard it again.

"I have been working for two years now believe me."

"How have you kept so sweet? Have you no boy-friend?"

"Oh, no, no." Christine burst into laughter. "I don't care. It's too silly."

"Then what do you do when you want to go out?"

"But I am not lonely, I have my sister." Christine grew animated. "She's still at school. And we have such fun together. Last Saturday, it was so beautiful, we went together to Anglesey to that castle, you know it, you can stay there all day for no more money. Do you know that castle, Beaumaris? It has real little rooms and passages truly and even a tiny chapel. My sister had one room and I lived in another on the tower top; imagine it. We took beds in of grass and in the dark passages we want to make lights. All that wall you can walk round and you can come down from our tower, but we have our own staircase up to the part we like too. Now we are saving our money to go there often for the keeper he never goes inside and he knows nothing. And we think to keep doves on my tower top."

"Why, that's wonderful!" the woman cried, as delighted as Christine herself. "Is there anything in the chapel now?"

"No, but—" A glorious new idea came to Christine. Oh, what a pity it was too early to wake Molly. "Why can we not make it again a real chapel as surely it was before! Then our castle would be perfect! Oh, Molly would be happy if you came too. Won't you? Where do you live?"

The woman suddenly pealed out laughing. "That's the very first question you've ever asked me."

"I'm sorry," said Christine, meaning it, afraid she had somehow stupidly broken the spell.

"I should have told you the moment I came climbing up your apple tree. I'm a boarder next door. As I said, I forgot the time and when I came back the house was locked. So I tried to climb in up the apple tree but it was too windy and there were no branches that side. I'm sorry. The only window I could reach was yours. I couldn't even get down again. Gosh, what a fool I felt. If you hadn't been such a dear, God knows what I'd have done."

"Why, I have been very happy that you were here."

"Oh, you are a pet," she said, leaning forward enthusiastically. The rocking-chair naturally threw her back again and she pushed at it impatiently. Christine regretted offering it to her, although it was really the nicest chair. "I've met few enough girls like you. Real innocents and afraid of nothing. Have you never noticed that it is precisely those who are innocent who are fearless?"

This was out of Christine's depth again and she began to be acutely aware that it would be breakfast time in a little while, and she had slept rather inadequately that night.

"I was in the A.T.S. Anti-aircraft girls in Hyde Park. Well, there was plenty to be afraid of there. I saw a few things, I can tell you, so I know what I'm talking about."

Christine goggled. So this wonderful woman was a war heroine on top of everything else.

"So long as there are girls like you and your sister defending Beaumaris Castle I shall never be afraid for England."

Phyllis Jean Bott sat back in her chair, discovered of a sudden the principle of the thing and began swinging contentedly. There, at last she had brought out a sentence which expressed what she meant without too much blah, and the girl seemed to have understood. What a dear thing, really. Playing houses in Beaumaris Castle at seventeen and too sensible to be ashamed of it. Happy with her doves. She wished she could believe that she had been at all similar at seventeen. What a pity the girl hadn't understood her question about the unicorn.

Christine was chewing over Bott's last remark, which certainly seemed like praise; could it be possibly true that an incredible woman like this found something praiseworthy in her, Christine? What, why? It was growing light. The woman was looking at her so radiantly that Christine couldn't help fancying the light came from her. She felt herself withering before such joy. She stared, baffled and beseeching, at the woman; dropped her eyes to her hands, those huge bony hands, which were gripping the arms of the chair as if they never intended to let go. Once again a power of stillness seemed to surround the woman.

"It comes from out of yourself," she told Christine, to her disconcertment, as if she had read her thoughts. "Only never let it out. Don't give yourself away to just anyone or anything, will you, sweet? You're too precious."

Christine stared at that face. She was very tired, she was very excited, she had also been quite frightened; she suddenly wanted badly to burst into tears and bury her face in that bony lap. She was saved from doing this by the sound of her parents' door opening upstairs. She knew exactly what they would do next. Her father would go into her sister's room, her mother into hers. Quickly she jumped up and began to clatter the kettle, to explain her absence from her bed.

"Great pleasure it would give me to ask you to stay for breakfast," she said, "but my father—"

"Oh, crumbs, yes, don't dream of it. I'd quite forgotten it was night-time," the woman said, blushing and leaping up awkwardly. "Heavens, how selfish I've been. Oh, I am sorry." The tea canister went flying. "Don't dream of offering me breakfast. It's paid for next door. You've been angelically kind anyway. Oh, I do feel awful about all this."

Christine only wished she would stop. It distressed her deeply to have her wonder woman bumbling about and apologizing. She turned from raking out the stove. "I hope you will come with me to Beaumaris," she said, "but even if not, I have loved to hear you. And can you kindly come this way for the front door I dare not open."

The woman followed her to the back porch, tripping over everything and apologizing nervously. Christine smiled at her, not daring to shush her, and opened the door. She stumbled out, her scarf trailing, chickens squawking in all directions. Christine wondered if she shouldn't make her stay for breakfast after all. She seemed suddenly a very pathetic figure. But just as Christine stood hesitating the woman changed again. She stopped, drew herself up, looked at the trees and then at the sky, and seemed once again the great ten-feet-high cloaked figure Christine had first pictured. As Christine watched incredulously, she stooped and picked up a clod of earth from the herb-garden, and smelt at it deeply. Then—so at least Christine remembered it afterwards—she suddenly started striding away towards the hill, something out of a legend, a giantess against the clouds, stepping over the fences and walls as if she barely noticed they were there.

2

I T T O O K B O T T four days, rambling about, to reach Bethesda.

She had lost count completely of the miles she had walked, the counties she had covered, the months she had been on the road. Not that she took roads if she could help it. The first thing she had done, after cashing her savings—she had never seemed to spend anything when she was in the A.T.S.—had been to take a bus until she saw country, when she had got out and walked. Unfortunately it had proved to be nothing more than Hampstead Heath and there were many miles of hateful London to be got through before she reached the real countryside.

When was that? April? It was the somethingth of September now. She wondered if her money would last through to Christmas. Oh, who cared?

She wandered vaguely across the landing to look at the hill across the road. It was nice and bare. She was lucky to find yet another bed-and-brek with such a view. Only, no apple tree this time. She'd have to be careful how late she stayed out. Unlikely to be another such hospitable girl next door either. She had seen a party of unattractive-looking young men in climbing boots going into the house next door, shouting stupidities at each other. Such parties abounded in North Wales; it was a pity, they spoilt the scenery and had no idea of respecting the silence of a mountain. Sometimes they would shout rude things at her when all she was doing was looking at them and wishing they weren't there.

She went downstairs to ease her feet in the landlady's sitting-room and see if the marks on the wall said anything. Undoubtedly they showed where the people had patched up a damp place. But, glancing at them as she came in, she had decided to come back and look at them seriously later on. They were oddly like a curious formation of rocks she had come across somewhere round Snowdon, and her palms still sweated when she remembered what that had said to her. No, no, don't think about it, don't think about it, she forbade herself. It was too good, too rare, to spoil by continually remembering it. She had spoilt the "Serenade to Music" by playing it four times in one day, years ago.

She was sitting in a chintz chair contentedly wiggling her toes and listening to the Welsh which came from the kitchen, when she slowly became aware that a small boy was standing in front of her gravely offering her a palm cross, rather yellow and brittle, of the kind children get in churches on Palm Sunday.

"Why, you must have kept that a long time," she exclaimed.

"It's for you," he said, still holding it out.

"Well, thank you." Good manners seemed to necessitate accepting it. Looking at it closely, she saw it was in fact an attractive object. The piece of palm had split and dried but it was beautifully grained. Unthinkingly she sniffed at it. Grass smell.

"Don't do that," the boy said sharply. "It's a cross."

Bott looked at him in surprise. "Sorry," she said humbly. "You're quite right. But it's such a nice thing in itself I'm afraid I forgot."

"It's Jesus' cross."

"Yes, of course. It's very kind of you to give it to me."

He smiled gravely and came nearer. "Present for you. I want you to have it. It'll help you. It shines in the night-time."

Crikey, how old? Three, four? Who ever said you should talk down to children? Bott felt out of her depth, as Christine had a few days before with Bott.

"Well, thank you very much."

"The clergyman gave it to me. Last, last Easter, we all went to the church, not with Daddy, he didn't want to come, but I went with Jane and Philip and we all had to go up to the—the—"

"Altar?"

"No, the place where you aren't supposed to go, beyond the golden angels. You know, right in there? We had to go, the clergyman called us." Dear little curly-haired boy, black eyes, smiling up at her, and don't think he's gabbling nonsense either. Bott listened respectfully to his account of the Palm Sunday service, thinking about the life-force that could be interpreted in so many ways.

"Daddy doesn't know I kept my cross. I put it in a special pocket of my rucksack so he wouldn't see it shining."

Bott noticed the word "rucksack", surely not usual in the vocabulary of a four-year-old, but was too interested in what he was telling her to take him up on it.

"Are you sure you want to give it to me?"

"Oh, yes, it's a present." He spoke excitedly, slurring and mixing his words, but his eyes stayed clear and intelligent, nothing babyish about them at all. Brilliant, beautiful eyes.

"It's a present, it will help you. Keep it in a secret place. Then you can take it out when you need it. But it's a secret, though. Daddy doesn't know. Keep it a big, big secret. I've got another. I won't tell you about that, it's my secret. This is yours now. Your secret. It will help you."

That was the third time he had said that. Bott looked at him curiously. "It will really help me?"

"Oh, yes, of course it will help you but you must hide it."

Seeing his anxiety, she slid it carefully inside her jacket. His face cleared. "There," he said. "A secret. All for you."

"Does your secret help you?"

"You mustn't ask about my secret."

He was reproachful in his gravity. Bott felt reproved.

"I'm sorry. But tell me. Why have you given me this wonderful secret?"

"It will help you."

"You think I need help?"

He looked surprised at such a silly question. "You must have a secret."

Obvious as daylight. Bott felt ashamed.

"But don't tell Daddy," the little boy said again, intensely serious, and then suddenly turned and ran from the room.

She was alone with her host and hostess for supper, (floury sausages), and felt vaguely disappointed. The child was absent at breakfast next morning too. Maybe after all he was only a village child. Speaking English? Odd. Though she had actually thought she detected an accent; but really how can you tell with a little child?

She was slowly hiking over the hill after breakfast, minding the stones and not thinking about anything else very much, when she heard a hail: "Hi there!"

Bott turned slowly under her pack, not liking being addressed either as hi or as there, and expecting to have to rebuff another gang of stupid youths.

A man was running—running! among these stones!—down the mountainside towards her. He waved gladly when he saw her turn and came springing down, all bright eyes and radiant grin. A funny little monkey of a man, but she recognized him as he came nearer. It was those brilliant eyes that gave him away. How funny for the father to look like the son, rather than the other way round. There was something distinctly childish about the very notion of a grown man jumping over rocks and enjoying it as much as this chap obviously was.

"Hi!" he said again breathlessly as he came up. "Are you still all alone?"

A curious thing for a stranger to say. Bott stammered. "How do you mean, still?"

"Well, you spent yesterday evening by yourself. Indeed, as far as I can see, you haven't exchanged a word with anyone except Michael since you arrived in Bethesda."

Officious man. Bott began to dislike him. She stopped smiling. He had only made her smile in the first place because he reminded her so of the dear little boy who had wanted to help her.

"I like being alone."

He was impervious to the snub. He stood there with his eyes sparkling, looking as if he thought he were Apollo or someone. Ridiculous, swarthy little man.

"We've been up to the summit once this morning," he said. Bott looked at him disbelievingly; it was still only a quarter to nine. "It's clear you're heading that way too. Wouldn't you like us to accompany you and show you the path? It's not very well marked."

At the word "us" she brightened for a moment, then realized with horror what he was suggesting.

"Oh, no thank you very much. I'm used to following rough trails."

"But maybe it would do you good to have company for a change," he insisted. "Do come with us."

He had a particularly unpleasant voice. American, mixed with something—something nasty; German, maybe.

"If I want company," she snapped, "I prefer to choose it myself. Good morning."

As she stumbled on across the mountain she realized he was laughing at her. She glanced back, and there he stood, just chuckling to himself, you could see it in his eyes, as he watched her tripping and fumbling her way along.

Well, it was too bad. She didn't see why she should have to be attacked by this old busybody just because she wanted to be alone. She really did want to get away by herself, badly, at once. She tried to hurry, to leave Bethesda behind. She wanted to think and, yes, she did want to be alone.

They were following her, there was no doubt about that. When she sat down at the top of the pass to eat her lunch, the little boy suddenly popped up from behind a stone and came running shyly towards her. You would say he had been waiting there for her.

Except for them, it had been a good morning. In fact she had forgotten about them altogether until this little fellow appeared. She was feeling tired and contented after her walk and wanted now just to be still and enjoy the mountain quietness.

"Hello," said the little boy, smiling up at her.

Irresistible. "Hello. How did you get here?"

"Oh, we came up," gesturing, eyes, face alight, "all the way up the hill. That way round. Where you couldn't see us."

"Oho, so you were following me then?"

"We came a long, long way, all the way up, and then down again, and up again. We walked—round there, and a long way." He looked happy enough though.

"Where's Daddy?"

"Over there. He had to carry me because we got stuck in some water and there weren't enough stones and I had to climb right up, right up on top of his back."

"Oh, what a shame! Fancy dragging you all these miles along a beastly pass like this!" Bott thoroughly disliked the man by now. "Aren't you tired?"

"Oh, no, it was a long way, and I didn't fall down once. But I had to climb right up on his back."

His beautiful dark eyes were sparkling with enthusiasm. Bott's indignation waned. Obviously he was delighted with his morning's hike.

"Oh his back! Never! Well, you have had an adventure."

He nodded, smiling with his eyes and his mouth serious. Now she knew where his father had got that trick.

"Goodbye," he said suddenly, and disappeared.

Bott thought vaguely that she ought to go with him and make sure he was all right. But it sounded as though his father were nearby. Imagine letting your little boy run around alone in such dangerous countryside. How sweet he was, though, really an exceptional child. She hoped he had come to her of her own accord.

*   *   *

Then they turned up again in the middle of the afternoon. She had been so lost in thought that she hadn't even realized they were there till the man called from just behind her, "Well, hello again."

She swivelled round, furious. There they both stood, with the same childish, confident smile, the same black hair blowing about. Bott wavered. How could you judge? Then she smiled uncertainly, at the boy really.

"I hoped you might have changed your mind by now," the man said. "There's such a beautiful view from the top of that rock face. Can't I persuade you to come up it with us?"

Bott gasped. "You can't take the little chap up there!"

"Oh, yes, I can climb up anywhere," the child said indignantly. "Look! Look at me." He scampered off towards the cliff.

"Hey, come back!"

Somehow they were all three scrambling over the boulders together, she and the man in pursuit of the little boy, who clambered on shrieking with delight. Before they were anywhere near the cliff they had collapsed on top of each other, and Bott discovered, to her great annoyance, that even she was laughing.

They did climb the rock face together, but Bott stayed with the child and avoided talking to the man as much as she could. She wouldn't have agreed to the climb at all except that the man had clearly so little notion of child care. In her days in the children's ward, Bott had heard about such fathers but had never really believed in them. She glanced wonderingly at the man from time to time, climbing above them, apparently quite uncaring about the others' progress. Really, it was a jolly good thing she was there.

The boy babbled on. Did she know there was a magic castle on top of this rock? Yes, a big strong castle with guns, and only special people could get up there. Someone had obviously been talking to him about Quebec. It was a wonderful castle but you had to be one of the very special people to get in.

They reached the main road again at last. This was the time to leave them, if at all. But at the crucial moment, the man said vaguely, "Bus should come along here in a while," and the boy launched into a perfectly enthralling story about the castle, with strong overtones of Quebec, but still, not bad for a little tot. They were on the bus before the man asked her, "You are going to Bettws-y-Coed, I suppose?" and paid her fare; as the bus wasn't going anywhere else, there was little she could do. She decided that if she saw any sign at all of habitation before Bettws-y-Coed she would leap out.

She should have done this at Capel Curig, the only village they went through. But she forgot all about her resolution until Capel Curig was ten minutes behind them. She had suddenly had the most splendid idea.

The little boy was going on so about castles. Why shouldn't he see a real one? Bott fidgeted with excitement. She couldn't bear to interrupt him; she was brimming over with her plan. She had promised, after all, to Christine, to come back and help her set up her chapel in Beaumaris, and it was a promise she had vaguely intended to keep. She had taken Christine's idea completely seriously, in a way, she prided herself, not many adults would. The girl had been confiding something real, she felt sure. What a good thing it would be to bring the children together. Not, admittedly, that Christine was a child exactly, but wouldn't she just adore this little Michael? It would do him a world of good, too, to mix a bit, to share his ideas and fantasies. Bott decided firmly that she must arrange it. Michael must join in the rebuilding of the chapel at Beaumaris. For the first time almost Bott addressed his father.

"Where are you ultimately heading for?"

"I don't know," he said smiling, disconcertingly. "I never like deciding in advance. And you?"

Bott faltered. "Well, I was thinking of going back to Bangor to see a friend."

"Good, that decides for me," he said. "I'm glad to hear something so constructive from you at last. I had been thinking of taking Michael to paddle at Llandudno, but Bangor will do very well."

Goodness, what presumption! And that cheeky smile just to add sauce. Bott almost flared up again, but she had so set her heart on her project that she controlled herself.

"There's another child I know there," she said, "a really sensitive, interesting girl, who I promised to go back and see. And it suddenly occurred to me that Michael might like to know her too? I'm sure they would get on. Michael makes friends very easily," she added with a sudden feeling that maybe she should try being a little diplomatic. For the man was frowning.

Bott was puzzled when he didn't reply. He was looking out of the window. She leaned forward to see into his face but it was too dark to read his expression. She said, "Don't you think so?" The silence continued. Bott's heart sank.

The sun was setting now through a gap in the clouds, throwing an extraordinary yellow light across the flank of the mountain, so that it looked like a piece of the sky. Bott forgot the man and Beaumaris and her own tired bones as she watched it. Then they lost it as the road went into a dark cutting. Bott realized that the man simply had not heard what she said at all. She would not have heard him either if he had spoken to her while she was sky-gazing. The mountain came into view again, brilliant against the dark sky.

The man said suddenly, "I want to meet this girl."

Everything he did surprised Bott more and more. She had been so sure he was not listening.

"She's just a schoolgirl—"

"I want to see what it is that has you so enthusiastic."

"Well, she's so full of ideas, and so is Michael, that I wondered if they wouldn't get on." It was as if that extraordinary break in the conversation had not taken place at all.

"To Bangor then I came," he said. He looked questioningly at Bott. She was more baffled by his face than by what he had said, which she assumed to be some Americanism. He looked intently at her, until she began to feel annoyed again, and then suddenly sighed and sank back into the bus seat as if he wanted to become part of it. His eyes were great black holes, and that posture gave him a double chin. Bott preferred to look at the landscape.

She couldn't concentrate. The silent sunken shape beside her began to irritate her. She turned to him again and said something more about Christine and Michael, but he neither stirred nor spoke and Bott stopped trying, angrier than ever at his manners. He just sat there, lining the seat, while his son played by himself behind them, all the way to Bettws-y-Coed.

The Griffiths had seen some queer customers during their six years as innkeepers at Bettws-y-Coed. Students, tramps, soldiers galore, and ten or a dozen characters whom they had reported, they were so obviously parachutists. (Pity they'd never heard the end of all those cases.) But these three, the couple and their child, they were odd by any standard, Mr. and Mrs. Griffith agreed. For a start, they weren't even married. Then look at their clothes. The man was apparently dressed in trousers made from a wartime blanket (the Griffiths had several on their bed, and could tell,) with a brand new, vivid green windjacket on top. It was the kind of thing one of the really dandy young climbers might wear, but with those trousers! And those shabby old plimsolls. They looked as if they had never been cleaned in their obviously long life. Probably that windjacket had taken all his coupons for months past.

The woman was no better. Fancy a self-respecting civilian woman going about in a filthy tattered old siren-suit like that; and just look at her hair, corkscrewing all over the place. It was a surprise to see the child looking as decent as he did, although, when he ran downstairs after supper, they both noticed how his pyjamas stank. But his parents, really, it was upsetting to see how low people would allow themselves to sink. Mrs. Griffith was mightily thankful when they asked for separate rooms.

Still, in another way, it was quite a pleasure to see two people enjoying each other's company so much. Or rather, it was interesting to watch the dark little man's animation as he leant across the supper table talking eagerly to the woman. Her reaction wasn't so easy to judge. Sometimes she answered with equal animation and their voices began to rise until Mrs. Griffith was obliged to ask them to remember the other guests. At other times the woman would suddenly go red with anger and shut up mum. Mrs. Griffith was sorely tempted to eavesdrop, but they had gone and sat in the window, the coldest place in the house and the farthest from the kitchen door. It began to get late, but they never looked at the clock. Mrs. Griffith started looking forward to going up to them and asking them if they wouldn't mind retiring. But she was cheated even of this, for towards half-past ten the man seemed to start questioning the woman rather seriously, and she began to lose her temper well and truly. Finally she stood up, knocking her chair over, and Mrs. Griffith heard her shout:

"Yes, you're a typical man, aren't you! Always wanting to push in, it's what I've been trying to explain to you all evening. I've told you and I'll tell you again, a woman wants her own peace."

And the man just smiled and watched her, and as the woman blundered her way angrily out, Mrs. Griffith saw him exchange amused glances with someone behind her. She turned and saw her own husband, shaking his head sympathetically at the little foreign chap.

Bott was seething. First the man had subjected her to a long tirade on what he thought of women alone. Then he had started to cross-question her about her private life and wishes in a way that would have taken nerve even from an intimate friend. He had tried to find out why she had not married. He had said—oh, the unbelievable rudeness—"So you fancy the idea of yourself as *vieille fille*, is that it?" She had pretended not to understand the French. That was when she was still trying to remain on good terms with him, for the child's sake.

She could not sleep. The man had managed to upset her thoroughly. She lay awake massing fierce arguments against him and in support of herself. So he reckoned she could not justify herself as an individual, living as she was! So, could he? Who was he, anyway? Some no-good G.I. too lazy to go home? Where was Michael's mother, and what were they doing, tramping round North Wales, as apparently they had been doing for months?

She knew what she was doing, all right. She was feeling out the enchantment of the country. She had never been to Wales before, and the strangeness of these barren hills had struck her. She knew the power of trees and growing things, but this magic of mists and mountains was quite new to her. But as she went around, touching and listening and exploring, she had had more and more strongly the impression that she was giving as well as taking. When she fingered the shape of a stone, for instance, searching out its latent meaning, afterwards the stone was changed. It was somehow richer. Coming back along the path she would be able to recognize her stone instantly. As she drew its strength out of it, she must, she concluded, be instilling something in return. The power of growing things, perhaps?

And this chap knew nothing of any of this, yet he dared to criticize her. Of course he had only been peddling the usual male line, of which she had heard enough in her life, so that you'd think she would be resistant by now. It was absurd to let this fellow annoy her so much.

When she had walked out after supper she had firmly intended not to say another word to him and to leave in the opposite direction, even if it meant going back to Snowdon. Before morning she had planned out a long speech for his benefit; and when they met on the landing before breakfast they discussed possible routes to Bangor as if last night's outrage had never happened.

He was still unwashed and unshaven when he came down to breakfast, and looked at least five years older than she had previously thought. He couldn't after all be any younger than she. He looked tired and worried and his hair was in a mess. Bott watched him doubtfully across the table. This couldn't surely be the same aggressive man who had been so offensive last night, or the agile little fellow who had skipped over the rocks, teasing her. Both he and Michael smiled radiantly at her as she came into the room and Michael called gladly "Hello!" Then the father relapsed into his gloom and put his elbows on the table. His nose shone with grease. He didn't eat his cornflakes and didn't speak.

But after breakfast, as she was packing, he knocked and came in, changed again, his face alight, holding out something in a paper bag. Bott raised her eyebrows.

"Go on," he said. "Open it."

This was something she had seen before in his son, too, when he had given her the palm cross. The same delighted anticipation.

She opened the packet and looked disbelievingly at him. "Toast sandwiches?"

"Sure," he said, the grin he had been suppressing breaking out at last. "Have a taste. See if it reminds you of anything."

Bott took a mouthful, still suspecting a practical joke. Then she burst into a splutter of toast crumbs. "Marmalade!"

"Marmalade," he assented, all sparkling eyes. "Oxford Vintage."

"But where on earth—"

"I made the toast downstairs," he explained. "The marmalade I've been carrying about with me for years, looking for someone suitable to give it to. It was a Christmas gift from somebody, but I don't like marmalade."

Bott sat down on the bed and munched contentedly. Marmalade was a treat however you got it.

"At breakfast," he said, "you had an 'I want marmalade' look."

"Considering you never raised your eyes from the table-cloth," Bott said, "that was pretty observant of you."

"And then when they cleared away the bacon," he went on, "you were looking so desperately 'I don't want dripping' that I had to do something."

Bott didn't know what to think. She felt she was being inconsistent. She had certainly meant to snub him properly, last night. Or have it out with him about the *vieille fille*. She had done neither; now here she was sitting on her bed with him, matily eating his marmalade as if he were the best of her comrades-in-arms.

"Is it good?" he asked anxiously.

"A real treat." Maybe he was trying to make up for last night. He was trying hard enough now to please.

"This is a great idea," he said. He had wandered over to her pack and was examining the padded strap system she had made. "I shouldn't think you'd feel the weight at all, the way you've distributed it."

"I don't," Bott said, flattered and boasting in spite of herself. "I've carried everything I possess on my back half round England and I haven't had sore shoulders once."

"Wow!" he said, and the look he turned on her seemed to be one of genuine admiration. Bott choked on the toast crust.

"I'm going to enjoy hiking with you," he said. "Meet you in the hall in twenty minutes' time?"

Bott nodded, and he went out with springy feet.

You got off that time, bribing me with marmalade, Bott thought. But I haven't forgotten. You wait, you little monkey.

3

GATZKOVIC COULD NOT help laughing to himself as he went downstairs. The woman was so easy to tease. Most people had their various subtle ways of showing that they were offended; but this miss had no defence tactics whatever.

He wondered about her though. He had not merely been playing with her last night. He had seriously wanted to make her think twice about her attempts at a self-sufficient existence. He had been watching her for several days, ages before she had even noticed his or Michael's existence. Without having managed to find out her name, he still felt he knew her very well. He had seen signs of the most intense emotions pass over her face as she sat staring or rambled down a hill; all for nothing, for nobody, all wasted. If she were questioned she would no doubt tell him that she had an interesting enough life, thank you. Probably true after a fashion. She had very likely had a few interesting experiences, living that way. But all sterile.

Who were they, these extraordinary Englishwomen? Even more interesting, why were they? He had seen dozens of them since he had been in the country, but had always tended to shy away from them, feeling that no woman goes around manless for choice. But this one, he had been intrigued by. These solitary English females were not usually such splendid big creatures; they tended to have a cast-off, downtrodden look, most unattractive. But this woman had a lot of pride, you could tell. Also she appeared to be enjoying herself. That was what made the difference, that was what made him want to pry; it was also that which somehow annoyed him.

How could any woman enjoy herself living by herself, for herself? It wasn't natural, it wasn't right. No, that was it: she hadn't the right. This woman was so closed up in herself it amounted to introversion. It was pitifully, heart-breakingly sterile.

Pitiful, that was what she was, and Gatzko pitied her from the bottom of his soft heart. Also, she was so delightfully easy to laugh at.

Bott had no idea that she was being pitied, and she was quite used to being laughed at. All her life she had been accustomed to seeing herself as a laughing-stock. At school; as a Girl Guide; in the hospital; in the A.T.S. At school, she remembered, they had called her "Fullie", surely exceptionally silly-sounding even for a nickname. The only thing to do was to keep all that mattered of yourself hidden. This was not as easy as one might imagine. She still had extrovert hankerings, she censured herself. Look at the risk she had taken emptying her heart to that little Welsh girl in Bangor. How she did hope she would have equal luck this time.

They all arrived in the pouring rain outside Christine's house on the Saturday afternoon. They rang and shivered and Michael grizzled.

Christine, upstairs sweeping her bedroom, looked out of her window at Bott, the raggle-taggle man and the howling child, and didn't recognize them. When she did, she nearly fell through the window.

She scurried down, fluttering and trembling. The door-mat jammed itself in the door and there was an embarrassing moment while she struggled with it half-open. Then she was able to cry gladly to the woman, "Well, it is you again! How happy I am to see you!"

"And I you," the woman said heart-warmingly. They both looked nervously at Gatzkovic and Michael, who were staring stonily at Christine. Bott fumbled in her mind for an introduction. She realized she did not know the name of either the girl or the man.

"These are two friends of mine who are so interested in meeting you," she said. She looked expectantly at Gatzkovic but he only went on staring rudely. He looked anything but interested. She shivered, and two cold raindrops rolled down her face. "They were on their way to Llandudno, and I remembered what you had told me about your plans to build a chapel in Beaumaris Castle. And—and so we've come to help you," Bott finished wretchedly, hating the man and his beastly brat who were making her look such a fool.

"And welcome they are," Christine said awkwardly. She hesitated. Her parents were in the front room. She didn't know how to get this dripping party of people into the house without their noticing. Nor did she know how to explain their presence if they did notice. "This is a lady who climbed into my bedroom last week...." "This is a lady and her gentleman friend...." Then Michael burst into another storm of tears, and Christine said impulsively, "Oh, I am sorry. Please come in." Nerving herself, she led the way into the front room. She said quickly in Welsh, "Mother, these poor people are very wet and cold and the little boy is ill. May I make them some tea?" In English she added, "These are my parents. Please make yourselves at home." Scarcely knowing how she had dared, she ran to the kitchen, shaking all over.

She had come back, that strange, wonderful woman! She hadn't just been a dream! Christine was so agitated that for a long time she couldn't even find the tea. But somehow—oh, she would never have wanted it to be like this—she seemed infinitely less glamorous, arriving all bedraggled at the front door towing two people with whom she was obviously ill at ease herself.

Gatzkovic settled in to an afternoon of boredom. He saw immediately by the china dogs on the mantelpiece, the way they were all sitting without lights on a dark wet day, the tea which was the first thing the girl's mind turned to, the reproving looks the parents gave him—this was just the sort of dreary household which depressed him most.

Michael caught his father's mood, and it did not cheer him up.

Christine's parents fussed over the child and tried to be polite, wondering whatever had got into their daughter.

Bott and Christine carried bravely on.

The afternoon was not a success.

Bott did, however, manage to secure a promise that Christine and her sister would make the outing with them all to Beaumaris tomorrow. She left as soon as she could after this, miserable with everything and dreading failure next day too. Gatzkovic did not try to speak to her again that evening.

But when she saw Beaumaris Chapel, with a rush of emotion she knew that she had done the right thing after all.

"Oh, what a wonderful place!" She stood in the doorway and gasped as people do in cathedrals. Michael and the little sisters crowded round her, looking raptly into the tiny chapel. Bott forgot the man completely.

"Come on! Christine, Molly! We must look for stones to build an altar."

"I saw a big one downstairs," Michael squealed, scampering off. Calling excitedly to each other, they started running about the castle searching for stones. They had all forgotten Gatzko. He sat grimly in a corner and watched them. Building an altar! Next thing, they'd be playing at holding a service in here. What was she after all, this woman, a nun?

Look at her galloping up and down the steps, leading the game, playing like a baby but her face all full of zeal. It disgusted him to see Michael mixed up in such a thing. It was dangerous, too, to encourage children to run on dark spiral stairs all full of holes and worn places, as these were. If he had any sense he would get up and stop it, or at least get Michael out. But somehow he hadn't quite the energy. He sat and scowled at them all, and they never even noticed.

This afternoon was everything that yesterday was not. Bott

had not enjoyed herself so much in years. The idea had been a wild success. The pact between herself, Michael and Christine was sealed now, that was for sure. She and Christine exchanged joyous and knowing glances.

Gatzkovic noticed them too and thought, I don't like the way this woman has managed to gain influence over that girl.

Probably the girl hadn't much personality of her own in the first place. How old would she be? About fourteen? Gatzko suddenly remembered his own daughter, far away in Arizona. She must be about ready to graduate from high school by now. Gatzko suddenly felt a pang of anxiety. Suppose her guardians had tricked him? Suppose they hadn't kept her on at high school in Flagstaff as they had promised? This was the first time he had even thought about her in months; he had had such implicit trust in the couple he had made her guardians, the Wilsons. Now suddenly he was suspicious. They could so easily have let her drop out of high school and put her to work, keeping his money. Then his daughter would turn out an uneducated moron like this girl.

He gnawed his finger-tips with worry. How old would she be, exactly? She was twelve when he left, in forty-one. Seventeen! She must be seventeen, coming on eighteen! Those Wilsons, they knew he wanted her to go to college, but how easy it would be for them conveniently to forget. Stupid fool that he was, he hadn't given Wilson any written instructions for Mary's further education. If he cabled them off now, Wilson, as Gatzkovic's lawyer, would be forced to obey them, wouldn't he?

At least if he did disobey Gatzkovic would have some legal ground to stand on.

It was September. There was barely time to enrol Mary in college before the term started. Thank heaven he had thought of it. It was watching these silly sisters that had put him in mind of Mary. He got up and yelled at one of them.

"Hey! Is there any way I can send off a transatlantic cable from here?"

His voice reverberated in the silent enclosed chapel. Everyone came scuttling down, alarmed by the force of his shout. At least he had managed to break up their churchy game. It was beginning to smell altogether too strongly of a secret society to be healthy. A churchy secret society. Although everyone was already gathered about him he sent up another shout: "Can somebody please answer me? I have an extremely urgent cable to send off."

"Why what's happened?" the woman asked.

"Never mind what's happened!" he raged. "Just tell me where the post office is!"

Christine said hurriedly, "In the town, but it will now be closed. Tomorrow you must send your cable."

"All right then, I'll telephone it. Don't tell me I can't telephone a cable. It's certainly possible in England if not in Wales. Let's get out of this place. I'll do it in Bangor."

Bott stared at him in dismay and disappointment. What on earth did he mean? He had been sitting there all afternoon perfectly quietly. Now suddenly he had urgent news to convey. It wasn't possible. He just wanted to butt in again, make himself noticed. Goodness, weren't there some things she'd like to say to him. Was going to too, but not now, not here, this afternoon was too good to spoil or to allow this man to spoil.

"Go anywhere you like," she said. "We'll bring Michael home when we come."

He stared at her. Angry or impatient or both? He said, "Michael is coming with me now."

"Oh, no, Daddy!" the little mite cried in consternation.

"I think," said Christine, "it will be very difficult to telegraph on a Sunday evening."

There was about eight hours' difference between Mountain Standard time and British Summer time. Maybe his cable would be in time to stop Mary setting out for whatever menial job she was doing. He did not argue any further; he simply gave Michael a fatherly hoist on to his shoulder, ignoring his yells, and marched out. Bott, too late, moved to block his path. She called furiously after him:

"I'd just like you to know you are the rudest man I have ever met."

He did not answer because he had not heard her. He had forgotten all about her. He was drafting his cable to Lawyer Wilson.

Bott felt sure she had seen the last of them. She tried to finish the decoration of the chapel by herself with Christine and Molly, but they were all curiously disheartened after the sudden departure of Michael. They tried for a while. It began to get dark and cold. Presently they trailed sadly back into the town to wait for the Bangor bus.

Christine and Molly said goodnight very nicely to her, and Christine begged her to write to her as if she were requesting some enormous favour from a film star. Such sincere admiration in a young person was flattering, certainly. All the same Bott felt tired and low when she went into her lodging-house.

There they were. Both of them, cheeky devils, smiling up from chairs by the fire as if nothing had happened. They had obviously been home some time for the man was in slippers and was half-way through a cigar.

"Well!" was all Bott could say, and "Did you get your cable off?"

He nodded, altogether pleased with himself and life generally. Now that he had got his precious world-shattering news out he was all delight and good humour again. It was all very well.

"No trouble at all," he said, "once I succeeded in obtaining your overseas service. Only problem was reaching them. Three cables, I gave them." Childish self-satisfaction. "That ought to have some drastic effects."

"Yes, that just about sums you up, doesn't it?" said Bott. "You always want to create a drastic effect wherever you go."

He smiled pleasantly at her. "There's not so much difference between us then," he said.

Bott was very angry. One after another, he deflected her neat barbs as if they were hairpins. It's because he's afraid of any serious argument, she consoled herself. He'll criticize others all right, but when it comes to defending himself he knows he can't. She suddenly could not face the thought of eating with that smug chuckle in front of her all the way through the meal. She went out of the room with hurried strides.

Gatzkovic finished his cigar, drank some of his landlady's tea and ate one of her fishcakes, refused her pudding and smoked another cigar instead at table while Michael ate. He took Michael upstairs, told him to put himself to bed, not caring overmuch whether he did or not, and went into Bott's room without knocking.

She was kneeling beside her pack raking ill-temperedly through it and throwing the contents on to the floor. There was blood on her hand. When she saw Gatzkovic she gave an enormous jerk and the bandage she had just succeeded in finding flew up to the ceiling, unrolling in great coils all over the room.

"You're in a mess," he said.

"And if I am," she snapped, "who is it who goes out of his way to mess up my afternoon, who stages theatrical scenes to distract me when he sees me getting interested in something which isn't him, who is as rude as he knows how to be, who picks on me when he doesn't even know me, who walks into my room without knocking and makes me jump?"

Gatzkovic winced under the torrent of noise, although in fact he agreed with her entirely that she had had a rough deal. As soon as she paused he said, "Yes, I'm afraid I've been a most irritating companion."

That stopped her, as he knew it would. She had probably expected him to abuse her or something.

"Well—not exactly, but—" she faltered.

"I merely thought," Gatzko said, "that you needed a little distraction."

"Really!"

"You seemed," he stopped and thought, and went on, "all wound up in anxiety. That's what I felt, anyhow. Preoccupied, worried. It worried me."

See her face change quite magically at the idea of a bit of sympathy, instead of disapproval, coming her way. She stared at him. She can't believe what she heard, thought Gatzko, and looked at her kindly, waiting for it to sink in. He continued, "I could see you were lonely, and maybe I was wrong but I thought you were unhappy too. Are you unhappy?"

She was pink in the face and flattered. "Well," she said slowly. Then she rallied. "Unhappy," she said, "no. Pre-occupied, maybe."

Gatzko was a trifle taken aback. Women usually loved a little pity, a chance to wallow in someone else's sympathy. And Gatzko could offer genuine sympathy to almost everyone, and indeed delighted in doing so. It really wasn't necessary to know the person especially well to feel sorry for them, you could start off right away; for Gatzkovic knew that everybody is at bottom unhappy. But this woman wasn't going to admit it. Gatzko felt mildly admiring. She most certainly did have a lot of pride. He also pitied her more than ever, for being obstinate as well as mistaken.

"But always, all alone!" he said. "What is it you're thinking to yourself all the time? Or are you fooling me, are you busy writing poems to carry back to your lover?"

She screeched. "My lover! That's a bad joke and I shan't even bother to reply."

Gatzkovic realized he had blundered, and decided to say so. "Now I've blundered," he said. "I was only trying to get you to talk."

She surely, surely can't go on resisting, he thought. No woman, no man either come to that, but is secretly longing to pour out their life story to someone, and is always looking for a sympathetic someone.

"Suppose I don't want to talk?" she suggested.

Gatzko wondered whether to try making her angry again. He looked at his watch. Nine-thirty. Oh hell. He had to see to Michael too.

Prepared to give the woman up as a bad job, he quoted,

> "What are you thinking of? What thinking? What?
> I never know what you are thinking. Think."

This did not have the effect he intended. He did not suppose she would place the lines, since he had already tried quoting "The Waste Land" at her; also, it said a good deal that there was not a single book among her belongings, scattered about. But he had assumed that she would tell from his tone that he was reciting. He was not expecting her to give him a look of deep interest and exclaim, "Why, that's poetry!"

Gatzko muttered and shifted.

"That's very interesting," she said, mulling the lines over. After a moment she suddenly began to speak, very fast, gazing out of the window.

"I know what it is. You don't really think I'm thinking anything and so you imagine I must be bored and it's your duty to awaken me to a more aware adult existence or something like that. Oh, yes, I see. You notice me looking at a hill and think I'm staring into space and so you try to get me to focus on something—you, for preference. Well, it's a lot of rubbish and if I haven't given you all the attention you'd like it's because I've been too busy thinking, that's what."

"What do you think about, then?" he asked in his gentlest voice. Rarely had he tried for so long at a time to be nice to the same person.

"Philosophy," she barked, and burst into screams of laughter. "You didn't expect that, did you? Serves you right!"

Gatzkovic tried to conceal his disgust and irritation. All the dislike and disapproval he had felt with her at Beaumaris came flooding back.

"Profitless activity," he muttered, which was mild compared to what he felt. But she went on screeching idiotically, and quite suddenly he lost his temper.

"So you are a nun then," he shouted. "A smug, conceited, introverted, wasted barren nun!"

She stared at him. Good, he had shaken her complacency. Yes, you could tell just how much she was shaken. She said, trying for indignation, "Oh, am I indeed! Well, for your information, I'm not even religious."

"A nun with no religion? God! What was all that for in the chapel then?"

"Oh, I don't say I'm an atheist. I believe in the power that makes the universe work, of course. But I'm definitely not religious. So perhaps the word nun is not quite apt." She was so angry she could hardly speak but she tried to bring the words out calmly.

"I see, you like to ease your conscience by believing in some nice, chaste, impersonal power, is that it? Read lots of George Bernard Shaw, I expect. Oh, this is sublime. You mess around in chapels perverting poor kids like mine, but you steer clear of anything dangerous, thank you. How sterile can you get? A churchy woman who's not even religious!"

"Did you say 'perverting'?" she said, still on her dignity.

"That's what I said. And that's what I'd say about all women of your kind. Or did you imagine you were unique? Somebody pretty special on the whole? Has no one ever told you about women like you? Well, I will. Or didn't you know what a race you are? Abbesses, matrons, female officers, lonely fiendish women, all as dedicated as hell. Oh, you've got plenty of company. It's one of the most common of womankind's temptations, I can assure you."

He was hitting home all right. Maybe she'd never been attacked in this way before. She hadn't the least idea how to reply.

"You're vicious, too. Yes, I do mean you in particular. Do you think I didn't notice what you were trying to do to those little girls today? You wanted to get Michael under your power, too, didn't you? That's what really made me angry. You'd have liked to make him into the pitiable, contemptible creature you've made of yourself. And don't you try whining that you've been an outcast from society since you were so high. It's up to you what you are, and I think you might as well jump into the nearest ravine, for all the good you are to yourself or anyone."

He went to get that child into bed. Bott sat on the floor staring at the finger she had cut and never remembered to bandage. After a while she heard Michael yelling dismally across the passage. Heavens, that man was in a rage.

For a long time she sat there. When the light went out at ten o'clock (turned off by the landlady at the mains) she never noticed. Her head throbbed. For a moment she could not remember whether he had not actually beaten her physically, as well as verbally. She listened to the blood pumping in her head.

After a while she went to the window and stared out at that dark wild hillside which she had so revelled in, only a week ago. How well she remembered stepping off the road on to it and shivering all down herself at the touch of the earth, and feeling the hill shiver too in reply, all the way down inside.

She had never dreamt that her way of living might be wrong. Nobody had even suggested it to her. Plenty of people had thought her peculiar, eccentric or even mad, but she had only laughed at that. It was so long ago that she had chosen the solitary way, when she was in her early teens, and she remembered that year, all the heart-searching and renunciation and dedication. "Dedicated as hell," she kept hearing the American's voice, "dedicated as hell." It had never, never occurred to her that dedication could be other than wholly admirable.

She stared at the dark sky, growing colder and colder. She

had meant to level a similarly attacking speech at him! She had meant to demand of him what he thought he was doing and what good he was. And what had happened? Why had she sat there meekly taking it? Why hadn't she counter-attacked? Why didn't she go right now and let him hear the other side of it, all the things she had been preparing to say to him for days?

Quite suddenly she felt a frantic longing to see the moon. It was so dark everywhere, there was not a single light on in the village and the electricity was off at the mains. If she could just catch a glimpse, one glimpse between the clouds, of that white wonderful radiance, she would be herself again, she would have strength to go in to that man and tell him what was what. It was absurd, irrational, but she no longer had much hold on the rational. She leant out of the window and looked hungrily at the place where the moon ought to be. She willed it to appear. Her final hopes seemed to hang on catching sight, however fleetingly, of the ugly, gibbous shape which the moon at present was. She stared until her eyes ached and a cold raindrop blew into them. Then she gave up. Feeling utterly humiliated, she groped her way feebly back across the room, stubbing her toes on her belongings. Oh, what a fool she was, what a wasted nunnish lost lonely barren fool.

She looked tired and elderly at breakfast. She sat hunched up with big miserable eyes fixed on Gatzko. He asked her kindly whether she was all ready to leave for Llandudno. She nodded meekly. Gatzko watched her with some amusement. She had so obviously been longing for so many days to ask him questions; now she scarcely dared even speak to him. That afternoon, as they walked along the front at Llandudno, out of sheer pity he began tossing her a few selected facts about himself.

His name was Gregor Gatzkovic, Yugoslav. He waited a bit, watching her goggle and swallow, and added that he was in fact born in Chicago, but he was only first-generation American and all his loyalties lay with his own Croatia.

"Ah, Croatia," mumbled Bott trying to remember where that was.

"I fought as a partisan," he said. (Goggle, swallow again.) "On both sides. I left the States in '41 when Germany invaded, although it was a Serbian government in power. With that silly little king. But at least they were anti-German. However they were wiped out anyway in ten days."

"Oh. I'm so sorry," said Bott.

"No, no, that was when the fun started. The Croats raised a flag of their own, or rather Tito did, you may remember, out in the wilds of Bosnia. We were at war with everyone. Chiefly Mihailovic, also the Germans, Italians and anyone else around. Even the Allies in the end, I'm sorry to say. But it was splendid at first."

"Mmm, I should think so," Bott agreed, bemusedly wondering who had conquered Yugoslavia finally. Gatzko seemed to have finished his story. She asked nervously, "Didn't you win?"

"Oh sure we won. That is, Tito won. But I couldn't stand any more of Tito by then. I've no objection to suppressing church, monarchy and feudalism, but I will not give my allegiance to a police state. I will not support power lust in any nation or any man, whether he's king, general or just my boss at work."

"No, no, of course," Bott said hastily, frightened at his anger.

"I stayed in Trieste when Tito left, but the city was more like a bit of New Zealand than a bit of the Mediterranean. A division of New Zealanders took it you know. Well, I was pretty disillusioned with everything around there by then, so I got out and eventually came to Britain. At least that hadn't tried to gain power over anything, or not this century anyway."

"You aren't going back to America?"

Gatzko did not answer. They walked up and down for ten minutes more and then he told her that he had had three sculptures in a show in Lausanne that summer.

Goggle, gasp, admiring eyes.

It was Michael she was longing to know more about now, but Gatzko didn't feel like discussing his origins with her, and merely smiled sweetly at her when she glanced curiously at the boy. He next tried once more to ask her a few questions, but either she had had a very dull life or she did not feel like discussing it either, for she stammered and hedged. But Gatzko must have been feeling expansive, for he found himself telling her, quite gratuitously, that he had come to Wales to study rock formations to make sculptures from. At that she nearly jumped into the sea with excitement.

"You mean you get inspiration from rocks? How marvellous! So do I! Have you seen Snowdon?"

"Yes, I found it disappointing in fact. I want to see Penrimmon next."

"Oh, I thought it was wonderful, but then I wouldn't have a sculptor's eye," she said humbly. "I expect Penrimmon is much better. I—I've been thinking about Penrimmon too."

"Then why not come along with us?" Gatzko offered, who must certainly have been feeling extraordinarily sociable. He himself wondered later at the effect those sea breezes had had on him.

She gave another excited start and said eagerly, "Oh, may I?"

Bott had never been in love, and so did not realize what was happening to her. Gatzko did guess, and vague scruples passed through his mind, but he forgot about the matter altogether before he had given it much thought.

4

MARY GATZKOVIC LAY in the swing seat on the front porch, watching the sun setting over A Mountain. For a moment the thick cactus bodies stood out black against the sky, squadrons of them, taller than a man, marching over the slope of the hill. Then they disappeared into the gloom, but it was impossible to forget they were there. They would be here too, right in the city, if it weren't for constant weeding and watering.

Mary wished for a breeze to swing her. She was too inert and too miserable to swing herself. That terrible cable! She could not believe it. It was too bad to be true. It was exactly the same feeling she had had when all those years ago her father had told her, so casually it hurt far worse, that he was going to Europe, that he might be back next year or the year after, and meanwhile she must go and live in Flagstaff and start high school. She had written, again and again, to the address he left her, but she was sure he never received her letters because the only one she had had back was posted from Italy and answered none of hers. Now, after four more years with no news whatever, suddenly a cable sixty-eight words long sent from England. England! What was he doing there anyway? Couldn't he, in those sixty-eight words, have given her some news, however brief, of himself? When it first arrived she had cried with relief because at least it was proof that he was alive somewhere. She read and re-read it sniffly with happiness, without understanding the words at all. Very slowly they began to penetrate, long after she had put the cable down, and then she turned sniffly for a different reason.

Severely and impatiently, but with no words wasted, her

father ordered the Wilsons to send Mary to Chicago before next Friday. She was to go to JOB. Mr. Wilson, after much frantic palaver with Information girls all over the country, had discovered that this meant the Jude O. Bergstein University. Mary stood swaying in the kitchen, holding on to the table. The rest of the cable was bitterly, brutally clear, so that it was simply not possible to misunderstand it. Each "STOP" was like a blow on the head. It was mostly concerned with business arrangements for Mary's college expenses. He had cabled one year's fees direct to JOB, with explicit instructions to his bank. Mary did not doubt that they were explicit to the last degree. He had also cabled the university.

The mosquitoes were humming round her but she did nothing to ward them off. Soon the crickets would begin, whirring away up there on A Mountain. Probably they would make her cry. They often had. It was because they always brought back Sedona so strongly to her that she found herself brushing off imaginary red dust, or sniffing for the sweet fertile valley smell. The desert smelt of nothing at all and Tucson merely smelt hot. But however strong her nostalgia, however vividly she conjured up the red rocks and the creek deep under the branches, there was one thing she could never succeed in remembering.

What was it, what was it, the great secret she had shared with her father, so long ago when they lived there together in the little wooden house he had built himself? What was it he had told her, what was it they had known together? Something to do with the source of the stream, wasn't it? And something to do with his sculpture? Yes, he had taken her up into the rocks and talked to her about it. Silly child she was, why had she not listened and remembered? There was another time too when they were digging together in the maize patch. Mary had been holding a prickly-pear blossom in her hand and her father had turned from planting maize and said—what? All she could remember was the feeling of mystery and his intense eyes looking at her and that prickly-pear blossom. Oh, now she so nearly had it, it almost came to her. She made a tremendous, superhuman effort. The strain was unbearable, but she surely must get it at any second. Try, try, remember, remember.

Mrs. Wilson saw her hands hanging limply off the arms of the swing seat and thought, She's gone to sleep again, and she knows it's time to eat.

But many, many times before Mary had tried to remember, and she had no better success now than then. So many, many times: that nearly-remembering, the struggle to reach it, the inevitable failure. It was like a recurring dream. In fact she did often dream it too so that even some of the episodes she thought were from her childhood may very well have been some past dream. Her memories and dreams were getting more and more confused. She knew the truth was that, far from being near to recalling the great secret, she was all the time further and further from it.

Tears welled up in Mary's eyes at the sheer hopelessness of everything. The more she tried to take hold of herself—to find something real, indisputable, to believe in—the more lost she felt, the more her mind shifted around. Where was her father? Where was Sedona? The two things her life was founded on, where were they? She had often been back to Oak Creek Canyon when they lived at Flagstaff but it had never seemed the same. Quite likely it was not the same. Maybe it was some other creek, in some other valley, where they had lived and guarded the secret. Maybe she had never made any excursion back to Sedona after all, but had only dreamt of it.

Something bad had happened today, she had had some bad news. Hadn't she? Mary found it difficult to attend to anything lately. No, she simply could not remember. She let her head loll over the back of the swing, hoping the tears would run back into her eyes and save her having to look for a handkerchief.

Mrs. Wilson peered out again at the limp shape in the twilight and thought, Look how soft and flabby she's getting.

It won't be a bad thing if sports are compulsory on the campus in Chicago.

Mary thought about her father leaping from stone to stone at Baldwin's Crossing. The last time she and the Wilsons went down there they had driven about for hours, along rutty dusty tracks, trying to follow directions given by the ranch workers, but they had failed to find Baldwin's Crossing. Everyone blamed Mary. She had lived there after all, hadn't she? Mary cried quietly in the back of the car as, tired and cross, they had made their way home through Cottonwood.

Mary could not see A Mountain at all now. It had disappeared just as Cathedral Rock and the Shiprock disappeared after sunset.

It was funny, really, the way she could still reel the names of all those rocks off. It was deceptive too. One day she would have to admit that she was forgetting Sedona.

Mrs. Wilson had to shake her to make her come in and eat. She had been calling her for the last ten minutes. She asked the girl if she fell asleep or what, and Mary said apologetically no, she was just dreaming.

Mrs. Wilson thought, and said to her husband that night, that it was a very good thing Mary was going away to a really big busy city, right out of this heat which was maybe enervating her. Hadn't he noticed how Mary seemed to be in a permanent state of lethargy lately?

Of course, they had both noticed it, and wondered if there was anything special wrong with her, beyond of course that she was still moping for her father. They had both tried all they knew to wake Mary up, to give her some interest in life. As it grew later, their talk grew more confidential. It was depressing her, Mrs. Wilson admitted, to have the girl always glooming around; never a smile, and constantly falling asleep.

Mr. Wilson liked Mary, of course, she was a sweet girl.

Sweet, oh yes, Mrs. Wilson hastily agreed.

But in a way he would be quite glad to have the responsibility off his hands.

After all, someone else's daughter is a terrible responsibility.
If only Mr. Gatzkovic would come home.

Oh, yes, if only he would.

They'll have had that cable by now, Gatzko thought gleefully. It should have shaken them up some. It was satisfying in
a way to be able to make his presence felt across five thousand
miles. That's what money did for you. He was glad now he
had left it untouched in America, instead of bringing it with
him to Europe. Wilson had told him he was crazy to set off for
a far continent that had a war going on without a dime in his
pocket; but Gatzko had stuck to his notion of leaving everything he owned in trust for Mary. There wasn't so very much
of it, after all. A bit of land, but what was land in Arizona
worth? It was not as if there were oil around; nothing but oak
trees and red rocks.

It was the red rocks which had brought him there.

He had seen a magazine issue on them, about a year after
his marriage foundered, when he was struggling in the depression to keep the Chicago business going and to work out
his own style in stone sculpting. It was just after he turned
against bronze casting, as too artificial. He was searching for
natural contour and grain. Nothing he could do in Chicago
seemed right. Then he saw the article on the red rock region
of the Colorado Plateau.

He went there as soon as he could take a week off from
work, although the journey itself, by a combination of Santa
Fe railroad and hitching, took him almost a week. He never
really went back to work. He sold up the business and persuaded the National Parks authorities to sell him a plot in
Sedona. He remembered the poetry of his second journey
there, taking little Mary; it was snowing in the Rockies, and
they were stranded in Colorado Springs for five days. He and
Mary went wild with excitement. They climbed Pike's Peak in
a storm when the routes were officially closed. The rest of the
world might as well not have existed. Even Colorado Springs

below was invisible in a snow cloud. Their day there had been something between a long joyous game and an artist's ecstasy. They camped in a hole in the rocks to eat their picnic and Mary made a snow-garden. She chased him up the mountain, riding an imaginary white horse, shrieking with delight. A crazy thing to do with a six-year-old child, very likely even illegal, but that time on the mountain was one of the best in Gatzko's life.

The same day that they left snowy Colorado Springs southwards, they were in brilliant sun and dry heat. The change came almost exactly on the border of New Mexico.

The longer they travelled the more the enchantment increased. They arrived in the far sacred valley of Oak Creek Canyon. It was sacred of course; long before it was American. But the Indians had all gone when he arrived. In fact the place was uninhabited except for a few lonely rancheros. Thinking back to that time was like remembering some book read years ago. It could not really be Gatzko building his own shack, cooking fish he had caught with Mary at the stream. It must be someone else, some character out of *Swiss Family Robinson* maybe. A rather adapted, lyrical version of *Swiss Family Robinson.* His life there must have been hard, it *must* have, but in retrospect he saw himself, twenty-five and strong to match, effortlessly floating through that dusky red light, master of the world, lord of the red rocks. He beckoned and his house appeared, a bit lopsided maybe, which ought to be testimony to his own handicraft, but he could not remember any of the more boring things which usually accompany housebuilding: timber sawn wrong, fingers hammered.

He dreamed red sculptures and they appeared, wonderful things, all the essence of mountains in them, the strata, the erosion, the unbelievable shapes. The first three years in Sedona were the most productive period of his career. Of course there had been many patient hours of chiselling and carving, but all he remembered now was his magical creations growing out of the stone or clay while he watched.

Was Mary still such a passionate gardener as she had been then? He was always tripping over her little beds and plantations; in every nook and hollow she had something growing. The fertility of the place was amazing. It didn't need Mary's green fingers to bring up an almost frighteningly outsize crop of anything you cared to plant. It was those Indians and their fertility rites, no doubt. Gatzko could feel them dense around the place. It was rather as if holiness were like some heavy vapour, settling thickly into low enclosed places, reeking along river beds. It was that eventually which had sickened him of Sedona. That sticky scent of holiness. In the end he had been glad of the excuse of the war in Serbia to get out.

All the same the Arizona venture had been a success. His relatives had thought he was deliberately ruining himself when he moved west to that unheard of village. But Gatzko had done far better there than he or his father had ever done in years of conventional business in Chicago. After a few months Gatzko took a job at Lowell Observatory at Flagstaff. Technicians were in short supply in that part of Arizona then and Gatzko found himself easily stashing money away. His family knew about this, but of course they did not know where the money was or what he had done with it. Let them think what they liked. When he contrived to make Isabel leave him his victory over the whole lot of them was complete.

Idly he imagined himself going back to Sedona, but knew at once that he never could. Sedona had gone bad on him.

He didn't know how it was he had stayed so long in Sedona at all, when travelling was really the greatest pleasure he knew. And almost his entire youth spent in Chicago! It seemed unbelievable now. He didn't remember being discontented with Chicago, either, until about '35. Then the wanderlust had struck him.

He gazed contentedly out at the dim shapes of these new hills. Penrimmon. He had seen plenty of better mountains, but the thrill of emptying his pack on to a strange bed never failed. His legs ached with walking. It would make a change to go somewhere by train tomorrow. The British rail system was not one he had had much contact with yet. Michael loved trains too.

"How would you like to go on a train tomorrow?" he asked him. Michael popped bright eyes up from under the bed-clothes, where he had been playing with something or other and pretending to be asleep for the last hour and a half.

"A real train? Really?"

"We might. I guess we could call ourselves train travel experts, don't you think?" Suddenly Gatzko realized that he had made a mistake. He had hardly ever been on a train with Michael. That long journey he was thinking of, on the Santa Fe, had been with Mary, not Michael. For a moment he had confused them.

"Riding on a train is the most exciting thing there is," he told Michael. "We'll have fun."

Michael bounced out of bed. "What do you have to do?"

"There are good train travellers and bad train travellers. Bad travellers get cross and tired very quickly. They're the ones who don't realize that the ride is most of the fun. And they forget to take any food and get hungry and impatient. We know how to pack up food to last us all day, don't we?"

"I'm going to be a good traveller!" Michael shouted, bouncing all over the bed.

"And good travellers know that you really have to be fresh for a long ride and they go to bed extra specially early the night before."

Michael snuggled down immediately, but his eyes shone with eagerness over the sheet. "Will it be a very long ride?" he asked hopefully.

"Yes, very," Gatzkovic answered, his own excitement mounting. "Hundreds of miles! It may take us all day!"

"Oh!"

"So we had both better go to sleep at once."

Portmadoc was a big station, and it must be quite close. They could probably get some express to take them right out of Wales. Gatzkovic had had enough of Wales, the mists and the drizzle and the endless rocky hills. It was months since he had been in a great city. Suppose they went right through to London. Only the fare worried him. Was there any way of riding tailboards in England? Michael would have to learn how to ride tailboards sometime, certainly, but was this the ideal way? Gatzko thought longingly about the great rail junctions at Chicago, where he had learnt the tricks. He could almost feel the peculiar jolting which resulted from clinging so close to the wheels.

Michael was dropping asleep. Dreaming about trains, probably. Gatzko switched off the light and went on leaning against the window, thinking about trains too.

He might have gone on woolgathering there all night but for a somewhat drastic interruption.

Suddenly the door burst open and the woman came hurtling in as if she had a hurricane behind her. Her eyes were completely round with excitement and her hair and clothes and arms were standing up in all directions. Gatzko found himself staggering back as if he had really been hit by a gust of wind.

"Have you seen! Have you seen!" she panted. "The Northern Lights are visible!"

"What's this, what's this?" Gatzko asked with interest.

"Didn't you see it too? But it's a marvel."

"Had a vision, eh, Cassandra? You certainly look like you did."

"Well, I just thought it was the afterglow from sunset. There was a red light in the sky. And then I realized I was looking north."

"Sure it's not a fire?"

"I've seen enough fires to know what one of those looks like," she scoffed. "Besides this was over the mountain. Look— look—I'm sure you can still see it—oh no, this faces the other way."

"Let's go and look out of your window."

He couldn't help catching her excitement. They ran together to the other room and stared out. Suddenly Bott gave a little gasp and fell on to the floor. Gatzko stooped down to heave her up and found her too limp and heavy to move. She clutched at him and gibbered.

"Hey, Cassandra, what's wrong?"

"There's—something—coming up behind the mountain."

In the starlight her face was grey. Gatzko put his arm round her and tried to support her. He peered curiously out through the dirty glass.

"There are some stars rising," he said.

"In the north?" Bott tried to raise herself up by the window-sill, weak and awkward with fear. "No, no, it's not stars. Look, there's Auriga a bit to the east. There shouldn't be anything there. It's not stars. It's eyes!"

Gatzko looked at the red sparks, gulped and held her tighter. A more frightening spectacle was her hand, clutching the window-sill so hard that the knuckles stood out like cogs.

"What is it?" she asked piteously. "Eyes—and spines—oh!"

Gatzko felt her muscles tighten and released her. She rose up before him at the window, a far more alarming sight than the red glimmer in the sky which was affecting her so strongly. She turned towards him. Talk about burning eyes and spines.

"It's the dragon," she said. "I should have known. The dragon of Wales who appears in the sky as an omen."

"Jesus Christ," Gatzko said. He fumbled for a cigarette. It was his turn to feel weak.

"Look, can't you see his claws and scales glinting? He'll cover the whole sky in a minute. Over there, see, that's his wing, where the stars are blotted out."

It was impossible not to be affected by the awe and delight in her voice. Gatzko looked, saw that a patch of sky had indeed gone dark, nodded and shivered.

Bott's voice vibrated. "He appeared above King Uther's deathbed when the whole kingdom was disintegrating and Uther was in despair. His wife had been abducted and he thought he had no heir. That night the Red Dragon appeared in the sky, but it was black, and Uther knew it meant death. And as soon as he had accepted that, it changed into a ship with a dragon prow and in the ship sat a crowned child, and that was King Arthur, Uther's son who he didn't know he had."

Gatzko listened in astonishment.

"Uther had to accept and rejoice in the omen of death, that was the thing. He knew the dragon was the dragon of Logres, that vanquished the white dragon at Carfax, when Merlin was a boy. The dragon—that one out there—is the symbol of everything that's good in the country. And as soon as Uther had made himself be glad of it even when he thought it meant death it changed into a portent of hope. So he was called Uther Pendragon ever after."

"Is this true," Gatzko asked, "or is it your own philosophy?"

"Both," Bott said. Gatzko wilted before such conviction. She was smiling down at him, her eyes full of fierce joy, a veritable Brunnhilde. She commanded him, "Look there! Look at him! Isn't he glorious?"

Gatzko could only nod. What, after all, was that great dark patch, if not a dragon? How could he say she was wrong?

"What does it mean? The dragon of Logres appearing to me?" she said wonderingly. She threw open the window and leant out, her lips working as if she were reading something. Her eyes opened wider and wider.

Bott herself was amazed at the things she had just been saying. She had never heard that interpretation of the old legend until she found herself telling it. She had not even known that she believed so literally in the story.

"What you mean, in fact," said Gatzko, "is that you have to surrender to fate, and this dragon or whatever is fate? What fate do you think it means for you, that you must surrender to?"

Gatzko said this innocently, simply because for the moment he believed in the story too and was going along with what Bott was saying. But to Bott, when she heard it, everything suddenly came clear. Surrender! That was what it meant! She must die, she must yield, she must surrender, and joyfully, for the sake of this poor fellow who saw nothing clearly. She flung open her arms to the dragon, and he parted those burning jaws, engulfing half the sky, and let out that old, old scream of victory which had rung out over Carfax, and from which, in Bott's opinion, British history dated. All on fire with gladness, Bott opened her throat and answered.

Appalled and stunned, Gatzko heard her jubilant prehistoric cry and dropped his cigarette. She was up on the window-sill, Brunnhilde to the life. She turned, the sky supporting her, nothing clumsy about her now, and looked exultantly at him. Then she jumped down on top of him, flinging her arms round his neck. Gatzko fell under her. His last coherent thought was that he would never have credited her with such strength.

It was just light when Bott climbed out. Guests were supposed to remain upstairs till the breakfast gong at seven-thirty but Bott awoke with the birds singing round her and the sun about to rise and knew she could not, for any rule in the world, bear to stay indoors one second longer.

She pulled her siren-suit over her pyjamas and looked out. It was bitterly, mistily cold. She went out on to the landing, where Gatzko's green windjacket still hung draped over the banisters where he had thrown it when they came in that night. Bott listened. Everything was still, as if waiting. The jacket seemed to glow across the landing at her. With a sudden daring movement she reached for it and zipped herself in. She went back into her room and the morning was all glorious outside. She breathed the cold in with deep gasps, sitting astride the window-sill, and started to climb down.

This was something she had often done, and ought, by now, to have lost its novelty value, but today she felt as if she were scaling a fairy castle; her breath kept coming out in great heaves of excitement.

She came down the bathroom drainpipe and jumped to the ground. The tops of the trees behind the house were in darkness but light was just beginning to seep through the lower branches. She set off towards them, hugging the green jacket round herself. She came to the trees and stopped. There was thick copse between them, with the dawn welling through. She longed to get past. She trampled up and down in the wet nettles looking for a gap. At last she found a tiny winding track leading into the copse. Holding the windjacket round her as if she were afraid it would fall off if she didn't, she tiptoed in.

It was dark in there. She felt sure she must, in that jacket, be shedding light as she went. Everything was magic and holy. But in a few steps she came suddenly to a great field, full of early light. Bott's excitement got the better of her at last. She bounded out into the field and started running across it, laughing and dancing and twirling and opening her arms to the sun.

Bott had never before been in a state of such complete joy. She danced and ran through the dewy tussocks to the rough stone wall at the far side of the field. She climbed on to it and sat panting and swelling with gladness until she did not know how to contain it without floating off the ground altogether.

Presently she realized how wet and cold the wall was she was sitting on. She climbed off and wandered back across the field, the trees dark shapes in the morning mist.

So here she was, utterly, totally committed to a strange Yugoslav who had told her to call him Gatzko. Gatzko—she could hardly pronounce the word. And never in her life had she been so happy. She felt she had never even known what joy was. This was something she had certainly not expected when she jumped into his arms last night. She had done it feeling more grim and dutiful than anything else.

She was relieved of a burden she had always carried alone, the burden of herself. It no longer depended on her what she

was or what she did. She could have floated away like a curl of
mist, she felt so light at heart.

There was a duty about it all the same. She knew what it
was. Perhaps she had known all along, all the time she had
been disliking and evading him. That poor man who knew
nothing, understood nothing, was certain of nothing; oh, she
could give him so much, show him how the patterns of life
fitted together, prove to him that there was a meaning to
everything and power behind all. She knew she could, she
knew she had to. What a wonderful task lay before her. All
the field seemed to open up ahead of her into a great vaulted
forest of light, which went up and up and on and on, trees
from before the beginning of time. Bott started running again,
but not from haste; she seemed to herself to be moving like a
runner in a slow-motion film. With a century between each
step she bounded forward into the light.

Gatzko would have slept late if Michael had not toppled the
two toothmugs he was playing with from the mantelpiece on
to the floor, at about seven o'clock. Gatzko shouted at Michael
and found he had a headache. It was beastly cold and he could
not find his windjacket. He got back into bed and told Michael
to tell the landlady he was ill and could she bring him breakfast in bed. He lit a cigarette and waited hopefully, thinking
about the express to London he was going to get that day.

Mary sat in the train eating a pecan log roll which Mr.
Wilson had given her at the station. She finished it and looked
for another, but it was the last. She gulped at her disappointment. Did they even have pecan candy in Chicago? Or did
everyone there just chew gum?

Her attention was suddenly caught by a fat, grained, white
thing lying on her lap. It was her own hand. Mary was
shocked. Was this what she was, then, was this how she
seemed to other people? She fingered her cheek; it felt strange.
To think that this was all others ever saw of her, that this was

what she appeared to them to be, a puddingy white human body! It was not so much an unpleasant thought as simply odd. But then the question arose, what did she appear to herself to be, if not that? Mary tried to think. She had got as far as visualizing a dark green light, glowing rather dimly, in a cave or a tunnel maybe, when she fell asleep, although in fact it was only three hours since she had got up.

By the time she reached Chicago her father, with Bott and a baby brother Mary had never heard of, were all in London. Michael still had not ridden a tailboard. Their journey to Paddington was legal, conventional and comfortable, with reserved corner seats. All three tickets were paid for by Bott.

5

THE VERY WALLS of Leadenhall Market smell of centuries of wet vegetables, Bott thought, as she found herself forced to inhale by one at close quarters. The passage was at most three feet wide but there were more people trying to push their way up and down it than on any normal sized London thorough-fare. Bott breathed deeply at the wall. Wet vegetables, wet bricks and something else which could be her imagination, but she thought was nitre.

She lingered a moment too long and found herself firmly jammed, as a very fat woman, very much encumbered, waddled by. Bott would have chuckled if she had had room to expand her ribs, picturing the scene if they really got wedged. By making concerted efforts in opposite directions they managed to get free, and the chuckle, a bit delayed, came out with a hiccup. Bott called over her shoulder. "I'm sorry. I hope your shopping isn't squashed?" The woman waddled on, too determined on fighting her way down the passage to hear. Bott did not mind. She wriggled clear of the passage into the main hall of the market. There, free at last to move, she did a little hop and skip and trod on a tomato.

"Oh heck," she said apologetically, and felt bound to join the queue at the stall it had come from. She looked frantically about for something on the stall she could possibly buy. There seemed to be nothing but carrots and tomatoes. She already had two pounds of carrots at home, a present from Mrs. Weingartner. "I was just looking for some carrots," she said to the stallkeeper, when her turn came. He had seen the tomato and was looking sourly at her.

The man's face changed. "Carrots, dearie? Well, you've

looked far enough. These are the only carrots worth queueing for anywhere in London."

"How splendid," Bott said enthusiastically, liking the man's cheerful face and his dirty apron and the stall. It was like a print of Old London, with street-criers and lavender-sellers, not like anything modern at all. She fumbled for the right change and wandered off down the middle of the hall. Yes, exactly like one of those really charming old prints that people hunt for in antique shops and treasure. The crowd made a pictorial unity but if you looked closely you found there was a story in each group of figures. That little child crying into his brother's knees, what was behind that? In the print they'd be the Abandoned Innocents, and that lady looking furtively about and clinging to the man would be their guilty mother. Only their clothes were wrong. They should be wearing black stockings and hats with ribbons.

Bott meandered out of the market and into Gracechurch Street, curiously examining the passers-by. People! Dozens and dozens of them! It was intoxicating simply to be among them. She could never get used to it.

Dimly she became aware that her arm was aching. She was carrying an awful weight. Gosh, she must have about five pounds of carrots there. Whatever had she done, given him the whole ten-bob note? Guiltily she remembered Mrs. Weingartner's carrots too. That girl across the road looked haggard, what was the matter, trouble at home, was it, or just the general woes of life these days? Bott had an urge to rush across the street and tell her that she was beautiful and life was good, but at that moment the bag which held the carrots began to split. Those carrots were behaving like a tiresome child, constantly wanting her attention. Bott gave them an impatient poke.

She could glaze and sweeten them to make a fruit tart. She was calculating how much sugar this would take when she was suddenly seized with a desire to make toffee for Michael.

Bott had never made toffee in her life. She had only the

vaguest idea of the ingredients, and those—syrup, sugar— seemed hopelessly unobtainable. Oh, but wouldn't it be lovely, she thought, to taste toffee again. It couldn't be good for Michael either never to get anything sweet. She decided to start saving up sugar. Mrs. Weingartner could almost certainly show her how to make toffee. Or she might even ask Gatzko himself. It was just the kind of funny thing he'd know.

Bott's feet clattered as she half-ran down Lovat Lane. Here at last were faces she knew. There were about six fishmongers in the lane, all of whom were her good friends and called "Afternoon!" at her. She ran into two or three of the wharf workers too with whom she exchanged a few bawdy jokes. Six months ago she would have been shocked. Now she enjoyed it. She had also come to like the smell of fish, which was just as well.

The whole neighbourhood knew her, as one of the only females between London Bridge and Tower Bridge (the other was Mrs. Weingartner). The harassed secretaries never came down further than Eastcheap and the fishsellers never really left the wharves. Lovat Lane counted as wharf country.

Bott went into her home; the lair, they called it. There was nothing else it could be called really, as it was only a bit of bombed-out office behind a shop in Lovat Lane. Gatzko and Bott had set up a makeshift camp here, tucked away in the ruins, using any old rubble that came to hand for furniture.

The shop was the only one in Lovat Lane which did not sell fish. It was very small, looked far more ancient than it could possibly be, was extremely picturesque, and had a deep brown sign covering half the façade and shutters covering most of the rest. On the sign was lettered elaborately "Dairy &" with the last word blotchily painted out. Gatzko and Bott had tried and tried to decipher what else the shop had been besides a dairy. Gatzko decided firmly that the obliteration dated from the Act making opium traffic illegal. It was a nice theory, if improbable. Whoever had painted out the last word had also decided that the first two looked a bit shabby and had carefully outlined them, with even more curls and flourishes. And since these obviously Victorian additions, the sign had not been touched.

Not only was the shop unique in Lovat Lane, as being a dairy instead of a fishmonger; it was probably unique in all London, if not in the rest of the world as well. The Weingartners seemed quite unaware that there was anything odd in living alone in the middle of the City of London, or that a shop, whatever it sold, might possibly benefit from a little window-display. The shop door appeared to be camouflaged as one of the enormous shutters. You had to know it was there to realize it was a door at all. It was actually an old stable door, opening in two halves, with big beautiful rusty bolts.

Bott went through this and through the shop into a little waste plot which had once been a courtyard, had been built on, bombed and reverted to being some sort of yard. Ramshackle brick buildings rose all round, housing dingy offices. Bott knew most of the people in these too. They were mostly two-man efforts, no smart secretaries, but seedy Armenians and Poles; quite friendly though. Bott waved at them as she went through. Gatzko referred to them all as "Mr. Eugenides, the Smyrna merchant". Bott had come to know "The Waste Land" almost by heart herself.

The office on the far side, which was the most ramshackle of the lot, was the lair.

Almost the whole house was gone but the ground floor office, which had its ceiling intact and was really perfectly all right, and the corridor, which was half-open. But at least it was sheltered and it made some sort of studio for Gatzko. He declared that the open side made an ideal studio window. Bott was always amazed at his hardiness. He would work in it for hours, and she couldn't spend five minutes there without freezing to death. He didn't welcome her in anyway, and his sculptures frightened her, with their twisted involuted shapes.

The lair had grown considerably since they moved in. At first they simply lived in the office. Then came the studio. Now

Gatzko was trying to make an extra room out of the bit on the other side of the studio. It had one sound wall, after all, even if the entire building had apparently collapsed just there. He had got hold of some bits of corrugated iron and said he was making a room for Michael, although Bott was rather sceptical about this endeavour.

Humming to herself, Bott dumped the carrots in the kitchen (behind the counter; she served through a pigeon-hole. Gatzko maintained that the place must have been a travel office) and went back to the shop.

"Oh, how glorious it is to be warm," she exclaimed, collapsing on to the stool by the counter.

"Cup of tea?" Mrs. Weingartner asked.

Bott couldn't resist. "Oh, yes please," she said, fumbling for the right coppers.

"See what your little boy built this morning," Mrs. Weingartner said, filling a cup from the huge urn which dominated the shop and kept it permanently full of sweet-smelling steam. The Weingartners had not managed to distinguish between the functions of a shop and a café. "He built an entire palace from the soap packets, look." She gestured behind the counter. "I don't know what I shall do if I need to sell one!"

"Oh, you shouldn't let him mess about with your things. I'm so sorry," Bott said anxiously, although she couldn't help admiring Michael's palace.

"Why? He never breaks anything," said Mrs. Weingartner.

"No, I'm the smasher among us," Bott admitted.

She sipped her tea and looked contentedly round the shop. It was so cosy here. She had never felt so much at home anywhere as she did installed on the stool in the little nook between the tea urn and the cereal shelves, nattering with Mrs. Weingartner. Quite often a fishman or two would crowd in too, for the warmth and a cup of tea, although Mrs. Weingartner's tea was as peculiar as everything else about the Dairy &. It was heavy, sticky, appallingly sweet and strangely scented. Gatzko had a theory about that too. He said that the

c

Weingartners must have been café owners in Central Europe once and still made tea as they would coffee, with hot milk. The shop certainly smelt like stewed Carnation; and yet, there was a curious tang, a pungent smell of spices, which never came out of any English tin. But when Bott argued he merely looked at her with amusement and said, "Well, of course. The walls of the place must be impregnated with opium."

It was one of the things which irritated Bott most that she could never tell whether he was joking or not.

She had found the heat and smell nauseating at first, but now she loved the place and everything about it. She loved the Weingartners, almost incomprehensible in their mixture of Yiddish and Cockney accents. Mrs. Weingartner was little and tubby and her husband was big and tubby, with a waxy white bald head. He stood head and chest above Gatzko. Gatzko had hailed him excitedly at first, as a fellow escaper from the Nazis, but Mr. Weingartner had looked blankly at him and said that he and his family had lived in this shop for ten generations.

"Well, you must have married and died young," Gatzko muttered to this, and Bott giggled, but Mr. Weingartner, sublimely aloof to such scepticism, did not even hear.

As far as they were concerned, the Weingartners were conventional, normal, good folk, engaged in keeping the Law and keeping shop. They did both very thoroughly. The shop was open until they went to bed at ten and open again immediately they got up at five. They saw nothing odd about this; the shop was their home, and they couldn't simply stop living there at night, could they? But not for the world would they sell anything on a Saturday. Once Bott forgot to buy bread and came to Mrs. Weingartner on a Saturday morning. She went away with her ears stinging from the reproof she got.

They saw nothing odd either about having an unmarried couple living in a bombed-out office at the end of their garden, which was just as well. Mrs. Weingartner had practically adopted Michael. On very cold nights Bott and Gatzko sent him to sleep with her. Gatzko had brought in an ancient paraffin stove, which roared cheerfully and needed far more looking after than Michael did. It was more use as company than as heating.

It was Gatzko who had discovered the shop and set his heart on living there. His enthusiasm spread to Bott. He had charmed both the Weingartners. He had spent so much time in the shop that he was as good as living there already. He discovered the office and spent a couple more days mucking about in it. He brought Mrs. Weingartner a present of flowers, and soon after brought in the paraffin stove and enlisted Mr. Weingartner's help in getting it to go. The next day he took Bott to see the lair. He did not tell her that he intended to live there; she was delighted with it, thinking that now he would have somewhere to work (the hotel they were living in in Paddington sternly forbade it). Bott had a long talk with Mrs. Weingartner about Gatzko's great talent and how frustrating it was that he had nowhere to work. Mrs. Weingartner was impressed by the story and deeply sympathetic with their troubles. She gave Gatzko a kitchen knife for his carving. (Gatzko was genuinely touched by this and used it for everything afterwards.) And Bott was pleased to find such a friend. She told Gatzko so.

"Don't you feel that shop is really a home?" she asked him. He smiled his odd I've-got-a-secret smile. Next morning she found they were no longer on the hotel books. She went hastily along to Lovat Lane and found Gatzko and Michael setting up house in the lair. They did not even listen to Bott's objections. She decided they needed a woman's hand in this. She went back to the hotel, fetched her things and stoutly moved in with them. It was true that Gatzko had not actually asked her to, and indeed appeared to have tried to slip away without her, that morning when she rose to find the room given up. But he had after all taken her to see the lair, and did not seem to object to her presence there once she was in.

The whole business had taken less than ten days. Bott had scarcely left the City since.

Bott realized she had been nearly an hour just soaking in the steam of the shop, drinking one cup of tea and chewing each mouthful as if it were tough meat. Mrs. Weingartner sat and watched her benignly. Bott stopped reminiscing, hastily swallowed the rest of the tea and hurried home to make the carrot tart.

Michael came running out from Mrs. Weingartner's bedroom as Bott went into the garden. "Come on, Michael," she said. "I'm going to make toffee. Are you going to help me?"

"Toffee?" Michael said bewildered. The poor little mite didn't even know what it was. Bott firmly took out the whole week's sugar and started to melt it in hot water. She cooked on a Primus on a shelf which maybe once held tickets for all over the world, as Gatzko liked to believe. She plopped in a lump of gelatine to melt and noticed, too late, that she had forgotten to unwrap the gelatine. She fished and stirred but the wrapping must have melted too.

"Has it gone?" Michael asked.

"Looks as if it has. Well, toffee wouldn't be toffee without the toffee paper, would it now."

"Paper is quite nice to eat," Michael said consolingly.

"Don't! Do I starve you as much as that? Let's make the pastry, shall we?"

There was no spare fat so they made it without. Michael was a good deal better than she was at mixing the paste and rolling it with a bottle, so she left it to him. He worked energetically, talking to himself. The pastry began to get somewhat grubby but after all it was going to be cooked. Bott turned her attention to the mixture which was to be half tart glaze, half toffee. She had put it on the counter while she boiled the carrots, and it had gone and set on her. Beginning to feel a little anxious, she divided it in half, and had to use a knife. However much gelatine had she put in, then? Or was the paper to blame? Frantically she tried to re-melt the toffee. She thought one put milk in toffee, but was really not quite sure; still, she had to do something to make it different from the rest of the mixture which she intended to glaze the carrots with. It didn't help that she had to cook in two burnt-out enamel pans rescued from a rubbish dump, which kept coming off in rusty flakes into her cooking. One had a hole just where a hole was most provoking, where she wanted to stir. She had mended it with a milk bottle top but it wasn't a great success. Bott dug a hole in the top of a tin of condensed milk and poured the lot into the toffee. It was setting stiffer and stiffer every second; the condensed milk sat in puddles. She had the Primus on almost dangerously high. No jelly had the right to stay so set so hot. Now the milk began to thicken too. Bott used all her force to stir it round. Sweating and panting, she held it up and saw that the milk bottle top had come off the hole. Perhaps it was just as well, after all, that the mixture was far too stiff to pour. In panic she dug the streaky goo out and plunked the lot into her hiking billycan.

"Now, Bott! Now look!" Michael called exultantly. "See, I've got it all in!"

Aghast, Bott saw that he had indeed got all seven pounds of carrots in. He had chopped them all. He must also have "got in" the whole three-pound bag of flour. He had used as a pie-dish the old tin bowl which served for everything from a mixing-bowl for Gatzko's clay to a sink substitute when they got round to doing the washing-up. Resourceful of Michael, but God in heaven, this was going to be the biggest pie ever made. Bott felt like the funny woman in a pantomime. She began to laugh.

"It's beautiful, Michael, absolutely beautiful! Far better than the muck I've been making. Wow! Whoopee! Let's see, what else can we put in?"

Laughing together, they started to hunt round the lair. Michael emptied in half a tin of cloves before Bott could stop him. Well, all right then. Bott emptied in two little bottles

Mrs. Weingartner had given her, which turned out to be the ancient remains of cochineal and vanilla essence. Quite suddenly Bott smelt something she knew. Toffee.

She rushed to the stove and realized that she had left the billycan on the heat. The mixture had gone all black and burnt and looked horrible, but it smelt deliciously of caramel.

"Why, Michael, it's come out right after all!"

Excited by such unexpected success, on an impulse she splodged in the rest of the gelatine and syrup. Michael was throwing cornflakes and goodness knows what else into the pie. She gave him a spoon of the caramel to suck. Yes, it was certainly delicious, if not quite how she remembered pre-war toffee. Giggling conspiratorially, they dug the black mess out of the billycan and stirred it into the pie, along with the cornflakes, cloves, grass stalks (grass stalks? heavens! she really ought to have kept a better eye on Michael) and seven pounds of carrots. It was becoming a marvellous dark red colour, thanks to the cochineal.

"This is going to be very, very nourishing," she told Michael. "We'll be living off it for a week."

Triumphantly they carried the great bowl across to Mrs. Weingartner's kitchen and asked if they could put it in her oven.

"Blimey!" Mrs. Weingartner cried. "What on earth is that?"

She never said "Blimey" quite right. The emphasis was wrong somehow and she always paused a little self-consciously, as if it were a phrase she had learnt. She sounded distinctly foreign saying it, although no doubt it was in reality quite natural to her.

"Just a pie we've been making," Bott said modestly.

Mrs. Weingartner sniffed suspiciously at it. She didn't seem to think it smelt as good as Michael and Bott did, but said tolerantly, "Well, we can try to bake it. There is nothing in my oven now."

Getting it into the oven was rather like manoeuvring a large ship into a small and awkward harbour. It was in at last, and they went back to the lair feeling pretty satisfied.

Bott hummed as she heaped all the messy pans and spoons together. That was going to be a job and a half, later on. Meanwhile it was getting dark, Gatzko would be in any second and she wanted to get the place warm for him. There was half an hour's work involved in lighting the stove and he did it more than his share of times. Bott wanted to give him something really nice, tonight. She did the stove, got the candles out, rearranged the bedding (which meant laying out the sheepskin more artistically and draping Gatzko's old Indian Navajo rug more decoratively across the draughty partition which separated them from the "new room" Gatzko was building). The sheepskin was their greatest pride. It was a sheepskin jacket come to pieces, given to Gatzko by a workmate. The leather was in such bad condition that his wife had refused even to give it to jumble. But Gatzko and Bott simply cut off the sleeves and laid the thing inside out on their bed, and gloated over it.

Bott lovingly rearranged these two objects and put yesterday's potatoes on to cook, scraping the worst of the muck out of one of the toffee pans first, and wishing she had some sauce or meat or something to put with them, to make shepherd's pie perhaps.

This, she thought, is domesticity. Me, domesticized. Still she could not properly comprehend what she had done. It was not easy to go back on nearly twenty-five years of resigned, even determined, spinsterhood. Longer, really, for even before she consciously called herself "the unicorn girl", the consecrated virgin (heavens! what a pompous little prig she must have been!) she had more or less accepted the prospect of a lonely life.

I've given in, she thought, prodding the potatoes. I'm exactly like all other women after all. There is a man in my life. She had to repeat it aloud to make it seem real. "There is a man in my life," Bott said.

"You said that," Gatzko said, "as if you were saying you'd found a fly in your cooking."

Bott jumped. "Oh, Gatzko! I didn't know you'd come in."

"No, you were stirring that stuff till it ought to be cooked by friction. It can't be good for it, whatever it is."

"It's only spuds," Bott said. "Oh, dear, yes, I do seem to have mashed them up a bit. Will you mind?"

"Of course not. I'll like it better for the extra loving care it's had."

"I'm sorry," she said humbly. "I wasn't giving it my attention. I was thinking."

"What about?" Gatzko asked, and changed his mind. "No, that's a question I don't ask, isn't it? You'll answer philosophy."

"Oh, don't," Bott said. "Please don't. I will tell you what I was thinking, if you like. I was thinking about you."

Gatzko did not answer. It had cost Bott a lot to say that; could it be he hadn't even heard? She turned towards him. He was sitting on the sheepskin looking at nothing. No, he hadn't heard. He gave her a jab like that about the philosophy and then stopped listening. Bott turned back and drooped into her saucepan. But as she poked the watery spuds disconsolately she felt his hand on her shoulder. She turned back and found herself looking right into those black eyes. In anyone else you would have called that expression tender but there was never any knowing what Gatzko felt. He stood scrutinizing her, blocking her light, but she could not look away. The light of the paraffin lamp shone through his hair, showing how greasy it was, and his face looked all oily and his jaw dark and he smelt fish and sweat, but his eyes were glowing and Bott in his grasp felt as limp as her mashed potatoes. Suddenly he kissed her, a lopsided kiss on the corner of her mouth. Her lip was caught on her teeth and it hurt, but she tried to respond. Before she knew what was happening the arm embracing her was shaking the saucepan, and Gatzko was saying calmly, "This mash has had enough and too much." She suffocated against his sweater, pinned between him and the cooking shelf, while he extinguished the Primus and turned the potatoes into another of the dirty bowls. Cautiously she felt her sore lip with her tongue. Was it really usual, this lopsided kiss she always got from Gatzko? Did other men kiss that way?

He reached for the tin plates, still giving her that amused tender look. "Let's eat this, shall we?"

"I'll call Michael," Bott said faintly, and wriggled past him to the garden, where Michael was playing. She had long ago given up trying to make him come in when it grew dark and cold. "Supper's ready, pet," she said to him. He looked up from his game, and damn it, he was smiling with just that same amused tender look that his father had just knocked her out with. She fled back into the lair.

Gatzko was laying forks and mugs out on the floor (there was no table). Bott salted and peppered the spuds vigorously and pushed the saucepan through the wire pigeon-hole on the counter, or as she had determined to call it, the serving-hatch. She put water on to heat for custard (no milk, too bad). She leant against the wall, looking through the serving-hatch and thinking fondly how cosy it was. The saucepan steaming in the middle of the floor, her man bending over it with his curly hair falling in the candle, dear little Michael running round chattering, bringing pillows to sit on. Even the battered brick wall looked mellow and comforting, and the light flickered up inside Gatzko's convoluted clay thing which stood against it—"Thinking", he called it. He treasured it. It was the first piece he had made in his new studio. He told Bott, one evening early in the autumn when he had been unusually affectionate, that it was a sculpture of her.

She had taken it as a compliment; tonight suddenly she was not sure. He and Michael crouched over the food in the ring of light, talking animatedly as Michael served out, but she could not understand what they were saying. She was frightened. She felt like a stranger outside, looking in at their warm

c*

circle. What was she doing, standing behind her silly counter watching them as if through a window, and why couldn't she hear what they were saying? With a whimper of fright she rushed round, tripped and fell against Gatzko, and buried her face in his smelly sweater. "Ah, come on," he said. "Don't eat me, eat your potato. It isn't so bad after all."

The kindness in his voice made Bott feel better. She sighed and settled her skirt, reproaching herself for being so neurotic, when Gatzko startled her again by saying, "Bring a little warmth with you."

"Me? Bring warmth?" she stuttered. But just now it had seemed that he had the warmth while she was out in the cold! She stared at him.

"Hey, honey, what are you looking so scared for? I only meant can you bring the roarer over?"

"Oh, I'm sorry," Bott said, uncertain whether she was relieved or disappointed. She carried the paraffin stove carefully across and set it down beside "Thinking". "I'm all nerves tonight," she explained apologetically. "Everything you say I think you mean something awful."

Gatzko looked at her with concern. "There, now. You mustn't be so afraid of me," he said. The lines of fear in her face were making grooves in his mind, twisting tunnels and furrows in the psyche, worry-knots in the brain. He studied Bott, feeling the shape of a new clay piece growing out of this. "Tree-roots" could wait for a bit. This interested him more. He could portray absolutely the anxiety in Bott's face; he could see exactly how it would be. He could almost see the teased, taut coils of her grey cerebral matter. He looked hard at her to fix the image in his mind. It was like taking an X-ray. That done, his original pity and affection flooded back. Had there been an awkward pause? He wasn't sure. He heaped potato on to her plate and put his arm round her.

"What did you think I meant?" he asked. "You don't think I'm such a monster really, do you?"

But Bott had felt that he was looking at her oddly and was

still uncomfortable. She smoothed her hair distractedly, wondering what was going on. She did not guess that he was merely considering the convolutions of her brain.

Gatzko went on, squeezing her slightly, "Such a tense bundle of nerves! What's the matter, honey? You mustn't be scared of me. I'm just Gatzko, gentle Gatzko."

He looked and sounded it too. Bott forgot that he had ever teased her. She could not remember what had frightened her so just now. He was kind and sweet, and she was a neurotic fool who gave herself the jitters with her own fantasies.

"Now. Stop fixing me with your glittering eye, and eat up while it's hot. Here. I'll fix you something."

Bott watched his thin dark shape as he moved about the lair. He gave her a drink, out of their dwindling supply of elderberry wine, in one of the mugs. This was a treat indeed. She took it gratefully and snuggled down on the mat beside the roarer. Oh, wasn't it lovely and snug here, wasn't everything wonderful, wasn't Gatzko an angel, a funny little dear dark angel. She smiled radiantly at him and Michael.

Gatzko said, "Wow, that had a rapid effect. You must have needed it pretty badly."

"Oh, not really," Bott said, ashamed of herself. "We've had a good afternoon. Haven't we, Michael?"

"We made," Michael said excitedly, gesturing and nearly knocking the candle over, "the big-gest pie in the world."

"Did you now! How's that for austerity!"

"Oh, it was an austerity pie, all right, just big," Bott said hastily. "I wonder how it's getting on. Michael, shall we go and look?"

All the fun of the evening had returned. She ran giggling out with Michael. Gatzko lit a cigarette, marvelling at her. One moment she sees a ghost, but give her a drink and a kind word or two, and she thinks she's at a funfair. He blew smoke rings at "Thinking", while "Fretting" came clearer and clearer in his mind. It ought to be metal really but he had none of the apparatus for metal. It was time he gave some thought to technicalities. Already, from laziness, he had made an un-warranted number of unfired clays. When he wanted anything fired he had to cart it over to the other bank where he had made friends with the foreman on a brickyard near Cotton's Wharf.

He heard laughter and bumping at the door, and in came Michael staggering under the pie, with Bott behind. He dumped it before Gatzko and said, "There!"

"Jesus," Gatzko said.

Bott was scurrying about with plates and knives. It was good to see someone so gay. He sniffed at the pie, which smelt vaguely of baking. "Hey! This smells terrific!" he shouted. "I want the half of it right now!"

"Me too!" Michael sang, dancing about.

"Why, I believe you really would divide it in two if I weren't around to serve," Bott said in amazement. "And you know what went into it, too, Michael. Oh, I wish this custard would boil, I'm longing to try it."

Ceremoniously, she cut the pie, and Gatzko and Michael craned over to see. The filling was a deep sticky crimson, and bubbled slightly. "Jesus," Gatzko said again, his appetite wan-ing.

"It's only toffee," Bott said anxiously, watching his face.

"Come on! I said I wanted the half of it! Toffee! I'd like to hear what our Chancellor would have to say to that. Wow, I didn't know I was so hungry."

Bott suspected he was pretending. But she tried a bit and was surprised to find it not bad at all. She grinned unre-pentantly at Gatzko. Bet he wouldn't be eating pie at all now, any kind of pie, but for her.

"You're a genius, Bott," he said. "I thought I'd eaten every kind of pie there is. I've had cherry pie, pecan pie, custard pie, apple pie with cheese and apple pie without, but I never, never ate a pie half so interesting as this one. Let's finish up that elderberry."

On a glass shelf in a coffee shop, in competition with the

cherry, pecan, custard and apple pies, Bott's toffee pie might not have done so well; but as it was, and with the help of a few drinks, Gatzko found himself sincerely declaring he'd never eaten anything so good. As he said this he choked. He managed to prevent himself swallowing something which turned out to be a piece of wrapping paper.

Bott and Michael looked guiltily at each other, and Michael started to giggle. "Oh, dear," Bott said. "I knew I should have fished for it a bit longer. It's the gelatine paper. I hoped it had melted. Oh, dear, I am so sorry."

Gatzko looked at her. He could imagine her, big, gawky Bott, rapturously stirring for him, whatever this incredible mess was made of; dropping in the paper, desperately angling for it, praying it would come up on her plate and not his. He started to laugh inside. How he had changed her from the stiff never-give-in manhating female he had met striding around the mountains. Now this was the kind of woman he could love. He decided to put "Fretting" aside until he could fix up a metal furnace. He saw a new sculpture, flat, squashy, full of smooth receptive hollows and recesses. "Submission". This would have to be clay, it would have to be stroked and fondled and fingered smooth. Not that there was anything strokeable or smooth about Bott, but never mind.

"Bott, honey," he said, and this time there was all the genuine tenderness in his voice she had ever hoped to hear, "I want another piece of toffee pie."

"Aren't you coming to bed?" Bott whispered, not to wake Michael.

"No, not yet. I'm going to work for a bit. You go to sleep."

"You'll be so tired."

"I want to work," Gatzko said obstinately. "I wouldn't sleep if I did go to bed."

Bott sighed and snuggled down under the sheepskin. It was always like this. Whenever he seemed in the least bit loving he would go away and work for five or six hours. Still she knew it was splendid really that she could get him in the mood to work, since that was after all by far the most important thing to him. He once admitted to her that he had carved nothing since he had been in England, until they settled in Lovat Lane. Apparently he had spent his whole time in England just moving about, tramping, with Michael. Just like her!

She could hear everything he did in his studio, although he seemed to imagine he was insulated from the world there. She listened to him breathing heavily and trampling to and fro; holding his breath while he shaped some intricacy, letting it out with a whistle.

She was cold and not too comfortable in bed. It was a very old sofa with the back let down. Dim red light of London seeped in, and far-away city sounds, but here there were no noises but ships hooting. The wharf clamour began in the small hours, but she had learnt to sleep through it. Lovat Lane came alive at about eight.

Her head was buzzing with the alcohol she had drunk, but the gaiety of the evening was gone. She knew Gatzko would not come to bed until very late, if at all. She felt a tiny bit sad. She was sure he had still not realized that it was against the very grain of her being to do what she was doing now: cook and fuss and keep house, and lie in someone else's bed, waiting, depending on him. That was how she seemed to spend her life now, waiting for Gatzko. She could not eat till he came in, she had to go out with him if he wanted, she had in fact to live for him.

She had to wait, too, for him to tell her anything. She had learnt at the very beginning how useless it was asking him questions. He had told her a few stories about himself and Michael in England. He had never told her anything more about his life before that. She never had found out who Michael's mother was. But if Gatzko was telling the truth about being a partisan, then he must have been born in Yugoslavia; Bott liked to imagine a passionate, transitory romance between Gatzko and some brave woman guerilla, in the hills of Bosnia.

She could hear him working furiously now, slapping the clay, stamping about. She began to feel warmer and better. After all she had already accomplished a lot, getting him working again. Some day she would change his cynicism. She knew there was a deep-down positive meaning to life, but she knew it instinctively. It was not a thing you could expect a man to seize all at once, especially when he was as convinced as Gatzko that the surface was all that counted.

Gatzko only meant to work a couple of hours, but when he stopped, exhausted, and went into the bombed ruins of the back of the office for some fresh air, it was beginning to be light.

6

BOTT WOKE GROGGILY to find Gatzko shaking her and whispering urgently. "Bott! Bott! Come and see! It's the brown fog of a winter dawn!"

"Eh? eh? what's up?" Bott muttered. "Is it morning?"

"It's dawn! The brown fog of a winter one! Wake up quickly!"

She climbed out of bed. It was dark and freezing cold.

Gatzko was shoving her siren-suit at her. "Oh, hurry up, put anything on. You'll miss it."

Bott shivered. "I don't know what you're talking about. Why've we got to get up at dawn?"

"It's the poem! It's exactly like the poem. 'Unreal City, under the brown fog of a winter dawn—'"

"Oh, I see! 'The Waste Land'." Bott scrambled into the suit, too cold to change her pyjamas for underclothes. "I'm sorry. I didn't understand what you were talking about. Of course I'm coming."

Gatzko could hardly wait for her to get dressed. They ran out together. This was the kind of thing she loved him for, when he got so absurdly excited about one of his notions. "The Waste Land" was one of his chief notions.

In Lovat Lane the lamps, which so looked like gas that they had never dared inspect them closely in case they weren't, had haloes round them. Gatzko put his arm round Bott's waist and they hugged tight together for warmth. Bott didn't know about "The Waste Land" but she thought this was poetry enough for her. The clock of St. Mary-at-Hill loomed out of the mist and dark tracery of plane trees over the old brick wall of the churchyard. She could just read the time, twenty-five past four. The famous brown fog was rolling about. "Oh, Gatzko, you were right," she said. "I feel as if I were setting off on a big adventure. Doesn't someone have an adventure in 'The Waste Land'?"

"There's a voyage by sea, and death by water and burning."

"That's it, that's it! Like an epic! Oh, don't you feel as if you were just starting to live an epic?"

She still whispered, although their shoes made an unavoidable clatter on the cobbles.

"One thinks of all the hands," Gatzko said, hugging her tight under St. Mary-at-Hill, "that are raising dingy blinds in a thousand furnished rooms."

"Oh, don't. This is so beautiful. I'm sure that doesn't come in 'The Waste Land'."

"No, it doesn't," he chuckled. "It's out of one of his earlier poems. Honey, I don't think you've understood 'The Waste Land' at all."

"All right, it's not an epic then. But this is. Oh, look, look at that!" She had turned her head and seen dim perspectives of bits of gutted warehouse wall and towers and steeples emerging from the darkness, a pink winter glow rising from them.

"Falling towers," remarked Gatzko. "Unreal. Doesn't it look unreal?" But she could tell from the trembling of his arm that he was as excited as she.

They came into Lower Thames Street and he caught his breath. He worked there every day, yet she could feel a thrill run down his body to be in it again. A few lorries were already there, a fishman or two clattering barrows about. The walls seemed blacker and lowered more than ever. Only the pavement shone with puddles of fish slime, reflecting the dark pink sky. They tiptoed on and Bott saw above them the Charringtons sign on the George and Dragon. "And in there at noon," she whispered ecstatically, "we'll hear the pleasant whining of a mandoline."

"Oh City city," and they stopped and breathed in the fish

and soot and Gatzko was hugging her so tight she had no alternative but to put her head on his shoulder, and they stared along Lower Thames Street as if they had indeed caught sight of the Celestial City in some epic story, and neither could think of anything more to quote.

Suddenly Gatzko shouted. "The river! We must see the river before it gets light!"

He took her hand and dragged her into a run. Laughing and panting, the back of her nostrils aching from the cold, she followed him splashing through the muck and up the dark stinking stairs on to London Bridge and there was the river.

"Oh, sweet Thames," Gatzko said.

It lay dark and foggy and full of carmine glints before them, and Bott forgot all about the poem.

Looking down at the water, she felt as if she were afloat on it. Yes, just she and Gatzko sailing away on their epic voyage, themselves all beauty and splendour of red and gold, but into this, this dream world of the river and the cobbles and the broken bricks. She held Gatzko's hand tight and leant over the bridge, inhaling the river smell. She tried to seize the moment. She looked at Gatzko for help but there was no telling what he was thinking. She took another breath of fog. It was like breathing solid light. All round them was brightness, a bright mist, an unbearable heady luminosity as they stood on London Bridge.

And now (Bott thought) they really did begin to float upwards. Towers, sails, bells, fish, winter, Gatzko, ecstasy. Up and up, they rose in the dawn, ascending on a still wind, borne on their own light.

"Oh, Gatzko! Look at the city all shining! I can see miles. There's St. Bride's!"

But he didn't seem to be aware of what was happening. Bott could see him below shaking a big body, which lay flopped over the parapet of the bridge. It must be her body.

"No, not there, stupid, I'm here, above you, Gatzko! Oh, do leave that silly great thing alone. Come on up!"

But he went on saying to it, "Bott, Bott! Come on, corpse, sprout!"

It was no use. She made an effort to get the body going again. If he wasn't flying with her she didn't want to fly alone. But it was several minutes before she could manage to operate her arms and legs, and persuade them to work together.

She smiled at Gatzko but as she did so knew she had not made a success of it. She could feel the smile come out twisted and unnatural, though she had intended it to show him how full of delight she felt.

"Okay, Bott? You don't look too good."

"But I feel marvellous!"

"Just old Hieronymo mad again, huh?" he said, and by now she was enough in command of her faculties to finish the quotation. "Yes, and London Bridge is falling down," she managed to say in her ordinary voice. Gatzko shook his head at her fondly and supported her back towards the bank. But this was more than Bott could bear.

"No! No! I don't want to hobble!" she shouted, pushing him away. As if it weren't nuisance enough to be on the ground at all, when she could have flown away for joy. "I want to run!"

"Let's run then!"

And they ran, holding hands again, until crossing the road they collided with a man hurrying along the opposite pavement.

"Stetson!" Gatzko cried, still holding Bott's hand. "You who were with me in the ships at Mylae!"

The man looked up with an uncertain half-smile, and then stared. Bott began to giggle.

"That corpse you planted last year in your garden," Gatzko went on to the man accusingly, "has it begun to sprout? Will it bloom this year?"

The man looked aghast, and fled past them in a near-run.

"Or has the sudden frost disturbed its bed?" Gatzko yelled

after him, squeezing Bott's hand. The man gave an apprehensive glance over his shoulder, and fairly flew towards the shelter of the underground. Bott and Gatzko both burst into uncontrollable laughter. They flung their arms round each other's necks, laughing until clouds of pink breath billowed out over the road. "Look at them!" Gatzko said. "Eliot's crowd flowing over London Bridge!"

Bott was so happy, and so glad to see him so happy, that she did not point out that there was scarcely anyone on London Bridge, and even in the poem it was nine o'clock, while it couldn't yet be five.

"Just look!" Gatzko said scornfully. "Miserable people. Let's wake them up!" He pulled her off again, running and capering and gasping with laughter till it hurt. Far from waking up a gloomy rush hour crowd, there was practically no one in sight, for which Bott was secretly relieved. There was no reason, no earthly reason she should contain her joy one second longer. Shrieking with delight, she broke away from Gatzko and ran towards the Monument. They were shouting like children as they chased each other round it. The empty offices down the long streets in every direction echoed with the noise. Suddenly Gatzko grabbed Bott and motioned vigorously towards Cannon Street. A policeman was slowly but purposefully coming through the fog towards them. They bolted back along London Bridge and plunged into the stairway down to Lower Thames Street, but in the corner Gatzko caught her and kissed her, an out-of-breath kiss. Bott kissed back with such passion that he recoiled. "Jesus, what sort of a crazy Greek Maenad have you turned into?"

"What's that?"

"A wild girl of Bacchus."

"That's just what I feel like!" Bott exclaimed. "And they used to antic around when they felt happy too, didn't they?"

"Once and for all," said Gatzko, "nobody is happy in the waste land. Will you never grasp that?"

He was pressed up close against her and had pinioned her

against the wall with his arms. She could feel it cold and wet through the back of her siren suit. She dared not move. She felt skewered against it anyway by the intense seriousness of his look. His play mood had vanished. When he kissed her, he was still intense and serious. She was never, before or after, kissed like that again. She thought later that it was maybe the only occasion, in all the time she knew him, that he gave her his whole attention.

It was a ferocious kiss, that went on and on. Bott, who had always imagined kissing as a pecking affair on the cheek, would never have believed a kiss could go on so long. But it was not so much the kiss that mashed her up as the way he kept his eyes open, looking almost desperately into hers with that fearful intensity, as if he were trying to tell her something. God, those eyes. It was like being speared on a couple of prongs. And culminating such a morning of heady rapture, it was too much, Bott was out of her body again into her myth of dawn and death and a black-eyed god. When Gatzko drew back she was mumbling "Burning burning burning..."

Gatzko was surprised and a little disappointed that even after that she should be so detached that she could go straight on with their quoting game. He could not have. He found he was shaking and still had to support himself against the wall, leaning on her and swallowing for breath. He went on looking at her. Hadn't she once accused him of never feeling any real emotion? He wondered why he could not, for once, see what she was thinking. Her eyes had gone cloudy and odd. Gatzko could not get his breath. He suddenly no longer felt young. He was gasping like an old man. He put his head down in her scarf.

She startled him by springing forwards, her arms round him tightly, almost holding him up if you please. "Gatzko!" she cried. "Gatzko! Look!"

He looked. She was staring ecstatically at the dirty wall of the stairway. "Look what's written there?" she said.

"It's—Gatzko, is it Greek? What does it mean? Is it for us?"
Sure enough, there in the soot were big chalked letters:

$$\grave{\epsilon}\chi\omega \; \pi\acute{\alpha}\epsilon\iota \; \mu\epsilon \; \tau\acute{o} \; \pi\lambda o\grave{\iota}o$$

"Yes, it is Greek," Gatzko said.

"But how wonderful, how right! Just when we were thinking about Greece. Is it only chalk? Doesn't it look as if it were written in fire?"

The letters did seem to be glowing meaningfully from the wall. Gatzko felt his own excitement rekindling. He looked closely. "Well, they do look a bit miraculous, you're right, but I suppose they're just something some Greek fisherman has chalked up."

"Some Greek fisherman...!" Bott stared at him all ablaze with wonder and joy. Gatzko always felt weak before her when she was like this. "Some Greek fisherman! Gatzko, do you realize what you've just said? It must mean something for us. I do wish we could read it."

"It's modern Greek," he said, "'I have gone by water.'"

"You don't mean you know Greek? Oh, you know everything."

Gatzko smirked.

"'I have gone by water'. What a strange thing to find written in Greek under London Bridge. It must be symbolic of something. I'm sure it's for us."

"Why, it just has to be." Gatzko's enjoyment of the morning and of the thrill of finding "The Waste Land" come to life had all returned. "We knew we were just setting off by water, didn't we?"

"Oh, Gatzko!" Bott cried, hugging him again for sheer delight that he had read the inscription on the wall and shared her myth, after all.

Gatzko hugged her back, laughing and thinking, 'I Tiresias have foresuffered all, enacted on this same divan or bed', but this time he kept the quotation to himself. At last he held her away from him. "Honey, all this has given me the biggest appetite in history. Let's go back and see if you can't fix me the biggest breakfast in history."

They walked back, arm in arm, through the magical winter pinkness. And it still isn't really dawn, Bott thought in amusement, although it's over an hour since he got me up telling me I'd miss it if I didn't hurry. She loved Gatzko for his craziness and squeezed his arm. There was full-scale bustle and clamour now in Lower Thames Street, a stink of fish, lorries unloading everywhere, "Morning, Morning" on every side. They were crunching through crushed ice on the road.

"You didn't go to bed at all last night, did you?"

"No, I was working so well, and then it was sunrise. If you like—" He looked at her, oddly shy. "Would you like to come and see what I was doing?"

"Why Gatzko, you know I'd love to! I only never come in there because I'm afraid you may not want me to see."

"I'd like you to see this."

"Anyway I think a man ought to have some retreat, somewhere he can go where his family can't bother him."

Gatzko did not answer. It was an idea he heartily agreed with, but he did not like her use of the word "retreat". He did not consider he was retreating when he went into his studio to work. He did not approve of the notion of a retreat at all. Getting out of somewhere, that was one thing, an entirely natural desire; but retreating, withdrawing inwards, there was something indefinably perverted about such a wish. He had got Bott out of it once. He hoped the emphasis with which she had just spoken was accidental. To change the subject, he said, "I'm thinking about that mighty big breakfast."

"Oh, darling, you know what there is."

"I'll start with hot cakes. Hot cakes and maple syrup and whipped butter. And a Texan steak with hash browns."

"Oh, dear, you do make me feel ignorant. I don't know what any of that is."

"And with the steak I'll have two eggs, over easy."

"Eggs! You'll be lucky."

They went cuddling and giggling into the Dairy &, which was already in full swing, billowing with sweet steam and full of dock workers taking their tea break. Mrs. Weingartner smiled amicably at Gatzko and Bott as if it were the most normal thing in the world for them to come in at five-thirty in the morning. "Do you know what you're going to get?" Bott asked Gatzko. "Toffee pie."

"Toffee pie! What a fine idea! If I'd known there was that on the menu I'd never have bothered with eggs."

"What do they eat in 'The Waste Land'? There's that typist who eats out of tins, but I don't remember anything else."

"Albert and Lil have a hot gammon. You remember that bit set in the pub."

"Oh, gosh, yes, that terrifically realistic sordid scene. You know, that poem's odd in one respect. Some of it, the part in London, is so true to life, and then there comes all that fantasy about the desert and the red rocks with no water, which can't be like anything on earth."

"Why not? I know that desert well," Gatzko said. "I lived among red rocks exactly like those for six years."

"You—lived among red rocks like Eliot's?" Bott thought he must be joking, but saw he was not. "But—where possibly— how on earth—" He smiled, and she realized he was not going to tell her anything more. "Oh, you are tantalizing," she said. "You're as mysterious as the one-eyed merchant with the load on his back that Madame Sosostris was forbidden to see."

He smiled more, and Bott could tell he was pleased.

She sang lustily as she got Michael up and made breakfast. She was thinking about cities and ships in the dawn. Only as the acorn coffee came to the boil did she realize that what she had been singing was alternate lines of "City of God, how broad and far" and "We joined the Navy". Gatzko was listening to her and smiling. Bott felt a fool and shut up, but a minute later, without realizing it, she was off again. She was too happy to keep quiet. Oh, what a morning this was, what an unforgettable morning.

Gatzko was happy too. He was pleased with his night's work and exhilarated from running about in the dawn. When Michael, cross at being woken so early, started to grizzle, he said, "Don't be dismal, baby! We're having a party!" Michael looked up eagerly, and Gatzko caught him by the hands and whirled him round until the little boy was as flushed and bright-eyed as his father. Then they both got dizzy together and fell in a heap on top of Bott, who was just setting the pie down on the floor by the coffee. "Wow, gorgeous," Gatzko said, digging a great hunk of pie out with his fingers and biting into it. Oh, well, Bott thought gaily, a few germs ought to add to the flavour. "Did I ever tell you, Bott," Gatzko said, "you're a wonder-worker at cooking." He corrected himself. "No, you're simply a wonder-worker." He smiled at her. Terrific woman she was. She'd learnt "The Waste Land" by heart all for him, although she didn't understand a word of it.

When the coffee was finished Gatzko stood up. Bott began to gather the plates together. "Leave that," he said. Bott looked up wondering at the tone in his voice. "You've forgotten your promise," he said. He took her hand and led her out to his studio. "There she is."

Bott gazed at the clay thing. Gatzko's hand was trembling a little in hers. Why, he actually cares what I make of this, she thought. It's what has really been in his mind all through this glorious morning. How awful. It matters what I say. Suddenly the words came. She understood more from Gatzko's look and touch and the note in his voice than from the sculpture itself.

"It looks soft," she found herself saying. "It can't be clay— can it?" She moved to touch it. Gatzko caught her in time, but it was the very reaction he would have wanted from her. Softness, strokeability, she had divined it, probably only instinctively, but it was that, exactly, Gatzko would have wished for. He caught both her wrists.

"So, how goes our odyssey?" he asked, and heard himself croak. "Have we reached Calypso yet?"

"Oh, yes," Bott said ecstatically, imagining Calypso as a port, some legendary city not far from Carthage full of taverns looking like the Dairy & and shining turrets on a hill—Wren turrets, of course. "Yes, we sailed in in our golden boat. I'll never forget it."

"Bott, you're so romantic, I'd better go to work before I catch it off you," Gatzko said, still holding her wrists. Bott was sure he didn't mean that crushingly. He merely still had that habit of talking cynically. But all would change now. She smiled joyfully at him. He kissed her a last time and went away to his work, back to Lower Thames Street, a junior fish-packer; in Bott's eyes, and his too, the most glamorous thing he could be. She thought about him, treading the mire and ice in that street where the sun never really came even when it did rise, carting his fish about. In her imagination the herrings and mackerel she knew he handled all grew long fins and strange gold spines, Calypso fish. "Oh City city," she muttered, picking her way back through the rubble into the lair.

7

MARY'S EYES NEVER left the lecture screen. Ardently she watched it and the professor's arm, waving about. She made notes. Her page was covered with things like "Perdita's *innocence*. 1611. Shakespeare can't imagine anywhere to be different from England. P. is *totally innocent*. Globe. 1616. Ophelia. Cymbeline. Note P's innocence. Perdita had to turn out to be a member of the aristocracy to please the aristocratic patrons but she is *innocent* (P.S. What is innocence? Perdita really knows a lot although she may be inexperienced. She obviously has the key to the secret which she knows by intuition because she is a pure virgin, and she is able to let the Prince into the secret which is why he cannot relinquish her. She is more than life and death to him because she knows the quiet still secret which is under the earth, and she has the secret of growing things which is why she can tell Polixenes with such certainty about the wrongness of gilly-flowers. She has the secret and she knows it consciously and is aware of it and does not ever forget it or herself so she can use it and so she is natural queen of everything—"

Mary read her notes aghast. She felt almost sure that the professor had not been saying anything like that. He was talking about Elizabethan theatre production for heaven's sake, and the difficulties Shakespeare would have had producing "The Winter's Tale". She must concentrate; she must. She energetically scribbled more notes. "The Bear can't really devour Antigonus onstage. Opportunity for a Clown. Comic. Other Shepherds' innocence ridiculous to show up P's wise innocence. Comedy usual in Eliz Autoly "

Mary wondered why her pen kept slipping. What were those

two unfinished words supposed to be? She could not remember although the ink of "Autoly" was not even dry. She focused all her attention on the lecturer. He was showing slides of various productions of that difficult scene with the bear. But at the end of the lecture Mary saw that she had written this:

"Perdita's mother after all is Hermione who can keep her very existence hidden for sixteen years. The key to everything is that there is secretly life inside the statue at the end, it makes a climax but it has been quietly going on all the time, Hermione's concealed life, a big secret which finally erupts to give the play a happy ending using the symbol of the statue which has life inside it.

"Perdita's life too is a secret. Also she does not know her own origins, she has lost her parents and birthplace but she goes quietly on growing like a seed nursing the secret and in the end she blossoms out too.

"Shakespeare made a mistake though to call her Perdita for she is not really lost at all, she has lost her father admittedly BUT SHE REMEMBERS THE SECRET."

The lecture was over. It was too late. She had not listened to a single word, and there was a pop quiz tomorrow. How on earth was she going to get marks in an exam on that? And what possible excuse could she make for herself? "I'm sorry, my mind just kept wandering along its own lines." "I'm sorry. That play just kind of set me thinking about my own problems and I couldn't stop." But then the professor might ask her, "What problems?" and that was a question she avoided at all costs. The professors were kindly, psychologically-minded people who worried about their pupils' problems, but they had not, thank goodness, succeeded in unearthing Mary's. Everyone called her reticent. But she had long discovered that if you got on all right in your sorority you were considered all right by the rest of the world. And Mary liked being in a sorority. But now, these notes! She really did have a concrete problem there.

Glancing at the other girls' notes as they poured out of the lecture room she saw that their paper was covered with diagrams of the Elizabethan stage and so on, which she did not even remember coming up on the lecture screen.

She would simply have to leave it for today and then hope and pray Su would have finished with her own notes. She could confess to Su at the sorority meeting that night. Su was not always sympathetic though. She was getting fed up.

There was trouble, too, with her professor, Mr. Fieldman. Mary could not think why he took such an interest in her, his dullest pupil. But he did, anyway, often summoning her to discuss her work, and always they finished up discussing her. Mary did not like it.

She got out into the street and shuddered with the horror of it. She never got used to that great hideous avenue, the unkind blocks towering over her with their filth and black angular fire-escapes. And if you had to go between two of them to get in at a side entrance, as she had to do to get to the lecture rooms, the restaurant, the social hall and almost everything else, you really felt as if the buildings were trying, deliberately, to crush the breath out of you. They lowered over every street, all alike, great strong blocks with hard outlines. Even the sky, the sky she could watch for hours in Arizona, the sky she had always imagined as a space, or as space rather, where you could go up and up and lose yourself. Not here. Here it was just another block, dirty and hard, as the buildings and the sidewalks and the whole cursed city were dirty and hard.

Mary walked past the YWCA, which was next door to the university, along the length of the eighth block on Wabash Avenue, and turned into 9th Street, heading for the El.

Why her father had chosen this college she could not imagine. Maybe it was a fine institution once. Now it was just the top three storeys of another monstrous city building. She supposed it was a good address: Wabash Avenue, right in the Loop. But next to the YWCA? Perhaps that wasn't there in the days when her father knew it. Perhaps the college had been on other premises altogether. She was sure there must be many more modern colleges in Chicago. Why, her secretarial college in Tucson had been nicer than this. Did her father know that it didn't have a proper campus at all; that she had to come all the way in from Oak Park every day in the school bus, from what passed as the "campus", a slightly more recent, long brick building containing accommodation for the girls in the form of four dorms. In front of it was a playing field, and all around was the unbeautiful district of Oak Park at Austin Avenue. Did her father know, or care, what a squalid life he had condemned her to lead? Most of the other girls seemed to think nothing of having to live out of town. They did not even seem to see anything wrong in the university building on Wabash Avenue. They said, there were few enough women's colleges with any sort of tradition, as JOB had, and it was terrific to come out of class and find yourself right in the city centre.

She came into State Street and walked down to Van Buren, to the El station. There was a church here, on the corner of State and Wabash, her own church too, Old St. Mary's. But it gave her no comfort. It was as monstrous as its surroundings. It would have gaped and devoured her as willingly as anything else in Chicago. She hurried on down State Street and mounted the ugly iron stairs to the El, shuddering at the noise as a train went past. She looked down State Street from the station and decided that what she was really feeling was that State Street hated her.

That was it! The city hated her. Yes, that was the most definite expression she had yet found for that sensation she was never free of in Chicago, of being crushed, bullied, battered at. Another El train came in; she forced herself to attend. Yes, this would do; if only she didn't get lost, as usual, on the Lake Street transfer.

She was meeting Scott in the downtown Mary-Ann Coffee Shop. He had promised to help her plan out her homework after each lecture, since he also was an English major at the Northwestern University. He had made his offer out of kind-

ness more than a month ago and abided by it. He was a really
nice boy, Scott, Mary acknowledged it, and these study dates
were probably her salvation, if she thought about it.

Mary walked towards the coffee shop, where Scott would be,
with piles of books brought specially for her to save her the
journey to the Northwestern University Library (JOB had no
library; instead it possessed the great privilege of being
allowed to use the Northwestern's, which was public anyway,
and where Mary had met Scott). She could imagine him, leaping up from the table he'd have been saving for her for the
last hour, with his cheery "Hiya!" Nice boy, Mary reminded
herself. The nicest.

As she came out on to the bank of the evil dark Chicago
River a gust of wind hit her. She fought her way down Wacker
Drive against it. It came from the lake, and was as much part
of Chicago as the Board of Trade Building. It pushed and
buffeted malignantly at Mary. After the months she had been
here, it had come to know her weak spots. It rasped at her in
places where she didn't like even to be touched, let alone
rasped at. Feeling bruised and worn out, Mary struggled more
and more feebly along Wacker Drive. Ten yards more to the
coffee shop and a couple of hours with Scott. Suddenly Mary
knew she could not face it. She went into the coffee shop and
Scott leapt up with his cheery "Hiya!"

"Hiya, hon," said Mary. "Look, I'm really sorry, but I can't
stay. Shall we make it tomorrow?"

"But Mary, honey! I've brought you these books. What's
wrong? Did you forget and go plan something else?"

"No—I—I don't feel well," Mary gasped. The hot sweet
smell of the coffee shop, a mixture of the stench of gallons of
salad dressing and gallons of sundae syrup, made her want to
vomit. "I have to go," she wheezed and bolted for the door.
She knew he would follow her. He was certain to. She broke
into a run. Whether or not he was following her, she was in a
panic; she felt hunted. She ran out on to the bridge and had a
vision of it opening up in the middle, quietly opening its jaws

and tumbling her into the maw of that foul river. Mary ran as she had only run in dreams. Across the river, but there was no escape, it was still Chicago on the other side, those looming blocks towering up and up. She must get up, out, away somewhere.

The wind chased her into a doorway. It was an office building of some sort. She had a choice now: out in the street again, or up in that elevator. She pressed and pressed the button for the elevator. Up, up. Floor 10. This was better.

Mary's urge was to get out, away somewhere she could breathe. She felt stifled by the sheer cityness of Chicago. Even the wind, down there in the street, was a city wind. She went quickly down the corridor. A man coming the other way stood by to let her pass; she must have looked as if she knew where she was going and was in a hurry to arrive. At the far end of the corridor was a door marked "FIRE". Without any hesitation Mary made for it. She was not really expecting to get out there, but when she tried the handle, it opened. Delightedly Mary stepped on to the fire escape. Ah! Here the air was more like air, less like some malevolent miasma. Mary raised her arms and stretched deliciously, rubbing like a cat against the iron steps.

The idea came, couldn't she go even higher? Here she was probably visible from the street and somebody might think there was a fire, or that she wanted to commit suicide, or something. She noted vaguely that the door she had come out by was self-locking, with no outside handle. She could not be bothered to worry. She set to work to climb on to the roof. The fire-escape proper seemed to start from this floor but there was a little black ladder which went up. Mary climbed it, feeling the weight which had seemed to want to crush her, down in the street, grow less at every step. She was filthy and her skirt kept blowing up. Steadily she mounted. At last she reached the parapet of the façade of the building. She turned around and sat on the top of it, her feet wedged into the ladder, and relaxed.

She was shocked suddenly to see the bridge she had just run across behaving exactly as she had visualized. Quietly, slowly, it parted in the middle, and the two halves rose, bristling lamp-posts, exactly as if the Chicago River were a fly-eating plant opening up to receive some other poor creature like herself.

It was by no means a new phenomenon for Mary, since the bridges in Chicago do this every time a ship passes, but she was shaken. She no longer felt at ease, perched on top of her ladder. She was still within sight of the river. She must get further up, further away.

Mary clambered over the parapet and jumped down on to the roof, and found herself in a strange landscape of grimy asphalt and curious metal edifices which were the water tanks, the elevator shafts, the heating and so on. Feeling better already, Mary picked her way forward among them. Here was a place, on the side of the elevator shaft, where she could get a foot up and then maybe wriggle her way into that little place, that metal ledge between it and the chimney or whatever that was. Heavens, but it was dirty though, and how awkward such a climb would be in a skirt. But that little nook looked so welcoming. There, she would be completely secret and hidden even if anyone came out on the roof, and she would be able to lie on her back and see nothing but the side of that thing and the sky.

Accordingly, Mary levered herself up, holding on to a wire which she let go in a hurry when she heard it humming. She crawled into her chosen corner. Oh, wonderful! Look what it led to! A little enclosed space she hadn't even seen from the roof just below, between three big round structures which were made of aluminium and so even looked comparatively clean and bright. Mary drew herself up, hugging her knees with satisfaction, and then sensuously, luxuriously, let herself spread out and flop, rubbing her body on the floor. She gave herself the treat she had promised herself: lay on her back and looked at the sky, feeling the grit on the asphalt under the backs of her hands. Her fingertips just touched the metal

D

round things like a delicate caress, and she heard a curious breathy little coo. That must be her sound. A happy-Mary sound.

Mary found herself gazing into a puddle. She looked down into the depths of it. She saw a far, far shimmering blueness, like looking down at a mist from some great height. Near her, comparatively close up, hung part of the side of a great globe, made of some dark substance or other but lit on the underneath by the depths of light below. Mary gazed down enthralled. She could not see the bottom at all, only the near walls of those two strange curved things and then—what? Down, down through infinity at least. At one of the lectures Mary had heard that infinity was calculable. But this was surely bottomless; so she was looking through infinity and out beyond it, maybe?

All recollection of rooftops, scrambling and cold weather had gone from Mary's mind. She stared and stared into the puddle, propped on her elbows. How strangely dark those things were near her, round the top. Then there was that beautiful misty chasm into the timeless. She looked and saw with a shock that she could see beyond this. Far, far down, unknowable distances down, light-years away, she saw clouds. Clouds, everyone knew, were only half-way to anything. When you looked up at high clouds you were not even seeing through the atmosphere, and when you looked down on clouds, why it meant you were at the very top of the mountain, with the valley a day's walk below. Mary knew a lot about mountains and valleys, after being brought up in the Rockies with a mountaineering father.

Mary looked and looked down through the clouds. She was afraid to dare to look into the timeless, but equally, she knew she must. This could even be the secret, if only she could see. It was blue and it was pink and it was a tantalizing haze of obscurity. And then at last she realized why the globes and the surface of the haze were so dark, and the brightness seemed so tormentingly far below. It was really below. The bottoms of the spheres were reflecting something; that haze was illuminated by something; and the clouds, the farthest and brightest things she could discern, were lit from below by something.

Down there, then, was a source of light, perhaps *the* source of light.

Mary strained and wriggled and writhed, trying to see. Suddenly, it came to her that this was not the way. Stillness was the way, and not sight but a sense beyond sight.

She tried again, and realized despairingly that in the trying she was defeating herself. But she must know what that chasm contained. She must know what strange country lay there, what secret of light welled up from that hidden source beyond infinity. It was not curiosity, but a certainty that this hidden source was her source, the source she had been for so long separated from. If she could only see. She knew she was nearer the secret now than she had been since she lost it.

She went back to look again at her puddle, to see again if she could make out what that secret place was which lay at the depths of everything. As she did so she happened to glance over the parapet into the street and saw with amazement that "down there" did not apply to puddles at all but to views of this kind, down into streets. Reality was not what she saw shimmering from the surface of inch-deep pools of water. It was a shock to realize it. She had taken it for granted that she actually was looking into the valley of the timeless, the valley she thought of really without ceasing, the valley where she belonged. The valley that was the essence of all valleys and contained the source of light and life and—oh, what was the rest of it? Already, looking down into the street, she had forgotten.

But it was not that at all. Here was reality, noisy dirty Kinzie Street. She went back to the puddle to make certain, and saw a shallow and muddy reflection of water-tanks, lightning-conductor and sky. Yet that, most indisputedly and only a moment ago, had been a crack into the timeless. Oh, Sedona,

Sedona. Mary moaned, hunting for her skirt. She also noticed that her blouse was gone, her underclothes too, either torn to rags or removed apparently. Her skin was knobbly with goose-flesh.

She squeezed out through the little passage next to the elevator shaft and dropped down to the roof. She climbed over the parapet on to the fire escape and down to the door she had come out by, only to discover, which she had already seen but had forgotten, that she could not open it from this side. Feeling discouraged, Mary peered through the bars at the door on the floor below. It was identical, and Mary felt sure it would be locked too, nor was there any reason to suppose the fire doors on Floors 8 to 2 would be any different. Fire escapes all over the city, down the front of every house, were the same, so Mary could guess how this would be. From the second floor to the ground there would be no more stairs but a hanging ladder which had to be unhooked and quite likely unlocked from a higher level. Mary did not enjoy the thought of doing this. She climbed back again over the parapet and searched for a way down from the roof.

Presently she came upon a little door, or hatch rather, on the far side of the water-tanks beside the lightning-conductor, and which was being used as a skylight or something; anyway it was open. Mary got through and dropped to the floor of a little place full of coils of wire and messy-looking pots of paint. Mary didn't have the energy to feel frightened; she merely felt weary and weak. This lumber room led into a long low attic full of bundles of papers, and the corridor this gave into led to the stairs. A flight down she found the top station of the elevator and recognized Floor 10. She pressed for it. When it came a man got out. He grinned at Mary.

"Keep you working late, don't they?" he said. Mary smiled feebly back and hurried to get into the elevator before he noticed the state her clothes were in.

As she left the building she made a note of it. Nearly on the corner of Kinzie Street, and a firm on the first floor called

"Kielers Continental Shipping and Transport". There was a pharmacy opposite with an advertisement for Schiaparelli in the window. Okay; she'd know it again. She set off back across the river and noticed that the dark sky was not merely due to murk and gloom. Evening was coming on. And that man had said something about she was working late. What time on earth was it, then? Ten past six, no wonder she felt cold; she must have been up on that roof nearly an hour and a half. She had missed the school bus too. Now she'd have to take the El home.

Passing the Mary-Ann Coffee Shop she glanced in, half expecting to see Scott there. A wave of emotion made her shiver when she saw that (of course) he was not. She could not tell whether this was relief, disappointment, nostalgia or nausea. She went on to the El.

If you had by any chance managed to forget where you were, this ride out to Austin on the El would bring it right back to you. First you rattled past the fourth-floor windows of the downtown offices, and over the grim streets west from Lake Street. No possibility of pretending to yourself that you were heading south on the Santa Fe. Then your mind wandered for a moment; and then, with a shock, there through the end of the coach you saw the city reared up over the plain in all its power and glory, its cluster of colossi seeming in truth to touch the sky. As you went on through Kedzie and Cicero it appeared to grow rather than diminish with distance. Even at the campus it loomed on the horizon.

8

MARY WAS DRINKING a cup of coffee from the coffee machine in the games room downstairs from her dormitory. That was where they usually held their evening sorority meetings. The cup was made of paper and was melting in Mary's hand. The coffee was extremely weak and she had forgotten to press the button for more creme. Altogether, Mary was enjoying it. She felt an immense sympathy, even an affinity, with that poor cup of coffee.

She was carefully sipping from the fast-dissolving cup when she heard one of the girls in a group near her say, "Well, the movie wasn't too interesting, but it had some very beautiful photography. It was all shot in Oak Creek Canyon...."

Mary's fingers slipped, Mary's mind slipped, slithered and tumbled and fell, slowly and gently, somersaulting over and over as gracefully as a diver. Deep and deep she plunged into the abyss of light, through the gold reflected from its walls, down and down towards the far shining source.

"Mary, hey, Mary, honey! What happened, she fainted? If anyone would bring some water she might revive—Oh, she is. Mary, baby, what happened, did you faint, are you okay?"

But it was nearly fifteen minutes before Mary could think in articulate form, in words, again. The girls and the dorm matron fussed round opening windows on her, bringing her aspirin, water and more coffee. She was a slow awakener at the best of times and it was a long journey now, up from depths of light towards the games room and the Austin campus. What finally landed her there with a jolt was hearing the dorm matron say, "Well if someone would help me support her I guess the best place for her is bed."

"No! No!" screamed Mary, pulling away. "No, don't send me upstairs. I want you to tell me again what you said just now."

"What do you mean, hon, who said what?"

"That's just it, that's what I don't remember. It was you, wasn't it?" Mary said desperately, turning to the girl next her. "Weren't you talking about Oak Creek Canyon?"

"Oh, no, that was me," another girl, called Sally, said. "Just before you blacked out or whatever you did I mentioned to Nina that I saw a movie made there. Is that what you heard?"

"Yes, yes, and then you went on, you said something else. Oh, please say it again. I'm sorry, Sally, I didn't mean to listen, but I couldn't help hearing. You said something really important connected with Oak Creek Canyon, didn't you, something about the—about that place. Sally, please. I just can't remember."

The dorm matron was there listening and everything and Su and all the girls but this was so vital that Mary didn't care if they did hear.

"No, Mary, I don't know what you mean. I didn't say anything more than just that, there was some beautiful scenery in the movie which apparently is a place called Oak Creek Canyon in the Rocky Mountains. That's all I said, isn't it?" Sally looked at Nina and Nina nodded. Mary cried out in desperation.

"No, that wasn't all you said. I'm certain. You said something more, about what there is at the bottom of the canyon maybe or something like that. It was that which sent me off. Oh, please, please tell me again. I've got to know."

Sally just kept shaking her head, looking more and more baffled and frightened by Mary's urgency. Mary felt herself starting to cry with frustration and disappointment. The dorm matron took Sally by the arm, pulled her away and whispered something in her ear. Strangely, Mary knew what she was whispering: "She's only becoming hysterical. I think you'd better efface yourself." Sally did efface herself. Mary felt weak with hopelessness. She could hear what the dorm matron mouthed to Sally; but when Sally talked out aloud about the secret—THE SECRET—Mary might as well have been deaf. Sally had perhaps been telling those very things that Mary had been striving to recall for so long—and Mary heard and forgot again on the instant.

Mary said yes and yes while they asked her did she not feel very well and did she have a sick headache perhaps and would it be that which accounted for her blackout and Mary must take care not to overwork in future. For a start she had better miss out on school tomorrow. Somebody gave her a handkerchief so she must have been crying openly. They put her to bed. Mary begged everyone she saw to try and persuade Sally to change her mind. But Sally did not come that evening. Mary cried and dreamt about a cactus blossom.

Scott was just preparing to have a shower before bed when Howard Seker, another freshman, yelled through that he was wanted on the dorm telephone. Scott put on his bathrobe and went to the phone, feeling vaguely apprehensive. It was Su, Mary's girlfriend. She said, "Hello, Scott. Did you see Mary this afternoon?"

"Well, yes, but—"

"Oh, you did! I knew you had a date but I wondered if she turned up. Listen, did she seem all right?"

"No, she suddenly went funny when she saw me and ran away, saying she didn't feel well—Su, what's the matter? What are you trying to tell me?"

"She fainted or something in the middle of the sorority meeting this evening and she keeps having these crying fits and talking nonsense. But she doesn't seem to be sick, I mean her pulse is normal and so on."

Scott gulped and drew lines with his finger on the side of the telephone.

"Something must be wrong," Su went on, "and I don't think it's anything physical. I should guess either she's in love with you, or else she's having a nervous breakdown for some other reason. And I want you to help me find out what it is."

"Why, sure, but you know I can't ever persuade Mary to tell me much."

"Not even you? She won't confide at all in me but I thought she might in you. If you tried to draw her out."

"Well, of course I'll try. I'd do anything if it would help her. Su, you don't really think she's in love with me, do you?"

"It's quite likely, and you ought to face up to it. I mean if she fell in love with you then you're kind of responsible, don't you see."

Scott drew more lines on the telephone and felt heroic.

"You really believe it's that, though? Doesn't she have any other worries? Her studies for instance? And she has home trouble, doesn't she?"

"Not now, I mean she's been living with her adopted parents since she was six years old and I'm certain she gets on well with them. But whatever it is, Scott, we have to find out and we have to help her."

"All right, Su. I'm glad you called. I was wondering what on earth the matter could be."

"Oh, Scott, honestly! And you didn't guess at all?" said Su, who was sure by now that she knew Mary's trouble, and thinking that men never did understand these things.

When Mary next met Scott he looked at her so oddly that presently she asked him what was the matter. He looked taken aback and asked, "May I ask you the same question first?"

"I had some funny dreams last night," Mary explained.

She wondered why Scott looked disappointed, although it was a relief that he didn't press her to tell him her dreams (that had been a fad of his, a few weeks ago). Scott, who had been thinking about her all night, wondered if there was something wrong with him, that she never would confide. He held her hand under the table, the first time he had dared to

D*

do so and the first time Mary's hand had been held by anyone. It was not a success. She was unaware of anything except that she wanted sugar in her coffee and for some reason could not manage to unwrap the lumps. After a while he released her hand, but by then her coffee was cold.

They talked about their studies, the rest of the afternoon, and about Mary's new evening job. She was a waitress in a downtown restaurant. While she was telling him a story about this, Mary quite suddenly remembered her father reading *Tom Sawyer* to her. She just remembered his laughing dark eyes. That must have been soon before he left; so she would have been twelve. Scott saw her staring at him with cloudy-liquid eyes and thought, with a mixture of emotions, Su, you know this girl better than I do. He leant across the table and took her hand again. Mary tried to imagine his eyes about ten tones darker and laughing at *Tom Sawyer*. The middle-aged couple at the next table nudged each other and shook their heads at the two young people who held hands so openly.

Mary wondered why her own eyes were blue, and tried to remember the colour of Nicky's eyes. Su's, she knew, were grey.

She saw Scott in front of her and remembered yesterday, if it was yesterday—no, the day before—and the shipping company office in Kinzie Street. She said, "Honey, this coffee's cold. Do you mind if I leave now and get some homework done?"

Scott said, "But Mary, you've said nothing to me all afternoon. Do your homework, of course, but then can't I see you again?"

"Sure," Mary said vaguely, thinking about that fire-escape and wondering if it was always open.

"Well, shall we go dancing?" Scott said desperately. He remembered his promise to Su. In his experience girls tended to speak more freely when they were out at night.

"Fine, why not?" she said equally vaguely, and Scott knew,

feeling depressed, that if this date were to come about he was going to have to borrow someone's car and drive out to Austin.

"Seeya," Mary said. She might as well have been addressing the waitress.

"Mary!" Scott said. He felt like taking her by the shoulders and forcing her to look at him. Her eyes were wandering distractedly around the room. He didn't need Su to tell him something was wrong. Mary's eyes came distantly back and focused on him again and it was once more that melting look. She was thinking about her rooftop corner. Scott searched around in his mind for somewhere they could go to be private. He was fed up with coffee shops. But it was far too cold to sit out in a park, or go down to the lake.

"Listen," Scott said earnestly. "I want you to feel you can trust me. I don't want you to think you're just another pretty face to me, although of course you are. I respect you as a person, as an individual. I am offering you my sincere friendship, and more if you want it. Mary, won't you trust me?"

He was saying the things he would like to hear said to him, assuming, or hoping anyway, that girls have similar feelings at least. She watched him while he spoke with the same serious but unchanging expression, the same liquid eyes. Now what? Was she going to cry again? Was she going to answer at all? Was she moved, embarrassed, pleased? Had she even listened to any of that?

At least she had not made another move to go. She sat still and looked at him. Scott finally decided the thing to do was to read all in the eyes so to speak and to gaze back. Mary had an extraordinary face. How come he had never really looked at it before, although they had been going out now for three months or nearly. It was all smooth and tranquil on the outside, but God knew what depths it concealed. We are staring into each other's eyes, Scott thought, and could not help feeling somewhat selfconscious. Not she. Scott wished he knew more about girls. No girl before had ever been in love with him. Without realizing it Scott had come to assume that Mary was indeed in love. But how peculiar it all was. Scott had never met anyone like Mary before. If she was unhappy, as was plain, it must be for far deeper reasons than just having a mad crush on someone (let's be impartial; let's say just anyone) as Su seemed to imagine. Mary, Scott thought emotionally, is a very complicated personality.

She went on looking and looking at him and Scott felt more and more emotional. This silence, this enigmatic gaze, was pretty plainly an answer to Scott's last speech. But he didn't really feel satisfied. He preferred to speak, to know, to have everything clear. This had led him, in the past, to say some rather unfortunate and committing things to girls, but now, he really meant it. He was just gathering his courage to speak again (although her silence was part of her character and was as beautiful as her face) when she startled him by springing to her feet, smiling a Mona Lisa smile at him.

"Okay?" was all she said.

Scott jumped up too, but dared not leave the table without paying the check, and Mary was gathering her things to make for the door. "No!" he cried, looking desperately round for the waitress and fumbling for the dollar-twenty the check amounted to. "No, Mary, it's not okay! I'm not joking, I simply have to talk seriously with you. Mary, wait, I'm just paying the check."

"I'm too hot," Mary said.

"Hot?" It was the coldest day he had ever known. Despairingly he waved his five-dollar bill at the waitress. Mary had her coat on.

"And I have my homework to do," Mary finished. "So thank you, hon. And seeya."

"Tonight at eight-thirty. I'll pick you up." If Pete would not lend him his Chevy he'd go out in the streets and steal a car. Mary went out without answering, but she'd certainly be at Austin, or if not, he'd patrol the entire city until he found her.

Almost ten minutes later he left the coffee shop, having succeeded at last in paying. It occurred to him as he walked disconsolately along Wacker Drive (Mary was out of sight long ago, of course) that he should have simply left the entire five-dollar bill and to hell with the change.

9

"IT'S SPRING!" BOTT shouted, throwing open the door into the yard.

"It's only February," Gatzko objected.

"Nearly snowdrop time! Anyway I can feel it. I can smell it too. Oh, come and take a breath. It smells alive."

Gatzko sniffed. The air was damp and extremely chilly and smelt, as always, of wet bricks and soot. "What's so spring-like about this?" he demanded. "Spring ought to smell of blossom."

"Oh, no! Not yet. This is a growing time, an earth-stirring time. Seeds get germinating now."

Gatzko grunted and went to work, feeling vaguely that such high spirits were unwarranted by the weather and that she had her horticulture wrong anyway.

Bott wanted to swing on the door. She had broken the hinges of three doors before she was ten, so instead she swung Michael round. He shrieked with delight. She left him with Mrs. Weingartner and went out, feeling too gay to stay in and clean up as she had meant to. She had an hour and a half to herself every morning between the start of Gatzko's shift on the quay and her own work in the kitchen of a restaurant for office workers on Cheapside.

Bott walked briskly along Upper Thames Street, heading only vaguely in the direction of her work, enjoying the dark, still morning, the start of the spring. It was extraordinary, this sensation she had of the air being alive. She felt it rippling round her, filling her with its own life. Yet, as Gatzko had pointed out, it was only a cold grey morning in February.

She stopped suddenly by the site of All-Hallows-the-Great

where the Wren tower stood alone among the ruins of the rest
of the church. Bare earth.

It was a shock, when the rest of London was lying under a
kind of lacquer of grey, trodden ice, which had originally been
snow. Looking down at the pavement as you walked you could
see far-buried grains of gravel beneath you, laid against slip-
periness in the snowfall of two weeks ago, and apparently
there for ever like flies in amber. There seemed never to have
been a time when the gutters were not snowdrifts, when
threats of ever more snow were continually being broadcast.
The sight of ordinary dark ground was enough to pull anyone
up sharp. There was an explanation, of course. Just here,
under the tower, snow could never fall; instead it would pile
up round the sides, which it had done. All the same—bare
earth!

Bott was on it with her shoes off in a moment. She stood
among the old stones and the bushes and weeds with bare feet
on the frozen ground, untouched and uncultivated for centuries, and a thrill went up through the soles of her feet and
made all her skin rise in gooseflesh.

That earth was earth still, even if it was consecrated. There
were little tufts of grass, hard with frost, only just alive maybe
but alive all the same. And Bott, when she stood there, had
felt a thrill and it was a thrill she knew. She, too, had been
separated from nature for a longish time—it was nearly five
months now since they came to London—yet still the earth
tingled for her.

Bott fell on her knees and started poking, digging, feeling,
touching the little plants and breaking up the hard soil. It was
not only packed down and caked with soot; it was also frozen
from the coldest winter Bott had lived through. Her hands
were soon numb, but she went on doggedly tearing at the little
clods. And whether it was that her fingers were too cold to feel
the grit and gravel any longer, or whether she really had
succeeded in breaking up the topsoil, she eventually had the
impression that the frost was softening where she touched. She

was starting a thaw; she was spreading the spring. Bott knew she still had the power of growing things. And it was the awakening of the year.

When she stood up at last, her hands were black and caked and her hair full of bits of plant and she felt lit up inside with a strange hidden light. And that deep throbbing. Was it the earth vibrating into her or her own heart making the earth pulse or both?

She caught herself thinking this and suddenly she was alarmed at her own imaginings.

Aloud Bott said in a rational and common-sense voice, "Dear me. This is perfectly good gardening ground. What a wicked waste that it should go uncultivated when the whole country is short of food."

Upper Thames Street was deserted. But her voice sounded so ordinary and human and what she was saying so reassuringly sensible that Bott went on.

"I do believe it might be a good idea if I brought some seeds along here. I'm sure this soil would raise vegetables if it were dug over a bit and given fertilizer."

Bott looked round with satisfaction at the site, planning her little vegetable beds and congratulating herself on her practicality. Then, "After all," she heard herself say, "anything may come of this spring."

And again she was aware of that deep-down throbbing and gave up the pretence of practicality. She was simply excited because she felt the stirring of the year.

She leant against the tower and took deep lungfuls of air and let her body and mind vibrate, and rejoiced in that almost imperceptible quivering which would bring life to the city, that poor ice-bound city.

She wandered on thinking about the stirring of life and feeling, as so often nowadays, buoyant with delight, until she could not really tell whether she was walking or floating or something between the two. These City mornings! In a lifetime of ecstasy, on and off, but more often on, she had still never encountered rapture like this which seemed to be just an everyday part of life with Gatzko.

She stopped again at All-Hallows-the-Less to stare at a little bush with brown buds. The brown skin was slightly transparent; Bott could almost see the new leaves straining at it. I must come back in a month or two, she thought, to see them finally bursting through.

Although theoretically she knew the one square mile pretty well by now she was constantly surprised by it. The other day for instance she had chanced to look the other way along Eastcheap as she crossed it and had thought she was having a vision. She was seeing the Tower of London caught by early sunlight. She had forgotten that the Tower was anywhere near. Now today she was astonished to find herself at the bottom of a little cobbled hill with a delicate white steeple, fairy-tale-like. Delighted by the sight Bott turned up towards it. When she got nearer she recognized it as a place she knew well: the bombed-out church of St. James Garlickhythe.

It had begun to drizzle. The spire was reflected in the cobbles, its little arches glistening there seeming to lead down into fairyland indeed. Everything shone with a pink light. Enchanted, Bott started to explore the ruins, and found that she could actually get into the shell of the church through what must have been the vestry entrance. She decided to bring Gatzko here as soon as she could persuade him to come.

She scrambled up on a heap of rubble on to one of the window-sills and stared down at the street. As it grew wetter, that wonderful pink luminosity increased. All the little brick alley seemed to glow and the reflections shimmered. Bott rubbed her fingers in a kind of caress over the beautiful Portland stone of the sill and saw what muddy marks they made. They were filthy. She was filthy all over, come to that, from grubbing in the ground and clambering around bombed sites. And it must be nearly time for work. Laughing, half at her own idiocy, half from sheer pleasure in the morning, Bott lowered herself down into the church again, picked her way out and hurried towards Cheapside.

That glow was everywhere. Too bad she really could not spare the time to dash down to the river. She just made it through to the kitchen of Tommy's Eating House by half-past eight. A customer in the restaurant drinking his morning cup of tea scowled at her as she hurried through, and Maria, the Spanish waitress, opened her eyes wide and said, "Ay Mama!"

"Oh heck," Bott said apologetically, "do I look as bad as that?"

Tommy himself was in the kitchen unwrapping strings of sausages. "Christ in Heaven, Bott, have you been for a swim in the Thames?"

"No—not quite—I found this darling little ruined church. Two darling little ruined churches, come to that, and I couldn't resist exploring. Do you know St. James Gar-lickhythe?"

"Well, forgetting your darling little ruined churches for a moment," Tommy said, "you'd better get in there and have a scrub. Because you've got yourself into quite a mess. And you'd better be bloody quick about it too," he shouted after her, "because Old Mac will be in wanting his breakfast any minute."

He turned back to his sausages grinning to himself at the vagaries of his cook. He could hear her singing and splashing and saying "Oh heck" in the back there. She wasn't much use as a cook but she was worth having around for the laughs. Old Mac came in and Tommy greeted him jovially. He looked at the trickle of water coming from under the door of the wash-place, sighed and started to make Old Mac's breakfast himself.

Bott worked hard when she did come out though. She ran and jumped round the kitchen getting and forgetting the salt and the flour and the ketchup. She seemed very talkative this morning and chattered away about the spring and some vege-table garden she intended to make in the ruins of one of her darling little churches. Tommy had to ask her to be quiet when the nine o'clock news came on. She knew by now, too, how much store he set by listening to that. Tommy could not really settle in comfortably to the day until he had been re-assured by the trivialities which the news inevitably carried now. He could never quite believe that the war was really over.

A song came on after the weather called "Jollity Farm", full of idiotic animal noises, with the unlikely chorus line of "Everyone says How-do-you-do, down on Jollity Farm".

Bott, who had listened intently and seriously to the nine o'clock news, her head bowed over the loaf she was slicing, cheered up like a child at this foolish song. She got it on the brain, wrong of course, and pranced round the kitchen all day singing "The hens go cluck, the pigs go hornk, the cows go moo, everyone says how-do-you-do, down on Jollity Farm." Maria giggled, and Bott went through it again, putting even more gusto into the animal noises.

While Tommy was making sausage rolls Bott came and stood behind him. "I say," she said, "those do look good."

"And with any luck," said Tommy, expertly rolling out the flaky pastry, "they'll even taste good."

"There, that's what I can never do, that layer bit. My pastry at home always comes out hard as wood."

"You want to put plenty of fat in, two kinds of fat. And don't moisten it too much."

"I usually make it without fat. We never seem to have any to spare."

"And you want to be very light on the touch with it," Tommy said helplessly. "Do the opposite to what you'd do if it was dumplings. Even if you're making short pastry."

"I see. But then, you know, Michael always wants to have a go, and he does bash rather."

"Oh, well," said Tommy, "there are a few things you have to put up with for the pleasure of having a kid about."

"Yes. I just feel," Bott said, "that Gatzko would like me better if I could cook nicely for him."

"Well, I think," Tommy said gallantly, "that Gatzko is doing very well with what he's got."

Bott beamed at him, and jumped away across the kitchen singing "The dogs go woof, the cows go moo."

In her lunch break she went to Leadenhall where she did most of her shopping (queues seemed shorter with plenty of stalls) and bought seeds. Her fingers trembled so with excitement that twice she dropped all her money under the stall. She bought spinach, turnips, parsnips and (rebelling suddenly against austerity) cornflowers. She also bought a sixpenny gardening manual. Reverently, as though it were in truth the treasures of the earth, she carried her packets out of the market, shielding them from the pressure of the crowd, just in case seeds were fragile. She wasn't sure about seeds; her interest in growing things, up to now, had been confined to wild life. A street clock said twenty to three. All her lunchhour had been wasted by those maddening queues. No, she couldn't do any planting today. Never mind, that would be a treat in store for tomorrow. The spring she felt within her wouldn't be over, after all. It was just beginning. Everything was just beginning.

Then coming back past St. Paul's she saw that hat.

Tommy, standing outside writing up the sandwich menu for tea, saw her coming and did not recognize her. The tall gawky shape was familiar enough, to be sure, but at first he only noticed the head, bowed over a bundle, wearing a brilliant orange, wide-brimmed creation. The front part was more a peak than a brim; it came down right over her face. Yet the top part was decidedly reminiscent of an officer's cap. Tommy stared incredulously at the thing. God, what a colour. It was enough to give you a headache. Then the head lifted and that radiant face grinned at him down the street and he thought of course, as if it could possibly have been anyone else.

"How do you like it?" she asked him.

"Bott, you're looking gorgeous. This isn't all in my honour, is it? Or is it your birthday or something? You seem to be carrying on some private fiesta."

"It's spring," she said, with another dazzling grin.

"So it is. Well, as you see, I'm just writing 'Sardine sandwiches' on here. So I'd be obliged if you'd go in there and make some."

"Sardine. How nice," Bott said vaguely, carrying her parcel in as if she were in a procession.

Tommy finished chalking up the menu. He polished the windows outside and went in. The whole restaurant was reverberating with a noise which he could not at first identify. Then he realized that it was Bott in the back interpreting the line "The sheep go baa, the cocks doodledoo." Conversation had ceased among the group of customers. They were all staring towards the kitchen.

He said to them, "I am sorry for this. It must be my cook." He went hurriedly through. Bott was strutting in the middle of the floor with Maria doubled up in laughter on a chair before her. When Tommy came in Bott wagged a finger at him and told him, "Everyone says HOW-DO-YOU-DO! down on Jollity Farm."

"Bott, for Christ's sake. Will you stop this bloody racket!"

Bott looked taken aback. She said, "Oh, sorry. Was I making a lot of noise?"

"You're audible all over the shop. What's the matter with you, for heaven's sake? You're behaving like a baby."

Bott looked distressed and tousled her hair. It probably felt uncomfortably smooth after having a hat on it. Tommy felt suddenly sorry for her. He said, "Ah, never mind. You're in love, that's all your trouble."

"True enough," Bott admitted humbly.

"Well, keep the old pecker up, hm? And if you could forget 'Jollity Farm' for the time being and cut me another plate of sardine sandwiches, that might be a good thing too."

Bott nodded and set eagerly to work. Within five minutes

she was humming under her breath "Everybody sings. The birds sing too. The dogs bow-wow. The pigeons coo."

Tommy smiled. It was good to hear anyone so happy, so long as she could keep the decibels down. He remembered his previous cook, a relative of Maria's, whose heartbreaking Galician folk songs were one of the secret reasons he had got rid of her, although she only crooned.

Bott was thinking regretfully that she would have to wait until August to see her cornflowers bloom. Were there any seeds which came up quicker? She saw the lair all bright and beautiful with a constant succession of her flowers. She saw Gatzko springing across the room among them, the symbols of her joy. Surely flowers were a symbol of joy. And she was brimming over with it. Yes, Gatzko would be springing about the lair, doing the stove or something. He always sprang in his movements. Then she would enter, bearing flowers, a great sheaf of them, a shaft of light and colour, that she had grown. Gatzko would turn, and the same light would shine back from his eyes as well.

Gatzko had got a piece of ice in his shoe. He was stacking crates inside the lorry as they were wheeled up to him and it was dark and the smell of years of fish slime was suffocating. He had been in similar lorries all day. He had been suffering the same stink, and wheeling the same barrows, and stacking the same crates, all winter. This was the penalty for being stuck with a steady job, instead of the casual labour the Home Office would not let him do. He exchanged the same chitchat and not very intelligent jokes with the same men all day, every day. It was good that the men were mostly such splendidly disreputable Irish Cockneys. But they were even better in their setting in the George and Dragon and the dialogue seemed to be much improved when there was a bit of beer splashing about.

The pile of crates was higher than Gatzko now. He groaned to get the top one on. That was another thing. He was tired of being called "Midget" and tired of exerting himself to do work meant for men twice his size. No job, however romantic, was worth this amount of effort. Okay, he'd had a crazy idea wanting to be a stevedore on the London wharves. But crazy ideas have to be acted out, unless you want a load of obsessions and neuroses. The bad thing is to keep at them too long so you get disillusioned. For instance, if Gatzko had quit this fish work three months ago he would never have found out how claustrophobic it could be. His pleasure in Lower Thames Street was largely spoilt from having spent too much time there.

Early this month there had been a revival of the old glamour when the first loads of strange things like whalemeat started coming in. But very soon Gatzko had come to realize that shifting whalemeat was really very similar to shifting herrings, and the smell, which had begun by being so magically different, quickly became just another kind of fish smell. And besides, whales were not sharks. They were nursery creatures; everyone knew about their foolish grins and silly spouts. They were made of pink rubber and floated in the bath. Now if the Government had thought of importing dolphins or sea-horses! But meanwhile, day after day, it was mackerel, cod, whalemeat, cod again and disillusion with the whole Thames-Mediterranean dream.

Gatzko thought about the Mediterranean. He thought about Phoenicia and Genoa and Marseilles and Piraeus.

And now he knew that this was the very highest he could reach and it was the moment for that humiliating experience, calling for help with the crates.

He was the only man he knew who could not lift to the ceiling of an eight-foot lorry.

If I change my job what shall it be? he wondered.

Something vaguely international. Banking, but then I would be the loitering heir of a City director, and I would depart leaving no address, Gatzko thought. I don't need to be a loitering heir to do that.

No, nothing white-collared. Hadn't he had enough of that in Chicago!

"Hey Midget, shall I take over for you?"

King old Big Alf had seen Gatzko's predicament and was saving him the embarrassment of going to the foreman. Gatzko, preoccupied with images of Naples and Smyrna, handed over without thanking him.

Airlines are so standardized, he was thinking. I could be a baggage porter at London Airport and never even know where I was. Dock work is better.

But Gatzko knew really that he was no longer strong enough for manual work like this. He, Gatzko, who had built his own house in Sedona, who, three years ago, had carried twenty pounds of ammunition seven kilometres across broken rocky hillsides, and been back before light, every night for a week, a week of hard daytime campaigning too. And that was effort wasted, looking back. His band of communist partisans had won their little war, perhaps, but it had only served to show them up, and to disillusion Gatzko with yet one more creed, communism. Feeling black, Gatzko slammed Big Alf's barrow across the pavement. Even that seemed heavy, and it was empty.

By five o'clock Lower Thames Street was so dark he could hardly see what he was doing. What an oppressive place it was, really. An abyss of a street. Gatzko felt it sucking at him, draining him; those foul fish fumes deadening his mind.

He thought he caught sight of a gleam of reflected sunset in a window and raised his eyes in surprise. It wasn't, of course; there was no sunset that grey evening. But Bott's orange hat shone out like a beacon as she came down the street, jumping over the puddles. Gatzko leant on his barrow and watched in delight and amazement. She reached him, all hot and pink from having walked from Cheapside to Billingsgate in five minutes, threw herself into his arms and panted, "Gatzko, darling, I've found such a wonderful place." Gatzko hugged her appreciatively. She was fairly radiating warmth.

"All right, Midget, you may as well go off," the foreman called, smiling indulgently. He, and everyone else, had stopped to watch the orange hat approaching. The whole of that stretch of Thames-side knew crazy Midget's crazy woman. Gatzko grinned at his boss, took Bott's arm and marched her away towards Monument Street.

"Well, Bott, let's hear the adventure! You found this wonderful place and there was the Tarnhelm, plus our old dragon, I suppose, and a pile of treasure, is that it?"

"Goodness, what marvellous stories you tell," Bott said enthralled, squeezing his arm and looking at him with adoring eyes. Gatzko felt better already than he had all day.

"No, it can't be the Tarnhelm. That's an invisible hat, you know, and you're looking a bit better than invisible, to say the least."

The peaked brim threw a reflected glow over her whole face. She shone at him. Gatzko squeezed her arm back and said, "I know! It's Don Quixote's golden helmet. And wow, you can count me as a conquest for a start."

"Gatzko, you angel. Now would you like to come and see my place? It's right by here."

"I'd like to go anywhere with Doña Quixote," Gatzko said. They went on, arm in arm, laughing a bit breathlessly though neither could have said what at. Bott led him to All-Hallows-the-Great and said, somewhat shyly, "There! Isn't it like a little piece of country in the middle of the city?"

As a derelict site it looked very much like any other derelict site, except that the broken stones about looked rather more weatherworn and the whole thing was more overgrown with weeds than most of the recently bombed sites. There were the hard-packed remnants of last week's snow at the corners of the tower. "Wow! Terrific!" Gatzko shouted, plunging towards it and leaping on to the remains of a wall. "Back to mother Nature, eh? Remember what old Bacchus used to get up to in the spring? Yippee!"

He leapt off the wall with his arms wide and began dancing

towards the tower through the old stalks and tussocks. Shrieking with delight, Bott ran after him. The rain began again as,
panting with laughter, they dodged each other round the
tower. It began to shine and glimmer. Even while putting all
her energy into her game of catch with Gatzko, Bott could not
help noticing how that wet luminosity of this morning was
rising again all round them. The sky and the bricks and the
earth she had bought seeds for were all aglow, and the air was
full of splinters of pink sleet. They spattered against her face
as she and Gatzko paused, gasping, watching each other warily
from two opposite stones. Then with a shout she launched
herself through the sleet towards him. For an instant she saw
the light shine back from his eyes in just the way she knew so
well, just how she had imagined this morning, and then he
turned and leapt away.

She never really knew where they went. He seemed to be
leading her through a maze of little alleys and over bridges
and along the stumps of walls of mile after mile of blitzed
London, and everywhere that incandescence. At one point
they ran along the narrow pavement of what must once have
been a tiny enclosed lane, but now as she stumbled after him,
the ground on her left fell away and she felt giddily that she
was running along the edge of a parapet with great stretches
of the ravaged city below her. Beyond this the arches of the
Blackfriars railway bridge stood up against the broken skyline,
and Bott caught a glimpse as she glanced dizzily up of St.
Bride's, white, untouched, perfect, rising into the evening
above the filthy bricks of the railway. Bott's head began to
spin until she was afraid she would lose her balance altogether
and crash headlong into the bombed basements below them.
She imagined that vista of the city turning and turning round
her as she fell.

Gatzko reached the far side, stopped and looked round. He
had gained on her in their chase. Now he was standing up
there watching her with such mockery, Bott thought, and
challenge, that she found herself suddenly furious. She

checked herself stumbling along and broke into a full gallop towards him. Cheeky devil! Leading her a chase like this round parts of the city she didn't know obviously just to tease. She came whooping towards him and he turned and ran lightly out on to Ludgate Hill, round behind Blackfriars Station somewhere, down another little dark turning and now she was catching up after all. The shops were all closed, even the station was nearly deserted. Gatzko looked like a running shadow, but she was almost on him and she could hear him panting and smell his fishy jersey. He dodged into an opening to avoid her, ran backwards and disappeared. Bott, leaping after him, found herself rolling painfully down a rubble-covered slope into the corner of one of those gutted basements she had just been looking down on. She fetched up with a bump against a wall, a bit of a chair and Gatzko. They lay in a heap breathing heavily and giggling, and then Bott tried to raise herself, fists ready to pummel him. Instead she found them both seized in those man's hands whose strength she always misjudged. His panting breath was in her face, and the more she struggled to pull away and get on top the more his weight pressed her down against the sharp broken bricks and the leg of the chair. His cheek rasped against her face, and she tried to remember when he had last shaved. Weak with breathlessness and laughter, she made one more effort to stiffen her body and fight, and found it instead arching to meet him with a strange catlike spasm.

She shifted against the bricks, trying not to let herself realize that she was extremely uncomfortable. Gatzko at least seemed perfectly content, stretched out looking upside-down at her with a pleased expression, though people's expressions are difficult to judge when they are upside down. Bott felt that life had reached perfection point. She wanted to prolong it as much as could be. She lay against Gatzko's chest and looked up into the rain. That same glow which had been with her all day! But now she felt it inside her as well.

It was a strange effect, less of a continuous "glow" which was the word she had been using to herself, than the light of thousands of little pink sparks. The air seemed to be full of them; her blood was pulsing with them, and they danced about, minutely small, somewhat as Bott imagined fire-flies. She remembered how she had noticed splinters in the light that morning too and had ascribed it to the rain driving. Now, looking hard, Bott could see, or feel, an infinitely complicated pattern, a real dance. She no longer remembered at all they were lying out in the dusk and sleet in a bombed site near Blackfriars Station. As far as Bott was concerned she and Gatzko were dancing with the spheres. She did not even feel it when Gatzko ran his hand down her stomach inside her coat with an interrogative "Mmm?"

She felt so stiff and odd and was so unresponsive that Gatzko sat up, alarmed. His mind had not been running along such exalted lines as Bott's. He had been contentedly lying back not thinking about anything very definite but feeling good and strong and pleased with life. He looked anxiously into Bott's face in case she had fainted or passed out with the cold. The wretched woman was lying there looking like a painting of St. Teresa in ecstasy or something. All she needed was a bunch of lilies in her hand. He shook her and she smiled, her eyes still rolled up towards heaven, and muttered something about the dance of the stars.

Gatzko, thoroughly annoyed, got to his knees and hauled her up too. What a woman, who goes into a metaphysical trance when she's made love to. He shook her quite roughly and yelled, "Bott! Snap out of that!"

Slowly she came round and gave him another sweet saintly smile. "Bott!" he yelled again. She said, "Gatzko, darling," in such an amorous voice that he was nonplussed. She gave him a loving melting look. Gatzko did not know what to think but since he had her by the shoulders anyway he hugged her. It seemed as well, though, to rouse her from her reverie, just in case his impression of a trance had been true, so he pulled her to her feet. As he did so a little book fell out of her pocket. He picked it up for her and tried to read the title.

"Your Short Guide To—" he read aloud, but the main word was printed in some dark colour and invisible in this dim red light. He felt vaguely that he had just been unfair to Bott, and since he was in a particularly good and gentle mood right now he wanted to make up for it. "Well, and what does our gorgeous Doña Quixote need a short guide to? Nothing that I can think of," he joked. She grinned and grabbed the book, wide awake now anyway. "No, no," he said, snatching it back. "I'm intrigued. Let's go somewhere with a bit more light so I can see what it is you're learning up."

It was her sixpenny gardening manual. "Oh, a real thriller you'll find it," she said. "Make your hair stand on end. Which, incidentally, it's doing now." She smoothed his hair caressingly. Gatzko smiled at her, feeling gay and terrific again and ready for an evening of celebration. "Let's go somewhere!" he shouted. "Let's really go somewhere and read your shocker. Let's go up Fleet Street and see what's going on."

"Oh, yes! Let's make tonight a special night."

They scrambled out of the ruined cellar towards the street, laughing as they slipped and stumbled.

"Do you remember that time we climbed the cliff face?" Bott asked. "Almost the first day we met, and we had to run after Michael, and he led us a dance all over the mountain."

"I think we were better at climbing then. Our powers are deteriorating."

"Oh, no, Michael was the best mountaineer of us three from the start. Yes, it *was* the first day we met, don't you remember? You followed me all over the mountain as a tease."

"It wasn't really our first encounter, as a matter of fact. I had been following you for days before that."

She broke away from him, astonished. "You'd what?"

"Sure. I saw you waiting at a bus stop in some village up there at least three days before you even noticed me. Then I followed you around, but I couldn't succeed in attracting your attention. So finally Michael and I were forced to ambush you on the mountain, and you didn't like that, did you! But otherwise I might have danced attendance on you from that day to this and been stonily ignored. So now I've confessed will you forgive me my prank?"

"Good Lord, Gatzko, I had no idea. I thought you were just playing a joke that day. Well, how extraordinary I didn't notice you. I'm dreadfully sorry I was so rude."

Gatzko laughed aloud. "Oh, Bott, and at the time you told me about a dozen times that I was being dreadfully rude."

"Well, so you were. But I thought it was sheer bad luck to keep meeting you all over the place. I must say I'm most impressed now I hear the truth."

She was all pink and pretty-looking with delight. Gatzko felt pleased at the success of his little bit of flattery. He put his arm round her again. He was shivering with cold after the bombed site episode and was surprised to find her as warm as she was flushed in the face. He said, "Hey, what a hot bottle you are. How come, after lying around in that icepit?"

"Oh, yes, I suppose that was quite cold," she said vaguely. "But walking always warms me up. Anyway I'm never cold when I'm happy."

"You're happy now then, are you?"

"Oh, yes! Tommy even thought it must be my birthday. Why, aren't you happy?"

"At the moment life seems temporarily to have brightened, yes."

She didn't listen. "Today's a real festival, in the proper sense of the word, isn't it? Look what a beautiful evening it is!"

Gatzko looked round, shivering, at grey wet Ludgate Circus.

"The light's all pink. A wonderful glowing pink and full of little dancing atoms."

"Mmm. I suppose you actually are correct about the atoms, but what's this pink light? It's sleeting."

"I know it's sleeting, stupid! That's where the light comes

from. Reflection or refraction or something. Can you really not see how everything's all shiny pink?"

"Well, hot bottle, honey," he said squeezing her, "I guess you're not only wearing a golden helmet but a pair of rose-coloured spectacles as well. Quite a combination."

Bott smiled at him, pleased to hear him so affectionate but wishing he would take her seriously. She really wanted him to see the beauty she was seeing.

"No, but joking apart, can't you see the buildings all glowing? All luminous?"

"Um, well. Monet thought rain was luminous in itself, didn't he? But I'm not sure how far I'm a follower of Monet."

Bott didn't want to talk about Monet. She knew very little about him, but was certain he was not what she meant. "No, no, this is something special."

"I have seen cities looking lit-up," Gatzko said. "But I wouldn't say London was one of them, right now. It needs neon and so forth."

"Oh, Gatzko!" Bott suddenly felt hopelessly sad. "You don't know one bit what I'm talking about. This has nothing to do with neon."

"All right, you tell me what it is."

"Oh, just—all these little things—bits of light. As if the atmosphere were full of little live particles all shining with their own light and dancing about and having a celebration."

"And all this is," Gatzko said, "is a freezing wet night in the middle of the bleakest winter since 1880 in austerity England." He pushed her against a lamp-post and turned her face up into the light. "When I'm locked up in the fog in Alcatraz Island Prison," he said, "if you come along too, hot bottle, life will be one long merry holiday. You'd have enjoyed yourself in a prison camp."

Does he mean that? wondered Bott. Do I really make a difference to his life? God knows I've been trying hard enough, these last five months. She stared up at him, and saw slivers of pink fire reflected in his pupils.

Gatzko's whole face was too numb for him to want to kiss her. He pressed his cheek against hers to warm it and said, "Well, how about this merry holiday, even without being on Alcatraz! Shall we start by painting Fleet Street red?"

"Pink," Bott said, and thought the whole universe was dancing with her and Gatzko as they set out on their Fleet Street pub crawl.

10

H o w G a t z k o l a u g h e d when he discovered, in the Black
Friar, that Bott's book was a gardening manual. The amusement it caused him even seemed disproportionate at first until
it occurred to Bott he was not trying to be unkind; he was
merely infected by the holiday feeling, which seemed to grow
minute by minute. All that evening they went from pub to
pub down Fleet Street and into the Strand, where, getting
hungry, Gatzko bought her sausage rolls in the Wig & Pen.
The bartender in each pub was nice, the atmosphere gayer,
they thought. By the time they reached Trafalgar Square they
were in a high delirium of delight. As this was how Bott had
been feeling all day it was hard to judge if she were drunk too.
When Gatzko wanted to jump in the fountains (not playing)
Bott laughed uproariously and thought how sweet and crazy
he was. He climbed on a lion's back and shouted poetry and
Bott adored him for his originality. A policeman made him
climb down and warned him against being rowdy. Gatzko said
yes, sorry, he appreciated that there was a war on. Bott
screamed with laughter and clapped and stamped.

"Now just you watch it," the cop said. "If you don't know
the English law against disturbing the peace it's time you did."

So Gatzko gave him that sweet smile which only he knew
how to do and which Bott loved in him perhaps more than
anything else.

"I truly am sorry," he said to the policeman. "But you know
how it takes you when you are really happy and you've
travelled all over the world and then you find a city that's
worth all the rest put together. You can't help celebrating."

The policeman softened, smiled, patted Gatzko's shoulder,

E

said it did him good to hear a friendly foreign voice in these hostile times and he was glad to welcome him to our country, but all the same, for his own good, please would he not climb on the lions.

Gatzko said, "I meant it as a compliment, not as disrespect, because I'm a mountaineer, you see. But I get your point, don't worry." And that smile again, baby Michael's smile. The cop walked away grinning and Bott and Gatzko squeezed each other and laughed in each other's faces at their triumph.

Bott's own happiness was multiplied from hearing Gatzko use her own phrase about celebrating, and speak about being really happy and finding a city worth all others. What was that if not confirmation of the hopes she had permitted herself during that glorious half-hour in the Blackfriars bombed-out place? Why else should he be really happy? Oh, the ecstasy of that mad chase, like some sort of bridal procession gone wild. She could still feel the tingling in her flesh and his too surely, and the myriads of frost sparks were spiking her, making her prickle all the way down, until she thought she must surely be sparkling like some tinselly Christmas tree.

The comparison with a Christmas tree brought her back to Gatzko again. "Do you remember our Mr. Noel?" she asked him. Instead of conventional Christmas decorations he had carved, out of zinc, a special Christmas sculpture which they had draped with tinsel and christened "Mr. Noel". But instead of answering this, Gatzko suddenly started steering her towards the National Gallery as if this was where he had been intending to go all the time. Bott panted along on his arm, and they stood reverently in front of the railings. "There," Gatzko said.

"Um, yes," said Bott, her ecstasy damped somewhat, although she enjoyed really being baffled by Gatzko. She liked it when he surprised her. All trace of his mad gay spirits had gone. He was looking up at this building with deep seriousness, and oh, there was light in his eyes again, not the excited reflections of public bar bulbs but that glow of his own which came into his pupils when he was seriously moved. Bott wished she knew what this place was, which affected him so much. She looked round and saw the policeman watching them with apparent satisfaction and then move off. Still Gatzko stared at this thing.

"In there," Gatzko said, his voice emotional, "are some of the most beautiful things this world has produced."

Bott did not dare to ask him what sort of things or what the place was. She said, "Yes, indeed," shivered and looked round. On the right was a building which interested her much more, a white church, looking very much like one of her dear City churches; Wren, maybe? A sign outside said "The service to-morrow will be conducted by..." (the name was too small to read from here). An active church, too. So many of her beloved little places were blitzed. She must come back.

"The Metropolitan has nothing on it," Gatzko said. She jumped. He was still looking at this great neo-Classic hulk. But he spoke with such reverence that Bott dutifully tried to appreciate it, and decided to investigate it along with the church tomorrow. His remark about the Metropolitan was un-illuminating since she did not know what that was either. She said, "I can't see much at the moment. I'll come back to-morrow."

He looked at her as if she had said something funny. "Very true," he said. "I hope you enjoy it."

Oh why could she never judge if he was laughing at her. To change the subject she said, "Meanwhile I want another drink, if it's still opening time."

"Good idea! We have ten minutes. I'd have let them run past and then wanted a drink. What would I do without a native of the place about?"

Not passionate maybe, but he gave her an affectionate squeeze, and she was contented. They marched away towards the Duncannon arm in arm.

Everywhere they went Bott's hat was noticed. People loved it. They said things like "I haven't seen a colour like that in years" and "Where did you find such a non-austerity trimming?" and "My dear, look at those stitches, did you make it?" and "Don't you know there's a law against bright colours these days, sweetheart?"

Now as they entered the Duncannon the usual chorus of whistles and applause started up and Bott and Gatzko squeezed each other's waists and giggled. Bott hummed, "Everyone says How-do-you-do down on Jollity Farm". A man near them, extremely drunk but looking pleasant, said, "It's a treat to see a woman looking good these days." But the woman behind the bar just stared.

As they came up for a last drink she said, "May I ask how much you gave for that?"

"Seven-and-six," Bott said modestly, hoping Gatzko would hear and notice her economy. He wasn't listening however.

"Seven-and-six? *Seven-and-six?*"

Bott shifted uncomfortably, suddenly frightened that seven-and-six was too much for a hat, instead of being a bargain. Bott had not bought a civilian hat for years. The barwoman kept on staring.

"And just where did you find that for seven-and-six?"

"Well, as you go under St. Paul's towards Cheapside," Bott began miserably, "there's a little shop—"

"I know! Good God!" The bartender, seeing her difficulty with his wife, had come up. He interrupted her, exploding with laughter. He could scarcely explain through his chuckles. Maybe he, too, had had a night of it.

"The blind workers' shop!"

And suddenly the whole pub was hooting with laughter. It was infectious. Quite what the joke was nobody knew but everyone there was laughing, Bott loudest of all. Somebody cracked a joke, saying the hat was supposed to be grey, but something had happened to the dye and nobody could tell because they were all blind! Bott did not think this was funny at all, quite the reverse in fact, but still she found herself aching with near-hysterical laughter.

Gatzko's own hilarity had ebbed away. He sighed and turned away from the counter and his mind drifted off to the Mediterranean. Trafalgar Square. He thought about the original place, Trafalgar.

The Duncannon sounded from outside as if it were New Year's Eve. A voice shrieked, "Don't you see what it was, before the brim was added? It's a renovated officer's hat."

That was the last straw. The idea that she might be wearing an officer's hat, let alone dyed orange, she who when she was demobbed was as much a Private as when she went in, made Bott so dizzy with laughter that quite suddenly she feared she would pass out. She stopped laughing and looked anxiously for Gatzko. He was not there. Bott felt herself panic. She pushed about through the crowd, to and fro between the bars, unable to think anything coherent except he's gone, he's gone, I've driven him away acting like a clown. No, no, not here, and this surely was his glass, half empty. Drunkenly she looked round for the gents'. She would have gone in if the bartender's wife had not turned all the lights off, crying "Time!" and started steering her customers out. Bott, unsteady on her feet, was swept into the street with a group of others, and there was Gatzko on the pavement looking meditatively into Trafalgar Square.

"Gatzko!" Bott called, feeling dizzy again, this time with sheer relief. Gatzko turned and gave her such a warm smile that she staggered; anybody might who got a smile like that. "Hello, Bott," Gatzko said affectionately. "Too drunk to stand up on about three pints of soap and water? Not bad." He put his arm round her to support her and shivering they made towards Charing Cross.

"I'm not drunk," said Bott. "I love you."

"You are drunk," Gatzko said, giving her that smile again.

Gatzko was in two minds whether to bother turning up for work at all any more or not. He had not told anyone yet he intended to leave. There was the question of references, but otherwise he saw no reason to bore himself any longer. Any of his mates—one of his new vocabulary of London words—he wanted to see again, he could whenever he chose, in the George and Dragon.

To hell with references. He could con himself into the kind of job he had in mind without. He could con himself into most things, come to that. If he wanted easy money, which he did not, or if he did not have scruples and conscience, which he did, he could probably have become a successful confidence trickster altogether.

Apart from this, which he was not considering as a future career too seriously, he thought he would like some work with a truly international flavour, and work—this was not so pleasant to face up to, but he was forced to now—that was not too heavy.

Bott had woken herself up with considerable difficulty and was cooking him some sort of breakfast, so although he had a hangover too he dressed as if for work and drank a cup of her tea. She said "Bother" and "Oh heck" and "Gosh, I do feel awful, but wasn't it fun," about a dozen times each. Gatzko sat on the end of the bed, rubbing his chin. It felt stubbly, greasy and had a certain flabbiness underneath, which was not a double chin exactly but was the kind of thing women worried about. He would be feeling depressed if there were not a certain holiday excitement about not knowing what was going to happen next that day. What did happen next was that Bott, who was groggily attempting to make porridge, tripped and upset the saucepan all over the Primus and the cooking shelf. It began to sizzle and blacken as she stood looking hopelessly at it. Gatzko extinguished the Primus for her and kissed her. She looked at him with big bloodhound's eyes. She was all in love with him after being chased and tickled and stoned up last night. That all went to combat Gatzko's potential depression. He tried the washing water, found it far too cold to touch and went out.

When he reached Upper Thames Street he turned left instead of right, simply to prove that today truly was different. He was out of the Fish Belt almost at once and found himself, rather to his surprise, in a Potato Unloading Belt. They had soon seen that the subdivisions of the City were as clearly defined as regions of London itself. By Blackfriars, after Fleet Street of course, you came upon the Fur Belt. Here two names out of three on office building doorplates were "Importers of Pelts" or "Furs and Skins" or something of the kind, with nice Waste Land names. But go up, say, Carter Lane to Ludgate Hill and you were in the Bible Belt. Bott did not appreciate the joke involved here; she had not lived in the real Bible Belt, U.S.A. For miles around St. Paul's every other shop was a religious bookshop, full of earnest women evangelizing each other's earnest shopgirls. How could they, how could Bott fail to see how funny they were?

At Billingsgate, of course, you entered the Fish Belt, the choice residential spot Gatzko had selected. Due north came the Big Business Belt. Gatzko this morning had chosen to go east. Potatoes, and then at the Tower, tourists. No, thank you. He turned west again through the Big Business Belt. Amusing also, in its way, to see these imposing buildings so empty and pathetic when the wharf he should be working on right now would have been alive and bustling for nearly two hours. Gatzko took King William Street, although it meant going towards London Bridge instead of away from it. He fixed his eyes before his feet and hurried along, gripping an imaginary briefcase. He passed St. Mary Woolnoth and regretted having missed its hourly chimes. But it wouldn't have been nine in any case. Everything was just wrong. He walked along Cannon Street, feeling tired and depressed and not really hoping to find the Cannon Street Hotel (he had looked for it often). He was a bit sick of this City of London dream anyway. Although Eliot, admittedly, knew quite a lot about that too.

He went down and looked disconsolately at the river, by Blackfriars Bridge, wishing the shops were open so he could buy some aspirin. It was neither dawn nor dark, wartime nor prosperity, winter nor spring, whatever Bott said, but it was damned cold. He came back from the river edge into Upper Thames Street and laughed aloud at the memory of Bott shyly showing him the place, just along there, where she intended to garden. Garden! God Almighty! Gatzko walked to the spot to have another look. The woman intended to come and dig in this, this black packed ground which must be fast on the way to turning into coal.

How they had laughed together last night over that little gardening manual she'd bought. They had planned delphiniums and asparagus and joked about landscape garden-ing, and a man they picked up had told them the only fertilizer worth bothering with was dried blood, and that had made a good joke too. But they had laughed in fun; now he found he was laughing bitterly. Just look at the place. In the half-light Gatzko saw, for the first time, that it was a church-yard of some kind. Jesus, that perfected it. And what a time to be thinking of cultivation anyhow, bleak, grim, frostbound without any of the glamour of midwinter. Gatzko felt bleak and grim all over. He wandered up into Queen Victoria Street.

Of course most people had their little games of make-be-lieve. Most of the world spent its time deceiving either itself or others. Gatzko was very careful to do neither. And if self-deception was to be dreaded, therefore detachment was to be desired. How could anyone be involved with—well, with any-thing, and not end up fooling themselves?

It was logic, but you try persuading Bott of it. The woman was in a permanent state of emotional involvement with some-thing, be it geology in North Wales, holding hands in the rain or keeping imaginary spring rites. God, what a fool the woman was really. She was incapable of understanding the necessity of keeping at a distance, of watching from a perch. She did not see the danger of weltering down there in the bog of your own personality. Gatzko could not help feeling a little tired at the constant effort required of him to keep her out of this.

Gatzko found himself looking at a gloriously flamboyant, scarlet-painted tie in a window. "Imported from U.S.A." it was labelled. It was about nine inches wide, had ships and light-houses on it and was perfectly beautiful. Gatzko discovered that he was considering buying it. Then he saw the sign at the top of the window display. "Spring is on its way!" it said. "Here, from America, for the first time, are signs of a thaw." It was like something Bott might say. Gatzko was revolted. He never wore ties. How, in the face of what he had just been thinking, could he ever even have contemplated such a compromise? Leave the mad spending and Easter bonnet cult to Bott. Gatzko walked on.

As he wandered past Blackfriars Station yet again, it started to snow. He went back towards Lovat Lane. Bott would be gone by now, and he could relax and talk with one of the Weingartners. He still secretly believed that one or both of them came from somewhere glamorously mittelEuropean. In any case it would be cosy there. Although Mrs. Weingartner had not succeeded in getting coal any more than any other Londoner, the Dairy & still managed to be snug. Probably that tea-urn was enough to heat the entire house.

He did consider going for a cup of tea to Bott's place but suddenly realized that he would rather go almost anywhere else. She was emphatically not cosy. Warm, yes, to a frightening degree. He had never at any point thought she looked cold, that was the first thing which had intrigued him, so long ago in Wales. He remembered her warmth last night after half an hour in a frozen bombed basement. It was phenomenal, even fearsome. If the lair were home to him it was for the sake of the Dairy & and the Weingartners; and not for hot Bott.

Poor old Bott. She tried so hard. If there was one thing she had succeeded in, incidentally, it was her relationship with Michael. For a moment Gatzko brightened at the memory of their snowman competition, last time there was deep snow (about ten days ago). Bott had tried then, too, and was

E*

resoundingly beaten by Michael. But then Gatzko's gloom returned. All that was probably just frustrated maternal instincts. It was worth remembering that at first it was Michael, not Gatzko, she had loved.

It was hours before the George would be open. Meanwhile he entered the Dairy & and settled down comfortably for a chat with Mr. Weingartner. The language barrier between him and Gatzko was almost complete (Mrs. Weingartner was marginally better). They got on very well together, talking happily at cross-purposes most of the time.

BOTT COULD NOT remember what, if any, food there was at home. Too bad; Gatzko would surely be just as pleased if she spent lunchtime admiring that building in Trafalgar Square he appeared to dote on so. After making one bloomer after another in the morning's cooking (and dear old Tommy had forgiven her each time, for the stars in her eyes he said) she rammed her new hat on and dashed along Fleet Street.

Yes, there they were, the delicate steepled church and the domed thing. Bott hesitated. One tempted her, the other decidedly did not. Then she thought she need probably only take a quick peep at the church and devote the rest of her forty minutes to the other. She went into St. Martin-in-the-Fields, and having enjoyed the wooden galleries and gilt for rather longer than she had meant was just leaving when a young curate came across the church towards her.

"You're a newcomer to our church, I think, aren't you?"

"Yes, I saw it outside and thought how perfect and sweet it was and I had to see inside too. I'm sorry if I've interrupted anything—"

"Oh, no, quite the contrary! We always welcome visitors in the hope that they will become permanent members of our congregation."

"Well, as a matter of fact, I'm afraid I'm not a churchgoer. I mean not to worship, you know. I do believe in some kind of supernatural force which I suppose corresponds to God—but all this doctrine and stuff, well—"

A blue-domer, thought the clergyman feeling depressed. God is in nature and I worship him under the blue dome of

the sky. Not Christianity, not Islam, but pantheism, is the
religion which has overrun the world.

He waited for her to say anything he had not heard before;
to his surprise, she did.

"I'm not in your parish; I live at Billingsgate. My husband's a
sculptor, you see. He needs a studio to work in so we found
this bombed place he could use." Bott gabbled out her ex-
planations, embarrassed by her unbelief and wanting to make
up for it somehow to this friendly young clergyman.

"A sculptor!" He was interested at last. "Really? Is he—um
—a very modern sculptor? I mean, might I have heard of
him? I—I'm rather interested in art."

It was sweet the way he switched off his clerical manner of
speech to say that. Bott smiled at him.

"He's modern, but he's quite unique, he follows no trend,"
she said proudly. "He has too many ideas of his own. He loves
beauty."

"Ah!" said the clergyman with such a deep sigh that Bott
could see that he was thinking how he loved beauty too.

"Gregor Gatzkovic. If you were in Lausanne last summer—"
Bott said casually.

"Gatzkovic, er. I'm not sure that I don't know the name.
Does he, er, ever show in London? You see I'm thinking of a
gentleman I know, a vicar of a neighbouring parish, who's
coming to see me tomorrow and is terribly interested in art.
He was complaining to me only last week that artists never
come to this part of London. I say, would you and your
husband like to come and meet him I wonder? He's taking our
midday service. Of course you won't want to attend that, will
you? No, but do come along afterwards."

"Why, how kind of you. I'd love to. I can't guarantee to
bring Gatzko, but of course I'll come."

He looked timidly at her, his face all aglow with admiration.

"A real sculptor! How exciting! I so wanted to be an artist
myself once," he said. "Art has always meant a great deal
to me. That's why I'm lucky in being attached to this

church; I can go into the National Gallery whenever I like."

"Oh, would that be the big thing next door?"

"Sounds like it."

"With a dome? My husband showed me the outside last night and said the most beautiful things of the world were in there." Bott was extremely proud to be able to say this. The only thing wrong was that she felt obliged to keep referring to him as "my husband" and Bott did not like telling half-lies. Although to herself it was no lie; but still. Fortunately, with mittens on the man couldn't see that she wore no ring. Would Gatzko mind if she took to wearing a ring? After last night?

The clergyman was saying, "This morning I had a quite impulsive desire to go in and look at Botticelli's Mystic Nativity. You know it?"

Bott shook her head.

"Well, if it is undoubtedly one of the most beautiful paintings in the National Gallery, and your husband rates the pictures there as the most beautiful in the world, that puts it pretty high on the list by any standard." He was back on his dog-collar tone but Bott was still interested. Gatzko seemed to be concerned in this somehow.

"Actually it was late last night I suddenly wanted to see this picture," the man mused, relapsing into his young ordinary voice, "it came before my eyes as it were. Very odd. I mean, inappropriate for the season. You'd think I'd have had enough of cribs and Nativities by February. But as soon as the National Gallery was open I went in, just to see that one painting. So lucky to work here."

Bott was trying to speak, and having difficulty in doing so. Her heart was thudding. She remembered last night, too. Finally she managed to say in a reasonable voice, "Can a beautiful picture ever be 'out of season'?"

"No, I suppose not. It's quite a remarkable painting. I do recommend you, if you don't know it, to go in and see it sometime."

Dog-collar coming back. Bott knew that in a few more polite

words he'd be looking at his watch and slipping discreetly away. Preferring to get in first, she said, "What a very good idea, I'll go and do that now. Goodbye, and I will try to bring my husband to your service tomorrow."

She left the man looking after her with a pleased smile as she strode out of the church and up the steps of the National Gallery. She had twenty minutes. That was easily time just to glance round, especially if she ran back to work. She had vague inhibitions about running in London, but she supposed she could sacrifice them if she had to. She loved running. In the country it was her normal method of movement.

She had never been inside an art gallery before. She took one look at the size of the hall and the staircase and knew that unless she enlisted help at once she would simply be wasting her time in here. She marched up to an old man in a blue uniform standing vaguely in the middle of the hall, put a sixpence into his hand and said, "Can you take me to the Mystic Nativity, please? I'm a stranger here and I'm in a great hurry."

The man gawped at her. "Oh, come on, do, please," Bott said impatiently, looking at his hand that held the sixpence.

She would have done equally well without it. The guardian knew that it was his day by the Front Entrance and he was not supposed to go upstairs at all, according to Regulations. But all he could think of was this huge and frightening woman standing imperiously before him. Impossible to do anything but meekly lead the way. "There it is," he mumbled, pointing, and stumbled away. He had to go and lean against the postcard stand to recover. When at last he discovered the sixpence it seemed like fairy gold.

And Bott was standing before the picture blinking, stunned. Here, apparently a famous masterpiece, was a portrayal of her own experience. The hushed excitement, the glow in the air, here they were, surrounding the Madonna as Bott had fancied them surrounding herself. Joy and light and solemn jubilation shone out from Botticelli's Bethlehem as they had from Bott's

City, and pink robed angels danced. Bott stood weak and shaking before the picture.

For this was a very odd painting indeed. Mary seemed to be weeping. She had a pale, thin face, with none of the contented tranquillity Bott was used to seeing in Madonnas. Her head was turned down over the child as if she knew there were something more going on than was apparent, and she was as white as a sheet.

Joy on earth, joy in highest heaven, the Christmas phrases sounded through Bott's mind. But they had a curious echo to them. Was it thundering in the picture? Joseph's old head was pillowed in his arms, as if he were sheltering it from something. The angels were as much grave as glad. A creature was rolling about on the ground, which seemed to be Death with a bat's face. The bat had a strange, knowing look. If Mary's head were raised would she have the same?

The palms of Bott's hands were prickling with sweat. She was now definitely frightened. It could be no accident that today she should find this painting with her whole story in it.

Suddenly Bott remembered the Dragon of Logres which had appeared the first night she had given herself to Gatzko. And she had thought then that omens always seemed to signify death, victory, bloodshed or the conception of a hero.

Bott had been standing goggling at the painting for three-quarters of an hour now, and still she stared. She had completely forgotten her intention just to take a quick peep and run back to Tommy's. This was far too important to leave anyway.

She remembered now what she had thought about on the night of the dragon. Joy and death in the wake of the great and wonderful event. And what was that event? In this case, the birth of a child. And in Bott's case?

It was bitterly cold in the National Gallery but sweat was breaking out all over her and her hair was even sticking to her face with it. She would have liked to sit down but was afraid that if she moved she might fall. Gatzko would have quoted Sweeney at her. As far as she was concerned she was not in any art gallery, nor even in London, but in the strange mythical world of a Renaissance Nativity.

She may have thought it was Christmas Night; Tommy thought it was half-way through her afternoon shift, and was very angry with her. He had almost decided to tell her to leave. He had put up with enough, God knew. Then she came in at last looking so ghastly that he forgot his annoyance. She must have had a row with that man of hers. She staggered as she came in and looked fearfully round, but plainly without seeing anything, with a curious paleness about her. It was difficult to place it; her face was the same old florid healthy face that bawled out nursery rhymes at you, but there was an extraordinary pale blue light in her eyes and her skin was shining with little spots of perspiration. She must certainly just have had some frightful scene, or had witnessed an accident, or was ill; anyway Tommy's anger vanished. He put his arm round her shoulder and sat her down at a corner table. She was trembling.

Tommy looked at those wandering pale eyes and felt afraid himself to see them. He brought a cup of tea and found his own hand unsteady. He put it in front of Bott and sat down opposite her. She seemed completely unaware of him or of what was happening.

"I say, old girl, are you all right?" he asked, attempting joviality. "You don't look too good."

Bott turned mad blue eyes at him. Slowly she seemed to focus.

"Aren't you feeling well?"

"Oh!" said Bott, as if surprised at such a question. Then her eyes dilated more than ever and she said, "No—perhaps—"

Tommy momentarily remembered the cookless kitchen where Maria was frantically running about trying to do everything at once all alone. But this was a lull time, usually the time when they were treated to a concert of "Jollity Farm" or an equivalent, or had to listen to ecstatic descriptions of Gatzko, Michael and something which was apparently known as the Dairy &. Tommy forgot the kitchen again. He was interested in this woman's peculiar life.

"Well, what's happened? You were all right this morning."

"I went into the National Gallery and saw a picture by—by Botticelli." She had succeeded in remembering the name because of the similarity with her own. Tommy looked blank.

She went on, as if she were amazed by the wonders she was telling, "It was last night really. We ran down to somewhere, some ruined place near Blackfriars, I believe, and—" She rubbed her eyes, looked piteously at him and said, "Oh, Tommy, I'm so scared."

Tommy was in his forties himself, and had lived through a pretty difficult time, all said and done; he knew what problems were. He could imagine all sorts of things to attach to this woman's anxiety. He said gently, "Can I lend you some cash?"

She looked more astonished than ever and was apparently on the point of exclaiming "Why?" She checked herself, laughed and said, "Oh, no, you don't understand. Sorry. Oh, Tommy, is this tea for me? You're so kind. Look, do you mind my unburdening my worries on you?"

"I only wish you would. My function in life has always been a shoulder to cry on. Sometimes I've even cried on it myself. Come on, dear. If you'd like to tell, tell. Something's wrong, isn't it?"

"No. No. Not at all. I mean yes. I mean something very marvellous is going to happen. Is happening now. I'm going to have a baby."

Tommy could not take this as the world-shattering news she seemed to expect. After all, what else did she think, since she was apparently living in good earnest with this man? Tommy said, "Well, now, Bott, what's the worry for? It's terrific news. Congratulations."

"Yes," said Bott. She looked at him differently. "Of course it is. I feel as if the whole world knew it and thought so too. Can't you see how thrilled I am?"

"Well," he said doubtfully. "You seem so upset."

"I'm glad," said Bott. "Glad, glad, glad, all the way down inside, does it really not show?"

She fingered her teacup. "This isn't just any baby, you know."

"Of course not," he said, thinking that the poor little brat was going to get a surprise to see what sort of household he was being born into.

"I mean, well. Tommy, did you feel anything special going on yesterday by any chance?"

"You seemed, ah, extremely gay. And you stunned everyone with a new hat."

"Mmm, yes, that was all part of it." The light in her eyes was fading into a pleased pearly shine.

"Did you know then?"

"It was that night it happened."

"What? Are you sure? How can it be?"

"Oh, I know. I'm sure all right. It had to be, after—oh, you don't know what I was feeling all day. I kept on thinking—Tommy dear, don't laugh, I'm deadly serious. I kept on thinking about spring and new birth."

"Spring?" Tommy couldn't help exclaiming. The snow had come back, heavier than ever. There were about six inches in the London streets since this morning.

"There, I knew you wouldn't understand," Bott said sadly. "I know, it was all frosty yesterday too. But it was the feeling. I could feel spring."

"But look here, Bott, you can't know straight away like that, next morning. It's not possible."

"I do know, though. I—I—well, I just know."

Tommy felt it would be indiscreet to press for details. He went to fetch himself a cup of tea as well. He had mentally given Bott an afternoon off. When he came back she looked at him—not through him, this time, but straight at him at last with shining eyes.

"All my life I've been empty," she said, growing excited as she talked. "Empty, alone, shut in, useless, although I didn't realize it. It was Gatzko who made me see it. He came to my rescue, if you like, he opened me up, deliberately I think. It had to be. All this was meant. I thought I was making him into something, I thought it was all my effort. If I seemed crazy just now it was because, well, because I'd just understood all this. Gatzko had to open me up because—because—I've got to do something. Make something. It's not enough just to be myself. I have got to produce, to act. And that something, I was just realizing today when I looked at that picture I told you about, is..." She began to speak in very slow deliberate tones, "the ... bringing forth ... of something, somebody ... bigger than myself. Do you believe in fate?"

Tommy mumbled into his cup. He did not believe in fate, fortune or anything else, but this did not seem the moment to say so. He had heard one should never contradict people in loony fits. He could not believe that Bott, whom he'd known so long, was really mad, but all this certainly sounded a bit loony. Not many people would have listened so seriously as he, Tommy, was doing.

"My fate," Bott told him, her jitters gone, her usual glowing self, "is to die in the bringing forth of a hero."

My God, so here was one of those women one hears about who believes she's going to be the mother of a future Messiah. What should one do with such people? Tommy stared wildly round the restaurant. But Bott seemed calm enough now. Only when she spoke again, her words sounded mad:

"I should have known to read the signs. I've had experience enough, God knows. To think it should take a silly young clergyman and an old painting to make things click."

"You, ah, have had a dream that you're going to die in childbirth?"

"Oh, no. I don't take dreams seriously. That's not how I've

seen things. Never have. But visions and intuitions are not so uncommon, you know. Don't look so scared."

That peculiar pallor had altogether vanished now. She was looking at him and laughing as if he were the oddity.

"Don't tell me you've never seen a sign? Never had a foreboding, a premonition?"

Tommy mumbled again.

"Because if you did I wouldn't believe you. Well, that's all I've had, but it gave me a shock because there was death in it. I understood finally from this picture, you see."

"What was this picture of, then?"

"It's a Nativity. A stable scene, with a Holy Family and angels and whatnot."

Aha, thought Tommy, I was right; future Messiah it is.

Now she was all radiant fearless joy. True, her eyes kept on roving about in an anguished way, but when she turned them directly on you blazing joy was what you felt.

"In this painting, this Christmas scene, were all sorts of peculiar undertones, symbols of death and strangenesses. And all the characters had this fearful look, as if they knew some dark secret. Yet as I said it was a Christmas scene. After I'd looked at it for a while I understood some things about myself. And I realized I was pregnant."

Bott was trying to express herself simply, for Tommy, though a kind listener, was maybe not all that intelligent, or at any rate not quite up to understanding the whole story. As it was she was afraid she was not expressing herself well. He did not seem to understand the glory and marvel, the great and mighty wonder, she was trying to convey. He only looked more and more anxious the longer she spoke.

"Well, I'm not worried if you aren't," Tommy said. "I admit it's all a trifle above my head—but you've plainly had a pretty harrowing experience, and you did look terrible when you came in."

"Oh, I just hadn't got used to the idea." She gave him a glorious smile. She looked like the Angel Gabriel herself now, a-brimming with infinite knowledge and infinite delight. Tommy could not sustain that look any more than the guardian in the National Gallery. He swallowed his tea and rose choking. Bott slapped him comfortingly on his back.

"Maria's rushed off her feet," he heard her saying in an entirely normal voice. "I'll do the washing-up. There seem to be extra big piles of it. Tommy, you're not going to go worrying about me, are you? I'm sorry you got the receiving end of my bit of shock."

Tommy tried to speak but could only cough.

"There's just one thing. Do you think I could have my early lunch tomorrow, please? There's a service at St. Martin-in-the-Fields I rather want to go to."

Weak with choking, Tommy nodded and wheezed.

When he closed the restaurant that evening he found that, thanks to Bott, he had succeeded in not thinking about his wife the entire afternoon.

Bott meant to tell Gatzko that night. But he whirled her out to the George, and they both got rather drunk again, and somehow the right moment never came.

12

As Bott set out for work, on her way through the shop she stopped, staring. There on the counter were two little mouldings, which—oh, she knew how his hands would have been moving as he made them—were plainly Gatzko's.

"Mrs. Weingartner," she said, "do you know anything about these?"

"I think it is Gatzko who spoils my candles," Mrs. Weingartner said. "He forgot to take them. I am afraid they will melt in here."

What temperature, Bott wondered in amusement, did Mrs. Weingartner think wax melted at? It was certainly not above fifty in here (the tea turn had not been going long). "Well, I'll take them if I may," she said. She put them in her bag (that dear old knapsack) feeling how Gatzko's fingers had dug and stabbed, sensing the emotion that had gone into them. Suddenly she was afraid again. She took them out and looked at them. What had he been thinking when he did these? She never knew what he thought. But they were beautiful. She had not known he could do miniatures. She wrapped them lovingly in her handkerchief (dirty old thing; hope it wouldn't mark them), and went out.

The cold air was so exhilarating that she felt happy again at the first breath outside.

She sang "Jollity Farm" as she went to work. Tommy greeted her kindly and asked how she was.

"As well as can be expected," Bott mimicked the hospital phrase, which she herself had used so often when she was at Poole General all those years ago. She grinned at Tommy.

"I'm fine. But you haven't forgotten my early lunch, have you?"

"You still want that?" Tommy said sadly.

"I'm afraid I'm adamant."

"Ah, well, there are a million things I'd rather do than argue with you, Bott."

Bott carolled, "Everybody sings, the horses too, the oxen low, the pigeons coo."

"Oxen low. Are you sure you've got the right song? Aren't you thinking of Christmas?"

"As a matter of fact," she said, trying to remember that name which was so like hers, "yes, I am thinking of Christmas." And let him make what he liked of that.

Bott arrived as the service at St. Martin-in-the-Fields was ending. The nice curate ran right round to the back of the church when he saw her, grabbed her and said, "Please don't rush away; the person is here that I do so want you to meet." And the person turned out to be another clergyman whose interest, and the reason for his friendship with the young curate, was modern art, but who was rather more senior and influential than the curate. He was vicar of a church on London Wall with a beautiful name which Bott immediately forgot. He organized exhibitions in the crypts of churches all over the City. He was arranging a group exhibition of sculptures now in one of them, and he was very interested to hear of her husband, who was, he gathered, a sculptor.

Bott could hardly believe it. How it would encourage Gatzko to have somewhere to show; and what might it not lead on to?

"Why, he'd love to contribute," she said eagerly. "And oh—gosh, how lucky—look, I've actually got something of his with me."

She fumbled to unwrap the wax mouldings. "I think they're just offshoots of his, made from candles," she said. "He's got masses of proper stuff at home; real, big sculptures, but this is his style."

"Well," the vicar said, looking grave and interested, "this is really rather remarkable. Don't you think it's really rather what we were looking for, James?"

And so on, the politely ecclesiastically concealed enthusiasm, but Bott could see what lay behind the small-talk. They were getting a group together, they were short of sculptors, and they wanted Gatzko. At the end they almost said so, in so many words. Bott talked away enthusiastically, glad to have someone she could let out her joy on. She praised Gatzko's work, she praised the church, she hinted darkly at "a miracle within" and asked the vicar to say a prayer of thanksgiving on her behalf; and she promised Gatzko's cooperation in their show. The men began to exchange glances. Suddenly she remembered Tommy's. She really could not be late two days running. She excused herself and hurried off.

As she panted in all aglow Tommy greeted her with a red face, and Bott stopped in alarm. "Oh, gosh, Tommy, *am* I late? What's wrong?"

Tommy went redder than ever and said, "Wrong? There's nothing wrong, Bott, why should you think that? Er, I'd like you to meet my wife, er Mrs. Mackenzie, er, my cook, Mrs. Bott."

"How do you do," Bott said, enthusiastically shaking the woman's hand, thrilled to hear herself called Mrs., and only wanting her pleasure to run up her arm and down in to Mrs. Tommy's—Mrs. Mackenzie's—hand. Mrs. Mackenzie gave her a cold smile and said, "How do you do."

Bott went gaily into the kitchen, thinking about love and joy and death. Maria looked up shyly and asked, "Do you know about the baby yet?"

"Know? Why does everyone keep asking me that? Of course I know." Humming "How-do-you-do" to herself, she began to get out the bangers and prick them.

"Do you want a girl or a boy?" Maria asked, who was plainly as excited about it as Bott herself.

"I'm pretty sure it's a boy. He must be, because—" Bott

stopped herself. How useless to try to explain to this sweet but dim Spanish girl about omens for the conception of a hero. And if she talked about the Nativity, goodness knows what misunderstandings that might lead to.

Mrs. Mackenzie came in. "My dear, I hear you're expecting. How thrilling for you."

"Yes, isn't it? I was just telling Maria I felt certain it would be a boy."

"You particularly want a boy, do you? Are there any children already?"

"Well, there's Michael—"

"And you feel Michael ought to have a brother rather than a sister. H'm." Mrs. Mackenzie's smile of congratulation had all gone. Now why on earth should she come into the kitchen and look disapproving just because Bott wanted a boy? Bott began to feel irritated.

"Michael can't be your child, can he?"

"Why not?" Bott said angrily. Normally she never tried to pretend he was, but somehow this woman had got her saying all sorts of things she didn't intend.

"My dear, you don't look like a mother at all."

"Well, I'm glad I'll never have to be your mother anyway," Bott exploded, and turned away to her bangers. Immediately she was sorry. It was hardly the most intelligent riposte to make, after all. But before she could apologize Mrs. Mackenzie had said, "Well, I *do* wonder *very* much about this child of yours," and left.

Bott, gloomily doing she knew not what at the cutlery drawer, began to wonder too. It was true after all that she knew nothing about motherhood. She felt the bigness, the tremendousness, of it, that was all. She remembered Mary's grey face in the painting, Mary pondering in her heart, Mary who knew that birth meant death too.

Bott was suddenly hideously afraid. How could she tell what the hugeness was which she contained? The seeds of something were growing in her, but what would they come up as?

Standing at the sideboard Bott was seized with a picture, as vivid and overwhelming as the nastiest kind of dream, of something monstrous coming forth, growing up out of the ground. She had planted seeds and they looked innocuous enough, and the stalks and the leaves but then the leaves unfolded and there was a head, a foul monstrosity of a head with a great mouth, and on a stalk and growing, growing out of her. . . .

"Bott! Bott! What's the matter? It's all right, you only fainted. Are you feeling all right now?"

"I—I—oh, how perfectly silly," Bott struggled to get up, but found she was too dizzy.

"You'll do better just to lie quiet," Tommy advised. Bott looked gratefully up at his sane, good, totally unmonstrous face. But then another one came in the way. Mrs. Tommy came looming over her, brushing aside Tommy's cup of tea he was offering. "No, no! Nothing to drink!" she cried.

"Well, please, as a matter of fact it might pull me together—" Bott said faintly.

"No, on no account, it's the worst thing you can do. And your tongue!" Bott found her head being dragged off the floor, her mouth pulled open and a great meaty hand thrust in. Bott yelled, choked as the hand grabbed her tongue in midyell and yanked it out of her mouth, and bit the hand with all her force.

Mrs. Mackenzie went calmly on pulling until she had got Bott's tongue where she wanted it, and said, "There, now she won't choke swallowing her tongue anyway. But oh dear, what a difficult patient."

Bott, feeling weak and defeated, lay on the floor with her tongue out of her mouth as Mrs. Tommy wanted it, afraid to withdraw it in case she got another taste of knuckly hand.

"There's someone wanting to see Bott," Maria reported from the dining-room.

"Well they can't. No, wait, I'll deal with this."

Bott heard her retreat, opened her eyes, tentatively put her tongue back where it belonged, and sat up. She saw the cup of tea Tommy had brought her still there, and looked hopefully at him. He gave it to her, saying, "I am sorry for the rough treatment. You must be feeling pretty rotten."

"Well, no better for that I must say," Bott admitted, and then remembered that she was his wife after all. "At least, I mean, she wasn't wrong, she just got fainting mixed up with epilepsy."

"Well!" said Tommy thoughtfully.

"Yes, I was a nurse you know. Oh! You don't think she *intended* to treat me for epilepsy, do you?"

Bott and Tommy looked at each other.

In the other room, it was Gatzko, who around two o'clock had woken feeling guilty, but unable to remember why. Was it just being abed when he should have been approaching his tea break? Or had he done something last night? He could not remember, but he did know that he still had the great story of the new job to tell Bott. He got out of bed and wandered around and missed having her make him tea, and found a scrawled list of names he had made the day before.

"Berne, Bâle, Lucerne, Turin, Genoa, Oz,"—Oz? That must be Michael, and who had he learnt about Oz from? If there was one place which did not tempt Gatzko to dream of it was Oz.

He put the list in his pocket and went across the City to Bott's place, still missing her tea and her orange hat. He had been to Tommy's once or twice. Nice Maria, who was all the nicer because she adored him, greeted him, but anxiously, he thought.

"Hi, honey. Is Bott around? Do you think I have a chance of prevailing on her to bring me a cup of tea?"

"Bott, she's—Ay mama, what was that?" (It was Bott's strangled yell.)

"It'll be her singing. Tell her I'm here, would you, honey?"

But it was neither Maria nor Bott who returned, but a strange and unpleasant looking woman, a proper old harridan.

"Good afternoon. I gather you wanted to see Mrs. Bott? I'm afraid she's unwell at the moment."

"Unwell? How do you mean, unwell? Did she fall downstairs or something?"

"Oh, no, but she lost consciousness, and we have only just succeeded in bringing her round; so you see you can't possibly, not just now, speak to her—"

"But what's wrong for God's sake? Has she got food poisoning or something?" (What had they been eating recently? Not much, as far as he could remember.)

"No, no, I don't think so. It's rather more long-term than that."

"What are you talking about, for Christ's sake!"

"Excuse me, I don't take kindly to being addressed like that."

And she was right, too; neither would he. Sweetly he said, "Oh, I am so sorry, but this is rather a shock; I wasn't aware she was sick."

"Oh dear me, that's hardly the word," the woman said with a gooey smile; "no, she's not sick, but she is—ah—expecting."

Gatzko stared at the woman. It was her turn, now, to be puzzled. Such revulsion and hatred (for Bott) were suddenly rising inside Gatzko that he was afraid he might really vomit. He turned and went just as fast as he could along Cheapside, away from Tommy's, from this ogress, from his own pet ogress in the back there in rapture over her embryos and seeds and growing things. He did not believe this tale of fainting. More likely she'd just gone into some mystic trance. (Remember that time in the bombed site, night before last? And that morning long ago on London Bridge?)

It was the unoriginality of it, as much as anything else, which so disgusted him. Babies! Couldn't she think of a more subtle way than that to tie him down? Isabel had tried it too. He dreaded what must come next. Or must it? Could Bott, dear eccentric English Bott, spinster eternal by appointment to His Majesty, sink so low as that? Would she start lecturing him about family units and stability for children, as his Chicago relations had?

She was certainly heading that way, come to think of it; what had she said yesterday—"Aren't we a cosy little three-some in our lair" or something of the sort.

Affectionately he remembered Sena. Her pregnancy had been one long bawdy joke in which all the guerilla band, including her cuckolded husband, had joyfully shared. When they disbanded she had handed Michael to him as if he belonged to him. Or, no, just that at any rate he didn't belong to her.

Sena had the right attitude. No one should belong to anybody. Come, see, conquer, okay, but then get the hell out.

"Has my wife upset you, Bott, or are you still feeling bad? You haven't sung a note all afternoon."

Tommy had taken over most of Bott's work himself, and put her on to the cushy job of making dripping toast. But she drooped and sat with her knife in the air, and when the customers saw the dripping toast they usually said, "Er, on second thoughts, make it a tomato sandwich."

"Oh, no. I mean, not specially," Bott answered. "Oh, I don't know. I think I just don't feel very well."

Tommy hesitated, and finally decided the kindest thing to do would be to leave her to it. As he went out he heard her resolutely strike up. "Everyone is happy, so are you; the piglets laugh and I do too." The voice quavered and died away.

Another plate of dripping toast came out, and Tommy looked regretfully at it, thinking of wasted rations. "Bott," he called, "would you do me a favour and transfer your energies to re-writing the menu cards? Maria can't spell."

"Oh, I'll spell anything you like," Bott answered, and the attempt at gaiety in her voice was pathetic, "but I can't promise that anyone else in the world will spell it the same way."

She hunted round the kitchen for a pen and finally found a

stump of blue pencil on the saucepan shelf. She took out the cards and wrote laboriously "PIE WITH PEAS 10d." and was amazed to see the words come out their ordinary, normal, foody selves. Somehow she felt they ought to be loaded with deep and dreadful meaning. But no, "BEANS ON TOAST 6d." was just beans on toast and carried no significance except that she was going to have to open the tin sooner or later that the beans were in.

She had had no idea pregnancy made you feel so ill so soon. Why, for instance, should it give you a headache? And backache? She wasn't going to go and have a miscarriage, was she?

She slid the card into its holder and wondered what Gatzko was doing now. Another card, "PIE WITH PEAS", and that was a point, she might take some of that pie home tonight to save herself yet more cooking. She felt so jolly rotten.

13

GATZKO WAS SITTING on the rug by the stove drawing maps of Europe with Michael when Bott came in. They both looked up, bright-eyed.

This was very unusual. He never came in as a rule until at least six, liking to take long walks around the place alone to get the fish out of his lungs, and if she got off early by some fluke, it was invariably her job to get the stove going and light the lamp for his return. But the lair was already warm (comparatively) and the floor was littered with scrawled maps and lists of long names. They had obviously been there for hours. It would have been human, wifely, right, civil, anything you like (Bott came to reproach herself) to ask a few questions: what's happened, where have you been, can I share the fun? She did not; instead she ran across the room to him, flung herself panting down at his feet (separating him from Michael and creasing up their papers, but she did not even notice this) and gazed ardently into his face. All she could think about was the baby. She was searching in her mind how to tell him. Within a few seconds she had forgotten that anything interesting might have happened to him, that he might have something to tell her, being home so early. She panted into his face and said, "Oh, Gatzko." There was a long pause while she breathed heavily and he could do nothing but breathe back, hypnotized by her big excited face so close to his. At last, after a long eager moment, he heard the words: "It really is spring."

Bott herself was horrified by the banality, the euphemism. She had such glorious tidings to communicate. It was the last thing she had meant to say although it was certainly what she felt. But far worse was to see his own eager look die down; his delight in whatever he was up to with Michael destroyed. Physically, even, he suddenly seemed to shrink. He became again that glum dark Gatzko she had seen so much of these last weeks.

Gatzko did retreat, did shrink. Was that all she had to say, yet again? She burst in like a prophetess, all aflame, the Bott he could admire; threw herself down before him, gave him a look that went through the back of beyond and uttered the one thing she could count upon to annoy him, that she knew he was sick of having heard about two dozen times yesterday, and that wasn't even true. The snow had deepened to nine inches during the afternoon.

Gatzko had half believed she was going to say something in Greek, or tell him of her discovery of an especially squalid tavern in some back street of Rome she'd just happened to pass. It was the way she had looked at him when she came in, so excited and expectant. Crazy, unfair, but he had imagined that she somehow had divined his mood and was going to say something in tune with it. Instead, what she said withered it utterly. He belched, the first time since this morning, but it did not help to restore his romantic feeling. The foul taste of last night came into his mouth.

Coldly he got up and took her gardening book from the counter, where it was leaning against the wire pigeon-hole. "Spring? Then I expect you want to get back into this," he said.

She took it, vaguely distressed, unaware what was wrong except that she had somehow failed to communicate the great news. She opened it at random and read: "Compost is used to enrich soil, thus feeding the growing seeds. It is waste matter broken down by bacteria into simple substances, rich in nourishment for plants. It is, in fact, Nature's own way of keeping soil fertile—the decay of dead matter, releasing vital minerals and chemical compounds—accelerated by the action of certain harmless bacteria under the stimulation of warmth. Compost can easily be home-made..."

The reference to growing seeds was the only one which registered with her. She looked up again at Gatzko, still longing to share the marvel that she had understood today, but saw him looking at her with such sunken hostile eyes that she could only stutter, "Oh, yes—thank you—I must read up about planting, mustn't I?"

She could see that at this moment he hated her, but she could not guess why. She still did not think of his map game with Michael. She had forgotten the unusual event of his being in before her, and still did not ask him any questions.

"Oh, haven't you done your planting yet? Somewhat snowy now, don't you think? I thought yesterday was the day."

"Yesterday was the day!" Bott burst out, in a renewed spurt of enthusiasm, trying to ignore his black angry eyes. "Don't be so cross. I've got such marvellous news to tell you."

"Like hell you have," Gatzko muttered, who had been expecting and dreading this.

"No, but listen. I think—I know—that—"

"Yes, all right, all right! That there's a wee tiny growing embryo inside you, all a-blossoming and a-blooming."

"Gatzko! Did you feel it too, then—like the night we both saw the dragon?"

"I just heard the glad tidings from that female hyena who wouldn't let me into your restaurant to see you."

"Oh, gosh, Mrs. Tommy. Did you come up there to see me? Oh, darling."

"What a lot of darlings flying about this evening. Is it Little Buttinsky who's making you so extraordinarily affectionate?"

Bott gulped, trying to make sense of his reaction. Didn't he want another child? He was fond enough of Michael. Anyway it was at least half his fault, wasn't it?

"Yes, I went up there around two o'clock but you were busy having fainting fits or something in the back there. I couldn't get past that monster woman so I got out."

F

"Oh, dear. Oh, I am sorry. She is a beast, isn't she? I've been suffering from her too. She wouldn't let you in? There, now, it would have revived me instantly to see you."

She was talking and looking at him like a schoolgirl with a crush on. Gatzko mistrusted such sudden, excessive affection. It was most likely those repressed family instincts which apparently were going full blast now. God, it was fearsome.

"But there's more good news than that!"

"Not twins?"

"Oh, Gatzko. Please stop being so horrid. Listen to what I've been doing for you. I've got you into a sculpture show!"

He jerked up. "You've what?"

"Yes, it's an absolute godsend. There's a group show being organized in the crypt of a church in the City somewhere which is all modern sculpture, just your very thing. I simply happened to chat to a curate at St. Martin-in-the-Fields, who introduced me to the vicar of the church, and he really wants you. By a stroke of luck I had these with me." She pulled out his candles. "So he saw what your style was like, and he was really truly interested. Isn't it wonderful? If you're in this show in the church (I've forgotten its name) it might lead on to—oh, who knows."

She talked on and on, putting more and more enthusiasm into her words as she saw his face tighten and become angrier and angrier.

He stared at her, kneeling foolishly with her orange hat still pinned precariously on and her gardening book open in her hand, grinning at him like a victorious school games captain and burbling about babies and churches. He felt so bitter that he tasted literal bitterness, beery bitterness from his belch of a minute ago. How could he tell her, now? Dreams, imaginations, are precious things.

And even now she wouldn't stop.

"Lots of people go into these churches, you know..."

"Yes! And with any luck you'll have me finish up a minister!" He stood up, black with fury. "Listen to me now, Bott.

Tell your friends in church that I'm not having anything to do with any church, crypt, temple, rite, celebration or what have you. And I'm not participating in any of your spring nature ceremonies either so you can stop yammering at me about your seeds and gardens too. You don't seem to have gathered that I don't take to anything culty or occulty. Well, you can begin thinking about it right now. Only for God's sake stop wishing these growing things on me. You'll give me cancer!"

Gatzko was so angry he could hardly see to find his wallet. When he did find it, there was dough on it. Damn her, she'd been using its metal edge for cutting pastry again. He took out all the notes it contained, and pushed it back under the counter for her to cut more pastry with.

"I think you ought to change your hobby," he said.

She was fooled by his tone, and looked up eagerly.

"Gardening isn't going to profit Little Buttinsky very much. You'd do better to take up knitting."

"Knitting! Do you think so?"

"Oh yes. Symbol of domesticized womanhood. It's what all women do when they get this hearth-and-home bug. Family stability, you know."

Of course she didn't know about Isabel's knitting. He left her gawping after him in dismay, still not understanding.

He only got as far as the Dairy &, since just to make things even better the pubs weren't open yet. He sat down on the stool by the tea-urn and buried his head in his arms. He felt blackly, murderously tired, tired of her, tired of himself, tired of London, tired of everything. "It's all hell," he said.

"There's something wrong, son?" Mr. Weingartner said sympathetically.

"Not something," Gatzko said; "damn well everything."

"I know," said Weingartner, "it's that woman."

"Your grasp of the situation is just fantastic."

Gatzko felt a hand on his shoulder and looked up to see Weingartner's bald head shining and smiling down on him, while, angel of benevolence, he held out a glass to Gatzko.

Scotch! The man had to be a wizard, not an angel, to conjure this up. He hadn't tasted any in years.

Gatzko said, "You ought to qualify as a life-saver."

"Is the quarrel very bad?"

"There isn't any quarrel. She's impossible to quarrel with. A good quarrel might shake her up some. Ask her how life is and she'll tell you God's in his heaven and all's right with the world."

Gatzko took another, bigger gulp of Scotch, noticing that it was a full bottle and that Weingartner had merely stoppered it, not put it away, and had poured himself a shot too.

"She's settling in to live here for ever. Guess what the latest is? Babies. She's setting up business as a mother goddess. Getting all fertility conscious. That's all she talks about now. Can you imagine?"

The level of the Scotch in the bottle continued dropping. Weingartner's greatest virtue was that he listened.

"She's trying to make a home. Put down roots, start a family. Put down roots," Gatzko said, "any kind of root, anywhere, and you've descended from the human to the vegetable level of life."

A customer came in for a cup of tea. Weingartner gave it to him, the tea-urn exuding a fresh cloud of sweet steam as he poured it, and pushed it across the counter. At the same time he pushed another whisky across to Gatzko.

"The truth is she secretly wants to be a vegetable. Cults, cultivation—she's making a garden in a churchyard, did I tell you? Jesus God, Weingartner!"

Mrs. Weingartner came in with her shopping, looked closely at Gatzko and said, "You have headache, haven't you? Would you like..."

"No! No Beecham's Powders! Out of the kindness of your heart spare me that!" Gatzko cried, jumping up in alarm. "I'm only stifling from sitting next your tea machine for an hour. And I'm dehydrated. Come on, Weingartner. I've got to get out."

They went to the George. Gatzko said, "Even these miserable dockworkers know better than that. Listen to them. How many different accents can you hear? Emigrant from everywhere, that's the way to be. That's the way I want to be."

"I am not an emigrant," said Weingartner.

"Well, you ought to be. You don't have to keep up that fool game of being ten generations a Cockney before me, you know. I don't go in for this traditions and ancestry rubbish. I respect the man who's had the courage to detach himself, not the one who bores on about his family vault."

Weingartner bought Gatzko another brown ale. Gatzko put half of it down without noticing it was a new drink.

"Why do you think I left the States? Because I was asked the question 'Where are you from' just once too often."

Two men across the room were bawling at each other; a quarrel or a funny story? Impossible to tell from their faces.

"What the hell does it matter where I'm from? There's something wrong with a nation whose primary interest in a man is his origins. A man is what he makes himself. Go on, go forward, for God's sake, not back to any origin. And not inwards above all. That's introversion."

Gatzko bought a round for himself and Mr. Weingartner, somewhat surprised at the way his thoughts were taking him. "Would you say Bott was introverted?" he asked.

"She has a strong character. Very strong."

"You never miss," Gatzko said moodily, looking into his beer. The fizz came from certain points on the bottom of the glass. Little bubbles rose in uninterrupted streams from these odd points, but in between the liquid was quite still. Now what curious property of bottled beer caused that?

"She's become attached to this place. Would you believe it? I chose it because it's a nowhere-place. A shack in your back yard in the only place in Europe maybe where everything from every country meets and nothing has any origins. With the exception, of course, of ten generations of Weingartners.

Now she wants to fool herself that this is where she belongs. Put roots down into it and into me!"

It seemed to Gatzko that he had been the last to stand drinks, but as he was somewhat hazy about it he bought another round himself.

"I still drink the other," Weingartner objected.

"Keep it. I need mine, anyhow. You can't imagine how she's let me down. She was so strong and independent when I met her. That's what I admired her for. Now all she wants is to get her claws into me, just like any other woman. She'll be wanting to marry me next!"

"But why not? I thought you didn't like a woman who is self-reliant."

"I don't like anyone who is reliant on anything. That's the way you start to get stuck into some comfortable rut—put roots down, there's a nice polite metaphor. It makes me sick. Have another."

"No, thank you."

"Well, I will. The same again, please."

"You will be sick for a different reason," Weingartner observed.

"How else can I get out? She's trapping me, I tell you, Weingartner, she's cornering me, she—she's making another of her damned gardens out of me!"

Weingartner took another mouthful of brown ale, two behind Gatzko, and looked meditatively at the excited glistening face, the head wagging (foreign fashion) as he talked, his hair shaking about in all directions.

"You don't want to have a home?"

"No I do not. I've had enough of homes." Horror-memories of his family and Isabel began to rise and Gatzko rushed on to forget them. "Don't you see how important it is to keep out of all things like that. You only end up deceiving yourself. Detachment is what you ought to aim at, and that means unattachment, doesn't it? Well, do you believe in domestic bliss? It's simply one of mankind's favourite frauds."

Weingartner didn't answer. Gatzko remembered Mrs. Weingartner, and realized that he must be drunker than he'd thought.

"I'm sorry," he said. "I was excepting you. Yours is no fraud."

Weingartner smiled. He was not, thank God, the kind of man who took offence.

"Well, you are exceptional altogether. I was thinking about everyday men like me. Or, to be altogether honest, I was thinking just about me. My ideal of life is to be moving. Moving, watching, judging, observing from a distance. You know? I ought to have been born a migratory bird."

"Do you think you will get this new job you want?" Weingartner asked. Gatzko brightened.

"I think I might enjoy to be an international telephone operator. What do you think of that? Wouldn't it be exotic? I'd be in touch with the whole world."

He began pouring out everything he had saved to tell Bott in a more or less incoherent flood of words.

"What do people say when they're talking to Italy? I would find out. Do you suppose a man's voice shakes when he calls up to place a call to somewhere say where there's been fighting?"

"Do they listen in to conversations?"

"That's another thing I wish I knew. Suppose I could overhear foreign languages. Wouldn't *you* be excited? Suppose I heard a language I couldn't identify? Can you imagine a bigger thrill?"

And on and on, the dreams, the magical names pouring out, beginning to leave syllables out of the long ones, eyes flashing, emotion growing. Weingartner began to consider how to get him away. It was so wretchedly early. An hour and a half to Time.

"What a job," Gatzko said gloryingly. "Connecting cities of the world. I have a daughter in one of the biggest, did I ever tell you? Chicago."

"Blimey, you have got a daughter? But you never tell me about her."

"Didn't I? She's at college in Chicago. I've just sent her there. I thought it would make a change for her. She was brought up among ranches, in the West." Gatzko thought fondly, even a trifle enviously, of Mary having herself a wow of a time in Chicago.

Weingartner saw his eyes grow liquid and said cautiously, "You look very tired."

"Do I? Not surprising. I've had a hell of a day." Quite suddenly Gatzko felt very tired, and intolerably sleepy.

Weingartner took Gatzko's arm and started manoeuvring him towards the door. But when Gatzko saw Lower Thames Street he jerked awake. "Oh City city!" he cried. "Oh, it's such a heartbreak. You don't know how I'd dreamt of this place. And now I find it's just like any other. That's what my life is. One constant series of disillusionments. Have you ever been to Jaffa?"

"No." Get him heading the right way at least, away from the river, or he might jump in.

"Don't. I went there looking for yids and kikes and olive trees. And what did I find? A horde of American nuns on a pilgrimage gawping at a British Victorian Gothic church with a cemetery full of crosses. One of them held up a crucifix and tried to bless me. So I pretended I was a Jew and took a swipe at her. I missed, and broke my hand against a gravestone."

He was weeping like a child all down his face as Mr. Weingartner hauled him into the lair. Bott received him with alarm, as he fell crying on her shoulder. She had been expecting a continuation of the row. Instead she found her arms full of crying, limp, lovable Gatzko, with Mr. Weingartner's round pale head above discreetly retreating and shutting the door.

She had spent the evening with Michael, unable really to play with him, distractedly turning over her gardening book and deciding she ought to make a compost heap, aware that she had broken the news badly to Gatzko. At last she had decided on a firm, realistic talk with him. She was ready to blame herself. She had found the lists of place-names he'd been making with Michael and had realized that something was going on which she was out of, and that it was her fault. Her little speech asking forgiveness and begging that they should share their secrets was all ready. But obviously it was not going to be like that.

She managed to get him on to the bed, all warm and crumpled and pathetic. Why on earth did she want another baby when she couldn't even cope with this one? He did not seem to know who it was tucking him up, and fell asleep before she could undress him. She made sure they had not woken Michael, and climbed in with Gatzko. She did not feel sleepy. She sat hugging her knees under the sheepskin, while a faint funny light shone round the paper they used as curtains. Snow-light perhaps? As her eyes got used to it she could see Gatzko's face all wet in the lines, and what deep lines they were too. The hollows of his eyes were black with exhaustion and his breath stank not only of beer. Something was wrong, something was very badly wrong. All right, she had made a mess of it so far, but now perhaps, was her chance to start again, to put his life right.

She found herself stroking her stomach and laughed at herself. Of course there couldn't be anything to feel yet. Oh, if only she had not so mucked up her attempts to tell him the news. How could she bring back that sparkling living Gatzko who chased and teased her and took after his son.

She snuggled down in bed, careful to keep to the uncomfortable side, the side that was the sofa back let down. As she moved Gatzko gave a grunt, shifted in his sleep and curled himself trustingly in her arms. Bott wondered what he was dreaming of.

When finally she fell asleep she dreamt of a hyacinth bulb. It was a lovely dream, but she awoke with the despairing remembrance that even hyacinths came out of "The Waste Land".

F*

14

IT WAS THE dismal familiarity of it which was worst. Those tepid little aches and pains, that miserable trickle. Bott would have preferred an appalling haemorrhage and convulsions of agony. At least she could have convinced herself, if nobody else, that she was having a miscarriage. But this! There was no doubt what this was.

She felt total humiliation, although nobody knew yet about her miserable mistake except herself. But how on earth was she going to face Tommy or Mrs. Tommy now—let alone Gatzko?

Everything had been a mistake. There never had been any mystic conception of a hero. Most likely there had never been any universal rejoicing the other day either, or dancing angels or sounding trumpets, and her consecrated union with Gatzko was just a bit of rough-and-tumble in a squalid ruin, and the Mystic Nativity painting was of another family, in another place and another time, painted centuries ago in another country.

No, nothing great or heroic was going to come forth out of her, Bott. She, who had the power of growing things, was herself as barren as a desert. She had produced nothing, done nothing, except somehow antagonize Gatzko.

"I'm going out to see to our garden," she told Michael. Her pleasure in it was gone, but she felt she must do something to be busy or she might break down and howl at the moon like a dog. Working urgently and with concentration, as she used to during air raids, shutting out all other thoughts, she hacked away at the hard ground. Snow fell on her while she did it; the tower only sheltered a small corner, and her feet and legs stuck out into the weather.

When at last she was too cold to nurse and pamper it any longer she went in to the almost as cold lair; but at least, in there, you felt warm, the paraffin lamp and its ring of light made you think you were sitting round a hearth.

Bott wondered whether Gatzko would come in to supper, and in the meantime made some tea anyway. It was not very nice without milk or sugar but at least it was hot. As they sat over this Michael said, "Tell me about our garden."

And without hesitation Bott began, "It's a magic garden with a high brick wall round it so it's quite secret."

This was far from being a description of the churchyard of All-Hallows-the-Great however you looked at it. Bott had already departed from the story of that garden.

"It's very early spring there now. There's been a frost and all the little growing things have been killed. But there are two people who live in the garden and look after it: a little boy and an old witch." (Why do witches always have to be old, Bott wondered?)

"The old witch lives in a cottage in a clump of trees. And the little boy—h'm, where does the little boy live? At the other side of the garden in a tree-house."

Michael's eyes shone with excitement. He asked, "What does the little boy do? Is he very naughty?"

"Naughty? Oh, yes, he's always up to mischief. But he's friends with this old witch. They have to look after the garden, you know. And right now they've got to do something to drive away the frost."

Michael looked doubtful. Bott tried to adapt her story to a child's tastes. "To drive away a great horde of enemies, grown-ups, who are trying to break into the garden, get over the wall. Invaders, you know. And they're the ones who've killed all the little plants with their beastly frost. The little boy was the first one to notice them coming. He ran to the old woman and warned her that there was an army of hostile grown-ups camped outside the wall. The garden, you see," she added on an inspiration, remembering their earlier game together, "is like that big courtyard at Beaumaris, in a castle. Do you remember?"

"Yes, of course!"

Bott went on, becoming uneasily aware that her story was taking on a somewhat Biblical nature. "They've got to save the garden and keep it protected and bring all the seedlings—the little plants—to life again. The trouble was that the seedlings' roots didn't go down far enough, so when hard times came, they all died. Now it's the task of the woman and the little boy to find something that has strong deep roots and would protect them all. So they planted a tree."

"But what about the enemies outside?"

"They wouldn't be able to get in with the tree there, they'd be so scared of it when it grew big. And when they sent frosts the plants wouldn't die because they'd have a tree with such deep roots."

"But where's the tree? Is it in your garden now?"

"Ah, now this is where our story really begins! The witch, you see, isn't a very good gardener. Or at least not very good at shopping. She tried to buy a tree seed, a kernel, and when she got it home she found it wasn't one at all."

"There isn't any tree!"

Michael began to look tearful. He was hungry and tired and Bott realized it was about time she concluded her autobiography and sent him to bed.

"No, not yet, and we've got to be terribly brave because meanwhile we've got to protect ourselves, and the enemies will get us if we're weak and start crying. They'll guess there's no tree and that we haven't any roots and they'll come climbing over the wall and smash up the garden. But luckily the witch can go out tomorrow to buy a new seed for a tree, and meanwhile I'm going to fry you a fishcake." She heaved herself up, took the teacups and went behind the counter. "Of course the tree is a big secret," she warned, afraid suddenly that Gatzko might gather that she'd been teaching his child Christianity, however involuntarily and disguisedly. (Had she been converted, then? When? How alarming.)

"A secret," Michael repeated mechanically. Poor little brat, everything had had to be a secret for him since age zero, with that father.

They were both hungry. It was amazing how a whalemeat fishcake could perk you up. Bott had fully intended to bed Michael down afterwards, but as she cleared away the custard (no pudding to go under it unfortunately, she'd been too upset to remember her shopping today) he gave her a wideawake look, a Gatzko look. "I know where there's a tree seed," he said.

"Do you, love? Well, tomorrow I'm going out shopping—"

"No, you aren't listening to me!"

Bott stopped clearing away, turned round and gave him her full attention. Why shouldn't he be treated like a human being? She knew plenty of adults who were far less intelligent than five-year-old Michael.

"The old woman doesn't know where to buy tree seeds," he reminded her, "and she got a bad one."

"True enough," Bott admitted humbly.

"So why can't the little boy go out to get it?"

Bott was dismayed. She had seized on the idea of a tree and had fully decided to plant a real one. That would be an ornament to the London landscape, and no mistake.

"It just costs sixpence," Michael begged. "You might buy a bad one again. But I know where to get a real magic tree seed."

Magic was a word she had taught him. It needn't necessarily mean anything in this context.

"What does it look like?" she asked. "Has it got little roots in a paper bag and twigs?"

Michael seemed baffled. "It's round," he said, making an oval in the air, "and there's a line in the middle."

A nutmeg, a walnut? Obviously infinitely precious, anyway. "Of course the little boy shall plant the tree!" she cried, hugging and kissing him and starting to undress him. "I'll give you sixpence and you bring home the tree kernel tomorrow."

"Shall I tell you what the tree looks like?"

"Yes, go on!"

"It grows up like this," he said, raising his arms solemnly. "With lots of big shiny leaves. And lights."

Obviously he'd seen a Christmas tree. "How nice."

"And at the top are two lights that can see."

"That can see? You mean we can see them?"

"No, lights that can see, like eyes."

"Good heavens. Some tree."

"It's a very, very big tree," Michael said, again solemnly raising his arms. Bott gulped. The story had run away with her rather—or from her. Michael seemed to know more about it than she did. Trying to join in again she said, "And there are birds on all the branches, aren't there? The phoenix and the paradise bird?"

Michael seemed uninterested in the birds. "Is the compost heap in the garden?" he asked.

Oh dear, what troubles one did run into when one started taking allegory too literally. "Yes, of course, why else should we be making it?" she said bravely.

"I don't think we feed it enough. Tomorrow I want to put my dinner on it instead of eating it," he said virtuously.

"You're the one who doesn't get enough to eat, poor pet! Bed now."

In bed he smiled up at her. "You've forgotten my sixpence already."

"Oh, here you are then. I'm dying to see the tree seed."

He just looked at her.

She wanted to pace round the lair, but for fear of disturbing Michael she sat where she was and tried to read one of Gatzko's books. It was, undoubtedly, a wonderful book, Virginia Woolf, but she could not concentrate. She thought she must be tired, and went to bed. She lay in a semi-doze until finally, impatiently, she jumped up realizing she was not asleep nor going to be. It was three o'clock, she saw, fumbling for the clock, and the bed was empty. She pulled on any old clothes and went out.

She walked and walked, skidding on the ice. There were no lights of homely windows. She went to the place where she had made love with Gatzko on that first night, and fell into a hole, a bit of basement about three feet deep but still quite painful. She extricated herself and went on down an alley to a wharf and saw a strange somebody, all hair and trailing clothes, in the reflected river light. "I've lost my baby and my man," she cried out to this character. "Now I've got to die." The shaggy person looked gravely at her and swayed past, staggering slightly, without speaking. Looking after him she saw him lurch into an unlit building which she had assumed was a warehouse. A weirdie, obviously, and no doubt he had thought the same of her.

She wandered hours longer and near St. Paul's, near Tommy's in fact, she met someone else. All these people were a surprise to Bott who had always thought the Dairy & contained the only inhabitants of this bit of London. He looked respectable and Bott turned to flee, but he spoke to her. He had a book and a torch. "Are you lost, can I help you?"

"Yes, no! I'm just frightened."

"Frightened? I'm not surprised. A lady shouldn't wander round these parts alone at night, you know. Are you being molested? All sorts of queer characters beset the neighbourhood."

"I know, I'm one of them."

"I'm a master at the Choir School, and also, you might say, a runner after God, a priest. I sometimes like to take a nocturnal stroll to say my office. Is there any way I can help you?"

"No! No, you're very kind, but you can't come, you aren't the man—oh dear I'm so scared—"

"Come where? Scared of what?"

"Down into the abyss, into the dark pit. That's what I'm

scared of. Deep down buried retreat, isolation, in myself. The descent into myself and it's black. That's death, isn't it? Or insanity?"

The gentleman stared at her. Probably he didn't come upon her particular problem too often in a school full of dear little choristers.

"No, it's very kind of you to offer, but I must go alone. Thank you, goodnight."

What a lot of hills there were in the City of London. Bott had never realized. She had not any idea, now, where she was wandering. Presently she realized that it was, once again, the brown fog of a winter dawn, exactly like that glorious morning which seemed a life's span ago. A life with no seasons except spring which had died. Bott went on to London Bridge and looked at the same view, so identically the same as when she had looked at it and shared it with Gatzko, and she laughed.

The raw air caught her throat and made her laugh turn into a cough. She thought of the old witch in the garden she'd invented with Michael and remembered that witches traditionally croak. She croaked, then, and leant against the parapet of the bridge and thought of Gatzko pressing her against it and telling her about their magic ship.

Distractedly she left London Bridge and went vaguely in the direction of the light, the sunrise. To her surprise she found herself climbing towards the Tower of London. She felt soothed to see it. It was so strong and steady and monumental, had stood for so many centuries. She made directly for it, fixing her eyes on those ancient towers. Sunlight shone on the vanes, although the sun was far from risen.

As she went past the moat she caught a glimpse of greenness within: trees, a courtyard, a garden? Not THE garden? She was seized with longing to get in, and stared hopelessly across the bleak moat and walls. She knew she could not. It was forbidden her, and not only because the Tower was not open to the public till nine or whatever the silly rule would be. She had lied, telling Michael that the witch lived inside the garden. She, like all other would-be entrants, lived hungrily at the foot of its walls, thinking about greenness.

She wandered despondently past the front of the Tower. There was a beefeater sitting on a bench looking at the river, meditatively munching a sandwich. Bott went and sat beside him and looked at the river too.

"Morning," said the beefeater.

"Morning," said Bott, and then, "At least—do you think it is morning?"

"Well, a grey one, going to be. Sun won't last. Never does, does it?"

"No, indeed," Bott agreed.

They both looked meditatively at the river for a while, and then the beefeater offered her a sandwich.

Bott began to cry.

She cried helplessly for about five minutes until she found herself subsiding on to his shoulder. This was so hard and prickly with uniform that she sat up again, sniffing dismally and feeling a fool.

"Now, dearie, eat that sandwich and tell me what the trouble is," the beefeater said, as solid and unmoved as the Tower itself had been by centuries of prisoners' emotion.

"My man didn't come home tonight," wailed Bott through her handkerchief. "I don't think he likes home very much."

The beefeater thought for a bit. "Is home nice for him?"

"It can't be, I suppose."

"Well, dear, what you want to do is to make a nice home for him. Make a real home and he'll come back to it, all right. You can take it from me that what a man wants at heart is a nice, welcoming place to come back to at night, and a nice sweet-tongued woman."

Bott took a mouthful of sandwich (not beef) and gazed wonderingly and hopefully at the beefeater.

"It'll win out in the end, you'll see, against whatever night-time attractions he's looking for. No, we all go through that stage. But what I always say is, if a man knows there's a comfy welcome for him at home, home is where he'll go."

He ruminated over his sandwich. Bott considered what he had just said, enthralled. After quite a long time he asked her, "Feeling a bit better now, are you?"

"Yes, thank you very much. I'm going to follow your advice."

He folded up the greaseproof paper and said with a final air, "I should think you'd better, and be off now and start straight away. Get him a nice breakfast ready, and yourself too. Eh?"

She nodded, dumbfounded and delighted. They rose and walked back to the Tower. "Believe me," the beefeater said, "home and family, that's what a man really hankers for, and drink and girls is no substitute, as you'll both find I don't doubt. So remember, a nice smile now!"

Bott gave him a nice smile. "Thank you *very* much. Good-bye."

"Bye-bye, dear."

Bott careered home, all full of new plans and hope. A hearth, a home, stability, gosh, if that was what he wanted no wonder he kept away from this. She stared at the lair. Dirty washing-up stood all over the place, the screening had mostly blown down, the bed was unmade and the whole place, though icy cold and draughty, stank of leftover food. She stared at it, and then burst into song. "Everyone says How-do-you-do, down on Jollity Farm." She felt stronger at once and set gaily to work.

The noise of her singing woke Michael. He looked at her, alert and amused, over his coverlet. She was, at that point, engaged in building a literal hearth from bricks out of the yard, though she had no chimney and no fuel.

"You're awake, are you?" she said to Michael. "I'll make you breakfast." Mindful of the beefeater's instructions, she doubled the amount of oats she normally used for porridge. It was amazing how it went down. Pity it was plain bread after-wards. Maybe with an open fire they could make toast.

"Eat your crusts, pet," she said maternally to Michael. She

was feeling maternal, though admittedly somewhat failed at the moment.

He shook his head. "They're for the compost heap. Don't you remember? We have to feed it. It hasn't had any breakfast. Besides I'm full up."

So they went and fed the compost heap, and Bott went to work. As she left him in the Dairy & Michael called after her, "Are you looking forward to seeing the tree seed?"

"Placing all my hopes in it," Bott answered.

She remembered her answer, and was stunned, when on her return Michael presented her with a small cardboard Easter egg.

15

MARY GATZKOVIC CARRIED a basket of hot rolls across the carpet to her No. 2 table. It was warm in here and the antique looking woodwork and the candleglow (but not candles—it was electric) made her feel pleasantly melancholic. This waitressing was one of the most agreeable things she did. It was a nice restaurant, not like that hurry-scurry coffee-shop Scott liked so much. Nobody hurried here.

Then she saw her English professor, Paul Fieldman, come in with another man. He grinned and beckoned at Mary. She took menus to them, suspicious. Was this a coincidence or something worse?

"Hullo, Mary," said Mr. Fieldman. "Can I introduce you to my friend, John Kirk. This is my pupil, Mary Gatzkovic."

"Mary," the other man said. "How nice to find such a beautiful name still in existence."

"Well, are you enjoying your job, Mary?"

"Excuse me, I'm on duty," she stammered, and left them with their menus.

They wouldn't give her their order straight but kept teasing her and horsing around. To mess her about they pretended they wanted things which had been unobtainable since the beginning of the war. She was miserable. When she wheeled the salad trolley across to them Mr. Fieldman said, "Yes, that was quite gracefully done. We came right across the city to be served by you, didn't we, John?" and snickered.

They both gazed appreciatively at her. Wretched, Mary put Blue Cheese dressing on both salads and then realized she had forgotten to ask them what they wanted. Grinning, Mr. Kirk said, "Blue Cheese is exactly what I was longing for." He looked at her professor, who still kept staring at Mary. "You're upsetting her. What a way to treat a new girl-friend."

"What are waitresses for if they can't be looked at?" said Mr. Fieldman.

"I may be your waitress here," Mary said. "But you might remember that I'm also one of your students."

"That gives me all the more right to be interested in you," Mr. Fieldman said, with a great big smile.

Three days later he came again, alone. He took a booth and looked at her. It was a disconcerting and fiercely intelligent look, no teasing this time and Mary was on its receiving end all through dinner. She spilt water and dropped forks and forgot sauces. When she gave him his check he tried to date her.

"Oh! Please no!" cried Mary.

"Why not?"

"I don't know," she said distractedly but truthfully.

"But the Sphinx is supposed to know everything. Did no one ever tell you you have the face of a Sphinx? The characteristic of the Sphinx was to keep a man guessing, wasn't it? That what you're trying to do? Keep this man guessing?"

Disregarding all rules about courtesy to customers Mary turned and ran for the staff rest room. When she came back there was a ten dollar tip.

As soon as she was free she left the restaurant and ran. She was intending to bury herself in her secret place on the rooftop, far from this hateful man. But although she searched half the night she could not find the street with Kielers Continental Shipping and Transport and the Schiaparelli pharmacy. At midnight she took a cab back to the campus and cried all the way. She felt sure she would never find it again.

The whole college knew, by the end of the week, that Mary Gatzkovic was dating her professor.

So she was not surprised, late Sunday night, to see Nicky coming towards her, coming, coming, filling the corridor, smiling at her. Mary tried to stand passively. But Nicky's smile was too bright and too sure and too friendly. Mary found she

could resist, after all. With a sudden movement that was sheer
heroism she bounded towards Nicky, pushed rudely past her
and shot off down the corridor.

"Don't you want a little talk, Mary?" Nicky called in surprise. "I was just coming to see you."

Mary did not answer. She was amazed to find herself capable of such action. But she felt so sick and shaky that she
could not eat or work. She had escaped this time, but Nicky
was always around. Mary went to bed at eight o'clock, ignoring the concern and enquiries of the other girls, and hid under
the blankets like a little kid.

Su was talking on and on about Shakespeare. Mary burst in
suddenly, "Of course everything is just like Shakespeare, isn't
it, even today."

"Is it?" Su said, surprised.

"I mean all these complicated plots just to overturn some
unfortunate king or someone. You know, you get these poor
innocent characters with Fate and all the rest of the characters
too against them, don't you? The heroines especially. I mean
Cordelia and those. It's so true. They never win. You watch
them all through the play going down gradually, and however
hard they struggle you just know they'll come to a tragic end."

"I hope you aren't saying that good is always bound to
lose?" Su said severely.

"No, but these weak good people. You always find them in
the plays all at odds with their environments, don't you? You
see them in Shakespeare's sophisticated urban courts and you
can just tell they belong to another order. Haven't you ever
felt that? That this isn't your world at all, that you had got
here by mistake?"

"Um—" said Su.

"I'm sure that's just how all Shakespeare's nice characters
must feel. That they're up against a whole, alien world. I mean
just look how peculiar it all is. The view out of that window,
for instance, with a massive great machine-built street. What

an odd thing a city street is, don't you think, Su? Don't you wonder how it ever came to be?"

Su had never wondered any such thing. She could only say "Um—" again.

"It's about as far from nature as it could possibly be. And yet, look, it's solid with people who are quite at home in it. It doesn't worry them. They're all the side characters, the clowns and courtiers and so on, who can somehow keep up and manage to stay in tune with their surroundings. I don't know how they do it, Su, I really don't."

Su pulled herself together and said, "Well, after all, a city is built by people just for themselves, so there's no reason why it shouldn't suit them."

"No, of course. I guess it's just me. I feel so—so prehistoric; that's what I feel. I'd like to be in a time when everyone worshipped the sky and the earth because the sky and the earth were what they saw in front of their noses. Everything was so real and simple and true to them, to the ancient peoples I mean. And if you really had a problem you just went and asked an oracle and the answer came out of the earth, straight from the horse's mouth."

"I shouldn't let that go too far, wishing you lived in the past," Su said. "You aren't and you can't."

"True enough. But sometimes I feel so at odds with everything and everybody, I think I'll just shatter under it. I'd like to sink to the bottom of some nice deep lake and never come up. I really would."

"Oh, Mary, come off it now, life's not so bad. We all want to help you."

"Yes! I know! Everyone wants to do things to me! That's why I'm scared."

She realized she had said too much and tried to turn it into a joke.

"I guess I'm just nostalgic for the Garden of Eden."

Su smiled uncertainly and decided that somebody, like Scott or Mr. Fieldman, ought to know about this.

16

GATZKO GREETED BOTT as she sat in the Dairy & with "Well, hey! That corpse you planted yesterday in your garden, has it begun to sprout?"

"Oh, Gatzko."

"Will it bloom next year?" he asked savagely, and went through into the garden towards the lair.

Bott looked into her tea. She was dreading the humble pie she was going to have to eat, the explanation, the pardon she must ask. She even dreaded the reconciliation that she thought she had looked forward to. She could not finish her tea. She handed it apologetically to Mrs. Weingartner and followed Gatzko.

He had found her hearth. "Now what the hell," he said. He didn't seem to notice his comfy home, that is, that she had tidied the lair and repaired the screening.

"It's a hearth to make you feel cosy."

"A hearth? With no chimney?"

"It was the idea," she said anxiously. Far off memories of Girl Guides came back. There, the camp fire had usually been imaginary, and the other Guides had never seemed to think this unsatisfactory. But when Gatzko turned to her she saw he was angrier than ever.

"Is this because you can't knit, so you've decided not to be a mother after all, but a vestal virgin? You can't be both, you know. Which is it going to be?"

This was the moment to confess, but she stalled. "Vestal, what, er—"

"The holy maidens who feed the eternal flame?" Sounded as if he were quoting again. "Not much of a success so far, is it?"

"Well, I've only just begun," Bott shouted. "Give me a chance. I'm doing it for you."

This Gatzko knew, and it only depressed him more. But he realized there would be a row unless he somehow swallowed his blackness. Bott never would understand what the Waste Land was or what it was like to be in it. Rows were what Gatzko feared more than anything in the world.

"Okay, okay," he muttered and plunged into his studio.

Somehow the moment had passed without anything but a little bickering to show for it. Bott stared hopelessly at the studio partition. Who knew when—if—he would ever come out to her again?

In fact he came out quite soon, scowling, clay on his hands and in his hair. The sculpture wasn't going well, obviously. Bott was nervously polite to him. He said very little, ate less and fell asleep on his face.

They never referred to the baby again. Bott wondered if he had forgotten, or guessed the fiasco. After a while she stopped bothering to wonder. He never had been interested. She also stopped relating her progress in her gardening schemes. He was not only uninterested, he apparently actively disapproved.

He was mildly surprised and relieved that the scene he feared so seemed to have passed by. Bott must be in a very bad way, if she was reduced to using tact. Had she ever been diplomatic in her life before? Had she ever thought of another method of attack than glorious frontal assault? He had no doubt she was doing plenty behind his back—the things she told Michael, for instance. But her self-confidence must indeed be wilting to be doing it behind his back at all. However, he did not care about the state of her ego any longer. She had grown to bore him and that was her fault. He was job-hunting and had no time to think about women.

Bott was scared even to speak to him, but she did not especially conceal her projects from him, except for one: the planting of the tree.

This impressive ceremony took place while Gatzko was in

the pub one evening. Bott was about to heat some washing water for Michael when he suddenly shook his head, half-undressed, and said, "No bath! Not now!"

"Oh, come on."

"No, that doesn't matter. We must plant the tree."

"Now? Must we really? It's dark—"

Michael found his little Easter egg and led the way firmly out. Bott hurried after him with his coat. He looked so solemn, marching into the night, that for a moment she fancied he was going to lead her to the walled garden of their story come true. He stopped, in fact, just outside the door by the compost heap. "There," he said, pointing.

"Oh, darling! But that's right in a corner, by the wall. The tree won't get any light."

"It must be near the wall," Michael insisted, "so the enemies can see it. And anyway it's nearer my bed."

Oh well, as if it mattered, it was only a cardboard egg. Why should she care? Funny all the same, she did care. She wanted the tree to have enough light. It worried her to plant it in a crevice, down at the bottom of this chasm between two broken walls. But Michael had set his heart on the spot, and obediently she began to dig, wondering again why she was taking so much trouble.

She talked as she worked. "Loosen up the soil underneath, you see, so the roots can burrow down deep. They must reach water. Go far enough down, you'll always reach water. Nothing can live without water."

"I could," said Michael. "I don't like water, not our water. It tastes of saucepan."

"Oh, this is different! This is magic, living water. There's a source far down that deep roots can reach and then the tree grows up big and everyone lives off the water, thanks to the tree. No, really, it's very special water. Perhaps you'll see some one day. It flashes all pink and gold and colours, and it comes spouting sparkling out, when once you've tapped the source."

"What does it taste like?"

"There's no other taste like it, it's the most delicious taste there is, and it's stronger than wine."

"When did you drink it?"

"When I was a little girl." Well, not so little, but never mind.

"Why don't you drink it now?"

"Don't I drink it?" Bott was shocked at the question. "How do you know?"

"I've never seen you."

Bott pondered, slowly and methodically burying the egg and packing the dirt round it with her fingers. "I gave it to your father," she said at last.

"But he doesn't drink it either."

"No." Bott felt suddenly bleakly sad. "No, he didn't want it, and he poured it all away." She realized how very cold it was, and that even if Michael was wearing his coat she was not. "Let's finish this now, pet, it's too cold for digging."

"Is it properly buried?"

"Yes, warm and safe."

"So it'll grow?"

"Of course it'll grow. A fine big tree, the biggest there's ever been." And you're believing that, she accused herself, you're telling him all that and believing it yourself, you grownup child.

"Then we must say goodbye to it. Goodbye, tree-seed, come up soon, grow big and strong and have two bright lights on top. Goodbye, tree, good luck." He chanted on and Bott decided she would have to stop this, or he would go on all night. She made one or two hesitant attempts to persuade him to come, but he sang on ignoring her. Finally she picked him up and carried him into the lair. He shrieked and kicked. The evening ended with tears and a tantrum. To get away she went and sat in the Dairy &, where Mrs. Weingartner, who had stopped serving tea, gave her a cup of cocoa made on her own stove.

Bott felt weary, weary and heartbroken, tired of trying and the uselessness of it all. That dismal little tale about the water had been so true, so beastly true. Everything she had she had given to Gatzko and he didn't want it, he had thrown it away.

She felt repentant for unloading her worries on Michael, giving him, no doubt, neuroses for life. She had not meant to. They had unloaded themselves, without her realizing, under cover of the story of the tree and the water. She saw now that that was a very thin disguise. Yet she had certainly not meant to tell any kind of allegory.

She had put in a tree because she loved trees, no other reason. She had grown up among trees. For a very long time, until the army in fact, trees meant more to her than humans. At twenty she left her village, sadly saying goodbye to the trees there which were more than half alive. They hovered between being trees and being giants, and this had been frightening at times. She did not realize how much a part of her life they had made themselves until she came to leave. She wrenched herself away, and found that the old lady she went to nurse, Miss Ridley, lived in a wood.

So much for the tree, then. All that allegorical stuff was unintentional; it had put itself in. What about the water? It was the first time for twenty years that she had thought about living water, a phrase she had so loved once. When she was thirteen she had had a vision of it, looking as she had described to Michael, cascading out of a cup and sparkling all colours. She had forgotten about it until she found herself telling Michael.

How real it had been to her then, the living water, as wet as wet. What a step downwards her insipid life-force was. It was like exchanging sunshine for an indoor thirty-watt bulb.

In fact it had been downwards all the way from age thirteen. Whatever had she been doing all those years? Instead of progressing, she had stopped. She had traded in living water for life-force, and generally deteriorated; and otherwise she was a girl, a middle-aged girl. No wonder Gatzko was fed up. She had a thirteen-year-old's mind—a stale, second-rate one by now—inside the body of a worn thirty-seven. It was the first time in years she had remembered her age. She stared disgustedly at her hands, dirty and cracked and old, with things on the knuckles—well, what were those?

She rubbed them in irritation. They itched. It must be these which had drawn her attention to her hands. She remembered now they had been itching mildly for weeks. So had her toes. Oh, what was the matter? Little hard lumps—she thought back to her nursing days—they weren't warts, were they?

She pushed back the cold cocoa so violently that it spilt, and hurried into the lair, clumsy with disgust. Michael was asleep behind his screen, thank goodness. She tore off her stockings and peered at her feet. Ugh! They were crawling with warts, great whoppers. They must have been growing there quietly for ages.

Bott tried to think about warts. She had never had any before but of course that didn't mean anything. They came when they thought they would, grew as they pleased and fell out if and when they thought they would (patients had told her). They were separate organisms, she rather thought, parasites, and except for very obliging ones their fundamental idea was simply to go on growing as big and as deep as possible. And if you rooted them up they grew in again. Mysterious, nasty things. Bott felt sick. Gardening was one thing; she hadn't meant to grow things on her own body. That was too much.

She lay in bed wondering what to do and decided to ask Tommy. He knew so much about her already it seemed useless keeping up any pretence at a private life. She needed a confidant, a friend, and it really didn't seem fair on Michael to expect him to solve all her problems. Tommy would know what to do. Yes, she must go to Tommy. She fell asleep thinking of him.

Tommy grinned when she told him her trouble. "There's always something, isn't there?" he said. "If you couldn't find anything else you'd imagine you were growing a hunch back."

"Oh, don't be horrid. I didn't invite the beastly warts."

"Didn't you? I wonder," said Tommy. "They're funny things, you know. They know what's going on in a person's mind."

Bott fidgeted uneasily with a milk bottle and wished she could believe he was joking.

"Of course there's only one way to get rid of them."

"Which is?"

"Funny—I should have thought you'd be the one to tell me," Tommy said. "Warts, magic and mystery—right up your street, I'd have thought."

"How d'you know that?"

"Perhaps you told me, perhaps a little bird did. Perhaps I just guessed."

"You're mischievous, that's what you are," Bott wailed, "horrid and mischievous and you won't help me."

"There, there," Tommy said, suddenly anxious that she might pass out again or something. "I'm just going to give you a lovely remedy. You wait for some moonlight and then you wash your prize warts out of a silver bowl. It's great fun."

"I haven't got a silver bowl."

"Oh, doesn't his lordship eat out of a silver porringer? I imagined he would. Or did he give it as a keepsake to the Queen of Yugoslavia?"

Bott burst into tears and Tommy realized his teasing had gone too far.

"I'm sorry, Bott. I'm taking out on you what's due to my wife. Don't cry. Or, yes, do cry. Let's howl together."

Bott raised her head and howled, her eyes screwed up but tears still running down the lines of her face from the corners. Tommy looked nervously into the shop to make sure there were no customers, gripped his knees and let out a little bass howl, for Bott and for himself and for the whole bleeding setup.

Gatzko was coming home after the pub closed one night when he saw Bott bent over her compost heap. He stopped, wondering whether to go on or go out again. Gardening by moonlight; that was the last straw. But then she did not seem to be gardening after all. She constantly stooped to something and raised it to the moon. He could see it glinting. He could hear her moaning and whimpering, too. Slowly and apparently in agony she bent and did something to herself, groaning. A whiff of decaying cabbage leaves came across to him, and she was standing over it; was that the reason for her groaning? God, what a stink, and right by the door too.

But what was she doing? She pulled herself up and raised her arms. He saw her hands against the moon, gnarled and twiggy. Drops of water ran off them. Then slowly she began to rub them together.

"Hey! Stop that!" Gatzko shouted, running forward. She turned towards him as if she did not recognize him, and for a moment he wondered if she were sleepwalking indeed. "Wake up! Snap out of that! I won't have you playing at Lady Macbeth. Snap out of it, do you hear?"

She dropped her hands and gawped at him.

"Ritual washing by moonlight! For heaven's sake, woman! Who have you been murdering? Though I can't see you doing anything so clean and healthy as a murder. What have you been up to—sticking pins into my wax image, or something even nastier? What's in this bucket—hey, it's not silver, is it? Washing out of a silver bowl by moonlight? Jesus Christ, Bott!"

"I'm not doing anything—I'm just trying to cure my warts."

"And where did you find this anyway? Oh, it's communal property of the coven, I suppose. Do you need a broomstick? Shall I buy you a black cat?"

"Gatzko, I'm not a witch, I'm not, I promise you. This isn't black magic. It's an old folk remedy."

"It's not going to take much more of this to make me tie you up and throw you in the Thames. That's what they did to witches, you know."

"But I'm not!"

"What do you call yourself—a wise woman? In popular parlance, that's a witch." He shivered, half angry and half really frightened. Women could get power of this kind if they chose, there was no denying it. He had had first hand experience of the evil eye, in Chicago. If Bott put her mind to it she probably could harm him. Though it was more likely a love spell she'd been brewing. "What are you trying to do to me?" he shouted. "What have you wished on me? Dreams and enchanted lusts? Or planted some witchy herb in my subconscious? Grab me with tendrils—aren't I guessing right? Well, even if you haven't, you'd like to, I know. And wanting is half the doing."

He stared at her. He could not bear the thought of going into that dark place which she had made her place, although he had discovered it and built it. He snatched her filthy bowl and ran out. It tingled in his fingers so that he could hardly hold it. He got on to one of the little jetties off Lower Thames Street, leant over the water and threw it in with all his might. It hit the surface with a splash, bobbed and floated, cursed thing. It glinted evilly at him, reflecting the moon.

Gatzko was thoroughly scared of her by now. If she really wanted to, she would find a way to grab him. Tendrils very likely. He could almost feel them. All women had these tendencies, of course, but she was surely worse than most. How could he get away? He paced and fretted up and down the jetty. The only money they had now was hers, and he would rather not have any than touch that. Why didn't the international telephone exchange write him to say he could start work that week? With a very little money—just his first week's wages—he could get out.

Bott stood looking at the moon until it went behind the building. Then she went in, so cold she could hardly open the door, and crawled under the bedclothes. She thought about her body, warts and hair growing on it without her permission while the baby she wanted refused to materialize. She wondered if she had indeed wished cancer on Gatzko, as he had once prophesied. Anything seemed possible. She put the pillow over her head, and it smelt mouldy. She imagined the mould spreading over her skin. When she fell asleep she dreamt she was singing in church "I am a foul pit of corruption. Selah." She woke to find it still dark, but the smell was worse.

"YOU MUST EXCUSE me if I'm being rude to take so much interest in you," Paul Fieldman said to Mary. "Only I've always been interested in primitive beliefs."

"Are my beliefs primitive, then?"

"Yes," said Paul. "You're primitive altogether. Your school work especially."

Mary didn't answer. She was used to him being rude to her. He seemed to enjoy it.

She had wanted to go home to Arizona for her Easter vacation, but she did not have the money. Just how she came to confide this to Paul she never knew. Maybe he discovered on his own. Of course she would have wanted to keep from him that she had anything to do with Arizona. But on Thursday before Easter she was sitting beside him in a cream colour Lincoln Continental heading south, deriving less pleasure than she ought from the glamorous fact of driving along Route 66.

To get out of it, she had tried to persuade him that she didn't enjoy automobile touring.

"And just when did you ever go automobile touring?" he had sneered. "Gasoline only came off rationing this year."

He did not come so often to her restaurant now (though still too often for her comfort). He said eating took his mind off her. But nearly every day he was waiting for her outside class in the Lincoln. (His own? Hired? Mary did not know how to find out, not that she cared.) Scott knew about him, of course, and was jealous, which did not help matters. How ridiculous could the situation become? She found herself on the defensive with Scott, protesting that she didn't love Paul or even like him. And it was very difficult to do that without giving Scott to understand that in fact she loved him.

"When do we reach Tucson?" Mary asked vaguely.

"Tucson? I'm not taking you to Tucson. We're going to see Grand Canyon."

"Oh!" squealed Mary. The word "canyon", any canyon, was enough.

"What's wrong with Grand Canyon?"

"I—er—oh, nothing. But I went there already."

"You could spend a lifetime at Grand Canyon and never exhaust it. I feel certain that whatever marvels they showed you there before you never saw anything like what we're going to see this Easter."

"Oh," Mary said.

"All the citizens of Phoenix have donated gifts. And on Easter Sunday these gifts are going to be sent down into the canyon with little parachutes, for the Indians at the bottom."

Mary failed to imagine this. "Are there Indians down there?"

"No. But there'll be police waiting to collect the loot and distribute it in the reservations." He grinned at her. "Sheriff's men, probably. This is what the Indian religion of gifts from the sky has turned into. I've brought you in on the end of a belief."

Mary said nothing but thought apprehensively about the canyon itself. Arizona was a big state, but still, it was perilously near the secret place. And Phoenix! Barely a hundred and twenty miles away.

"All beliefs turn out to end in something, you see. Gods and goddesses through the centuries culminate in the men and women of recent times—at least, in some of the more archetypal specimens, shall we say. Did you know, honey, that you are one of the purest archetypal specimens I have ever seen. Diana, Freya and Mother Earth herself—that's you. The elemental she."

Mary shook her head, amazed at the idea that any goddess should finish up as herself and feeling sorry for the goddesses.

"Of course polytheism was rather silly," Paul said. "All gods are only facets of Man and all goddesses of Woman. There was a problem about this crops and sowing business. The Greeks solved it by having two goddesses—Ceres and her daughter Persephone. One is the goddess of growing things, but it is her daughter who does all the work, constantly bobbing up and down to Hades to carry out the job of death into life each spring. Of course they are one. Every spring Persephone goes down into the earth, into Hades, to be united with Dis, that is, to die."

"No! No!" screamed Mary. She felt the spasm, the darkness coming, the sucking.

Paul accelerated into a rest area and pulled up. "What's the matter?" he said. "Did I upset you? Honey—hey, Mary!"

Mary's body was arched stiffly over the back of the car seat; her mouth was open but she did not breathe through it. Her hands flexed a little and then hung limp. Her body arched more and more and her head fell over the back of the seat. Paul watched her. At last she collapsed, down among the pedals of the car controls, heaving and gasping.

"I don't want to go to Grand Canyon," Mary said. "I'd rather go to Tucson."

"Why? It's a dull little town."

"It's not! It's a city, the oldest desert city, and I have family there."

"No you don't. Only guardians, and you don't want to see them, do you?"

"How do you know that?"

"Honey, I know everything. At least exteriorly. Listen, honey goddess, Persephone, I don't in the least mind you paying the odd visit to Hades. That's quite in order. But how hot is your mythology? You won't go and forget, will you, that Persephone always comes back?"

"I don't know," Mary said miserably. "I don't mean to forget things."

He gave her an intense look for a few minutes until Mary felt sure that his mind must have wandered. Hers would, if she tried to concentrate on one person so long. Eventually he said, "No, I'm sorry, we are definitely going to Grand Canyon. I want to see your reaction."

Mary thought she could climb out of the hotel and run away—where? Where were they? She had not taken notice. A small town, some white board houses she remembered, a mile or so of petrol pumps. Could be anywhere. She could even, come to think of it, just walk out and go. But she knew she would not, either climbing or walking. She had given up trying to escape.

They arrived at Grand Canyon in the evening. Mary looked in bewilderment at the stretch of blue nothing, while a woman on the terrace beside her said encouragingly, "Yes, it's beautiful, isn't it?" Beauty was a word that had passed out of Mary's vocabulary. It did not apply to her lost canyon, therefore she had ceased to think about it at all. She stumbled back into the big hotel, feeling baffled and bewildered, but relieved that this thing obviously had nothing in common with her canyon.

But Sunday morning was different. They went out of the hotel into true Arizona heat and sunlight. A big buzzing insect flew into Mary's face and made off angrily into the sky, trailing long black legs. The car door was too hot to touch and Paul had to open it for her with a handkerchief. Mary wished for sunglasses but did not say so, knowing that Paul would immediately spend an hour choosing and buying an expensive pair which she would lose at once.

He drove her to a lookout point on the canyon rim but Mary could not see the canyon. She was distracted by the sweet herb smells, the colour of the stone and the light, and above all by the prickly-pear cactus. Every plant here was one she had loved and probably tried to cultivate at one time or another in Sedona. At least the rocks were yellow, and there were none of those weird eroded shapes, she thought; until she saw a cliff of red rolled rock across a break in the canyon rim.

The lookout terraces were filling up. All Phoenix seemed to be coming to see their gifts parachuted in. Paul drove further along, got out to investigate, and came back delighted. "There's a choice shady spot with a tree, and quite a good view. I suggest we install ourselves before the natives invade."

Again he tried to make her take an interest in the view, but it was too big. Mary blinked at it and turned away, and saw with a surge of nostalgia a lizard by her feet.

Then, "Oh!" she said, and, "Is this the actual canyon?"

She was looking down into a sheer cleft.

"This? No, it's not a canyon at all, just a split in the canyon wall. It probably only extends about a quarter of the way down. You'll have to lean out to see Grand Canyon itself, I'm afraid, but the shade compensates. Look, you can see Bright Angel Trail winding down there opposite. It's the only way down, it's a mule track."

Mary could not find the trail. All she could see was the abyss plunging down at her feet, brilliantly lit where she was, at the top, and then suddenly black. But as she looked further in the darkness seemed to lessen. The deeper she looked the more light there seemed to be, as if there were another source of light at the bottom, not the sun. Although she leant precariously over the fence she could not see the bottom, only, far down, the golden cliffs glowing. Whatever Paul might say, this canyon was already too deep and great for her comprehension.

"There go the parachutes!"

Her eyes aching as she looked back into the glare, Mary saw two or three little white specks floating down away out in the main canyon, turning and eddying and then just hanging.

"The hot air must have carried them clear of the cliffs."

So sweetly, so gently, they fell, gifts from the gods, or surely, if Paul was right, the gods themselves, descending into hell, themselves their own offerings, belling and sailing and falling.

More came after them, and then on the left too, a host of little white points. The crowds cheered at each new volley. Then one came over the edge of Mary's own little rift. Down it went, Persephone in her white robe, into the darkness and then into the light that shone from far below. Mary craned further and further to follow it and of course now she thought she was it. It was like flying in a dream, so tantalizingly slow and delicious was her fall. Mary moaned, aching to see the far source which made the cliffs shine.

Paul caught her skirt as she toppled over. The bystanders shouted and ran to him, seeing him struggling to pull back a girl who had apparently fallen over the fence. She was surprisingly heavy and had already slithered a long way down the rocks. When she realized that she was being hauled back she struggled feebly.

Paul drove her back to Chicago well satisfied with his experiment, and more interested in her than ever.

What is the way out of this? Bott wondered. Is there any way?

This was the second night she had lain alone under Gatzko's Navajo rug, smelling corruption. Where did he go? He didn't look as if he slept, when she saw him, which was rarely.

She could feel the black pit closing over her. She was going down into it, down into the abyss of herself, as she had predicted to the St. Paul's choirmaster. The daylight was receding fast.

I must get out, she thought. How about a bit of willpower. If it is myself I am falling into I can surely get myself out again, if I will it.

She turned over, cradled her head in her arms and set herself to will herself out. She shut her eyes and thought flying. It required an impossible effort but presently she was flying, not very steadily, the concentration behind her eyes her only support. She could feel her eyeballs moving and her eyelids screwing up and unscrewing each time she sank suddenly or managed to raise herself a few feet. She thought she must reach the ceiling soon, but oh, it was so far. At last she did, and now surely it would become easier. She could fly, she could do it this way, she could raise herself, yes, and maybe Gatzko too.

Then as she hovered just below the ceiling, she was possessed by an idea of feet walking. They were not her feet, but a man's, very dirty, cracked and bruised. Slowly, as if the walker were having even more trouble than she was, each foot dragged itself up and set itself down with a little wince. Stumbling and hesitating the feet plodded on, sometimes climbing over things and often tripping. Bott watched fascinated, and then realized that her flight had halted. She was back where she had started, in bed, and she would not now, nor should, escape by flying. That was not a right way. She must follow the way the feet were walking, the slow, hard, dogged, earthbound way. There was no easy escape.

Bott wanted to scream and beat her fists on the pillow, as Michael would. But when she had raised her hands and opened her mouth for this she found she was exhausted. She fell face down in her pillow and thought of nothing but total blackness.

Gatzko in fact spent his time trying and failing to forget Bott. Her memory hung over everything. He couldn't get away from her anywhere in England. Too bad: so he must leave England.

He paced about on the wharf, worrying. He didn't like breaking his own resolutions. He had quite intended to leave all that money for Mary, for ever, never to touch it himself but to start all over again from scratch as if he were really poor, the wildpiece he saw himself as. It was a failure to go back to past caches.

He thought about Mary and suddenly wanted to see her again. He visualized her as she would be now, tall and willowy, beautiful, dancing, dancing all the time and giving parties in her college room. And going around Chicago, having fun. He had heard something about shortages and rationing even in the States, but he didn't really believe it. There would certainly be more fun in Chicago than in this dreary city, which seemed to be enjoying rolling in its austerity and rations and generally low-keyed living. How—why—had he stuck it so long? Suddenly he was tired of being a down-and-out, tired of squalor and discomfort. He wanted to be back where the money was, back where life was, back with his young daughter who had (thank God) never had a chance to grow into this fatal habit of practising austerity.

"Hi, hon," "You're *so* welcome," he could hear them, those sweet Middlewestern voices. Mary would not shout at him or lecture him or cultivate compost by his pillow. She would not pull ruses to get him into church and/or clumsily seduce him. He ran and skipped to Lovat Lane and rummaged for some writing-paper. It was dark with all the screens up and stank. He did not notice Bott watching him from her pillow with worn eyes. He went into the Dairy & but it was tea-break time and there was not really room to stand, let alone to sit and write. He went back into the lair, impatiently pulling down a bit of the screening, and began to write to Mary. "Hi, hon!" the letter began.

Bott leant on her elbow and looked at him writing so energetically, his black head bobbing, and supposed listlessly that he was writing to a woman. She considered him again and knew, quite simply, that he was writing to his daughter whose name began with H—or else with M;, yes, that was it. M, a short name. She could not remember if he had ever told her about his daughter and she did not bother to think very hard. She knew he was writing to her, that was all, and if he had not wanted her to know, that was too bad. Because she knew exactly what he was writing, watching him across the room as he scribbled excitedly.

He was asking her for money to come and see her. He mentioned Michael but she, Bott, was nowhere in the letter.

G*

He sealed it up, addressed it and put it out for post—for Bott to post. The dear innocent! He could never remember to be mistrustful.

Bott could have steamed it open but she did not bother. She knew what was in the letter. However when he was gone she copied down the address. She put on a skirt and went out to the post.

She was beyond thinking over her actions; she could only get on with them. She supposed she was technically "heartbroken" or "in despair" or something, but she did not feel anything but cold. She went into Westminster Abbey, into the cloister, and sat on the frozen stone and looked at the snow. She took out her pen—a mouldy old ex-government ballpoint that hardly wrote—and paper, another piece from the same block Gatzko had used. "Dear Mary Gatzkovic," her letter began. The writing there was quite small and neat, but when she came to post the thing she had to pay extra on weight.

Mary just could not believe it. When she saw his writing she had actually flinched, fearing some new, terrible command. But he was coming! He wanted to see her! He was coming from London to Chicago especially to see her! That is, if she could afford the fare from her college trust fund. How surprising he should bother to write her about it at all. He could have done it through the bank. He must really be wanting to make it up. She felt as if she had heard news of rescue coming. She must, she would afford it even if it meant leaving college altogether and getting a job. She had completed nearly a full academic year. But she would have done anything—she would have jumped off the top of the Board of Trade Building, where that mammoth Corn Goddess stood, if it would have brought her father quicker.

And there was this other letter. Mary knew she was stupid, and that no doubt explained why she found it quite incomprehensible. Also she could not read most of it. Without particularly thinking about the matter she found she had decided to take both letters to Paul. She could not account for such a decision. Recently she had discovered—after the Grand Canyon episode in fact—that she disliked Paul more vigorously than anyone she had ever met, and that included Nicky.

Bott went every day to the Trafalgar Square post office to see if there was a reply yet. So, probably, did Gatzko, but when they first moved to Lovat Lane he had entrusted her with the job of collecting mail, and just in case he still held to this, she went. She did not worry particularly that he might get her letter. He would only leave it lying around the lair if he did. He seemed to know even less than her about deception.

On Sunday she went in and as she stood by the Poste Restante desk, knew quite certainly that this was a waste of hope and of effort. She was fooling herself. She could not keep Gatzko, whatever miracles this girl performed, and she could not escape the black abyss.

She left the post office and went into St. Martin-in-the-Fields, but all her joints seemed locked and she could not kneel. She gripped the pew and stared at the altar and felt the darkness coming.

The woman next to her was in the middle of a hymn when she was startled to hear a deep voice croaking beside her. She looked round and saw a great haggard scarecrow of a woman leaning urgently forward, apparently addressing a little negress in the pew in front. "Fool! Adulteress! Wretch!" the big woman spat.

The Negress jumped and dropped her hymn-book. The woman went fiercely on, "Yes, you've lost him, and destroyed him, and destroyed yourself, you know that, don't you? Shall I tell you what you've been to him? A parasite. You've clung to his back wherever he went until you sucked him dry. Satisfied now, are you?"

Bott's neighbour signalled to the curate. He came scampering up and she jabbed wildly towards Bott. "It's a madwoman
next to me," she whispered. "She's insulting the black lady in
front."

The Negress was struggling to get out from the middle of
her row, giving terrified backward glances at Bott who still
gripped the pew as if she hated it.

"He was a good man, a kind man, and if he's bitter and bad
now it's your fault," Bott accused. The curate leant forward
and touched her arm, and the great gaunt face turned slowly
towards him. He was shocked to recognize it, after a minute.
The frightful eyes and slightly dribbling mouth belonged to
that nice, enthusiastic woman who a few weeks ago had told
him about her husband's sculpture.

"But I wanted to save him! I thought I could," she wailed.
One was used to such things at St. Martin-in-the-Fields in
moderation, but this would not do, she was shouting and upsetting the congregation. With the help of the woman next to
her he managed to get her out and into the crypt. "I am a foul
stinking pit of corruption," Bott cried. "Loathsome things
grow out of my flesh that I have fed with my blood. Look."
She stuck her hands out in front of him.

The other woman had gone to get the police. He only had to
hold her for a while. He put his hand out soothingly towards
her and she caught sight of his wristwatch. "That can't be the
time! Twenty past twelve?" Bott exclaimed.

"Ah, yes, er—"

"Goodness, I had no idea! Gosh! Poor little Michael is waiting for his dinner. Wow, that stew will be boiled dry—gosh,
and if it goes up in flames he's in there. Help. Goodbye, I must
fly." She leapt up and rushed for the stairs.

"Hey! Excuse me, don't go, er, you mustn't leave, er,
Mrs.—" He ran after her and caught her with both hands. She
shook him off easily, she was by far the stronger, and hastened
away with skirts flapping shrieking, "The dinner! Oh gosh!
The dinner!"

The curate rubbed his fingers ruefully, and watched her flying down Duncannon Street.

"Well, what a splendid thing. It's a chance in a million," Paul said, sounding pleased.

Mary was suspicious. "What's it to you? You don't know my father, do you?"

"Not yet. But this is really worth looking into. It could be a very interesting experiment indeed."

"What do you mean?"

"Well, we'll bring your father over, that goes without saying. But this other letter! It's obviously from some woman who has a reason for wanting to come too—she's the child's mother, probably."

"You aren't going to pay for her to come over? Paul!"

"Of course. How can I not? What's this if not a classic opportunity of relieving human misery?"

"But, Paul." She searched for words, making silly shapes with her mouth and unable to concentrate on anything but Paul's grin. At last she pulled herself together. "That's not your real reason, is it? What was that you said just now about an interesting experiment?"

"Oh, yes! The way I see it, this is really an opportunity in more ways than one. See, here's this interesting couple in some kind of predicament that's probably worth examining. And here am I with the chance of extending that predicament and observing it under my very eyes, without even having to leave my hometown. It would be a crime to miss it."

"But that's horrible! I want to see my father! I don't want to observe him in a predicament with a woman."

"Maybe you haven't made human beings your particular interest, as I have. Gratification of infantine wants, is that really all you're after? Aren't you interested in your father as a man? I am, if you're not."

Somehow he had managed to make her feel guilty. "You're a hypocrite!" Mary cried, "and you're callous."

"On the contrary," Paul said, "I'm proposing to carry out a magnanimous and expensive act of kindness towards a bereaved woman."

"But she's mad. She must be. That was a mad letter."

"She may merely be frantic. Don't judge in advance. What a little girl you are," he added looking fond and patronizing, "a little immature girl. It's a lucky thing I'm around. Little girls need uncles."

Mary looked dismally out at the street.

"Anyhow I don't think they should be separated. For the child's sake, you understand. We can simply leave them in London if you prefer."

"No! Oh no! I can earn money for one passage, at least."

"Leave it to Uncle Paul." He sounded so extremely self-satisfied that Mary wondered if he wasn't behind the scenes somewhere even in this matter of the letters.

"Meanwhile, honey, it's bedtime. You need your beauty sleep," he said and started the big car. He pulled slowly out of the parking lot, looking as though he thought he had a movie camera trained on him. Mary wondered how he could even imagine she would sleep with this hanging over her. She would have liked to spend the night studying the two letters, but Paul had them in his pocket and she was afraid to ask for them.

A nice letter. Gatzko nodded with pleasure. Just what he had hoped for. A nice, sweet, welcoming letter, not one word of reproach. And practical too; he was to pick up his ticket from the American Express. Good girl, good girl! Her writing was a bit careful and laboured, but maybe she had been a little nervous.

It was hard letting him go. It was hard seeing Michael lose interest in her and the garden as Daddy began to confide more exciting things. He did not confide them to her. He ran and bounced about the place, his eyes bright as she had not seen them for months, and she had to pretend that she did not notice and had no idea what it was all about. She had not the energy or desire to do anything, even to please Tommy. She sat about brooding, and Tommy began to wish that he had not become so involved with her that it was really difficult now to sack her.

It was terrible the night before he left. Gatzko packed his things in his studio, imagining as he always had that in there he was invisible and inaudible. He and Michael whispered merrily in the main room of the lair, and shouted gaily in the studio. They ran to and fro with bundles and belongings. Bott lay in bed for warmth and listened to the squeaks and the bumps and the rustlings next door. Gatzko kicked her brick hearth impatiently aside as he trampled through with his other pair of trousers. It never had been lit.

Once he came springing over to the bed and then stopped, for the first time looking embarrassed.

"What is it, darling?" Bott said from her pillow. "Aren't you cold? It's such a cold night. Hadn't you better have your rug and drape it round you?"

He brightened at such an easy way out. "Well, maybe I had," he said. Bott heaved herself up and unwrapped it from her. He took it and scampered away, making the most minimal effort at pretending to drape it round him.

"Oh, it's too big," she heard Michael's clear voice. "It'll never go in."

"Yes, it will. I've done it often. We wrap the other things in it—there."

Bott listened, wondering vaguely whether the mould that the rug was covered in would dry out in America. She imagined America as being a warm, dry place. Gatzko would tan very dark there. She could not get any pleasure somehow from reminding herself that she would be there to see it.

He did not want to go to bed at all, that was plain. After midnight Michael got tired and began to cry. Bott felt too listless to move and left it to Gatzko to soothe him and tuck him up. Bott was so tired that she dozed and had nightmares, but whenever she woke she saw Gatzko standing around smoking, the lamp lit and his eyes shining.

After this had happened several times it came to her that this was the last time she would wake up and she must say goodbye. But how, without making him suspicious?

"Well, let's hope for good things tomorrow," she mumbled. Gatzko looked startled and turned towards her, dropping his cigarette.

"I'm planning a super-duper dinner," Bott went on, as if explaining herself. "Cheese curry." She could not make herself think about what she was saying. He looked so sweet standing there with curls of hair everywhere and his travelling clothes already on.

"Cheese curry," Gatzko repeated, and said gallantly, "Mmm! That sure does sound delicious."

It was the first time he had used such a nice tone towards her since goodness knows when. But of course he knew he would never have to eat it. And she knew she had neither cheese nor curry powder in the house and had no intention of buying any. She dropped wearily off to sleep.

She woke and did not feel awake. Stiffly she crawled out of bed. The lair was empty. They must have taken the very first train out. Nothing was left of them but a lot of cigarette stubs and wrappings on the floor.

Or wait a moment—what was this? There was a piece of paper under her pillow. She pulled it out and blinked at it. It was a drawing by Michael, a huge man with hanging arms and eyes with scored rims. It was an incredible thing. Bott stared at it, quite baffled. Then at the bottom she saw in Mrs. Weingartner's hand, "This is THE TREE. For BOTT from MICHAEL with love."

But Bott was too empty to cry.

18

MARY WANTED TO be alone, to think out this extraordinary turn of events. Was Paul friend or enemy? Nothing was clear any more. Last night he had laughed at her for her suspicions and then, apparently quite seriously, advised her to accept him as the friend he said he was. "I'm just giving you a bit of fatherly counsel, in default of a father. I'm a decade or so of years older than you, even if you are prehistoric in character. Make all the world your enemy and that's how it'll end up."

But even while he was saying it she had disliked him.

She could not think. The traffic noise stunned her. She could not help listening to every car that went by, in case—in case what? Her father was in it? That was another place where it hurt to think. He was not merely coming to rescue her, he was bringing an entire rescue party consisting of a mad English-woman and her baby. Mary felt harassed and ready to panic. She left the library, forgetting her books, and took the wrong way out of the building. Instead of coming out at the side and turning on to Wabash she found herself looking straight into the rear parking lot of the neighbourhood market. With little whimpers of relief Mary ran across to dive into the market. Here, your persecution mania would need to be something really extreme for you to feel hunted. Mary took a grocery chariot and started wheeling it contentedly up and down the aisles, between the shelves of strange foods Mary had never seen, except, she supposed, when she served it cooked in her restaurant. It all seemed to be pretence food: imitation this, substitute that. Real food—wholemeal bread, cheesy cheese, shell eggs—had gone out with the war, apparently never to return. The shoppers jostled in their queues; nobody took any notice of Mary. She wheeled her empty chariot about a bit more and then suddenly felt sick of the smell of food. It was the delicatessen counter, she thought. She ran out of the store, her chariot squeaking and trundling in front of her.

In the parking lot the other shoppers were cramming what looked like several months' provisions into their cars, as if they were preparing for siege, but Mary's chariot was empty. She went on wheeling it up and down the parking lot. She lent on it and squeezed the handle, oddly comforted by it. She had once seen a little girl talking to her dolls' pram. Mary addressed her chariot, as she walked slowly between two lines of cars. "Will everything be all right when father comes? It will, won't it?"

She looked anxiously about, half-expecting the answer to appear written in the sky, and saw an unfriendly car registration plate. KN7759 it said nastily at her, ILLINOIS. Frightened, Mary trundled her chariot on faster. "Won't everything be like it was before? I mean he knows the secret. He told me in the first place. He'll tell me again, won't he? Won't he? Or will he be so angry I've forgotten it that he'll never speak to me again?"

Mary pulled the chariot sharply round at the top of the lot and almost ran back towards the exit. "Or perhaps he's forgotten it too? I mean maybe he was tortured by the Nazis or brainwashed or anything." Horrible visions filled her of her father, tortured and wrecked and mindless. She gave a little scream and clutched the chariot for support. "Maybe I won't even recognize him!" This seemed so likely that Mary stopped, appalled, and a car that was trying to leave the lot hooted at her. She was supposed to go meet him at La Salle Street railroad terminal. She could almost see herself, lost in that crowd, while the train came in and the passengers hurried away and presently there was no one left, only Paul and Mary. Mary would cry, knowing her father had come and gone and she had failed to recognize him.

Bott walked all day round and round the lair, feeling as if

she were haunting it. It was very cold and she had forgotten to buy any more paraffin. Also she could not remember now how the thing worked. After a while she came to like the cold. It satisfied her somehow.

The place was desolate without Gatzko and Michael and their stuff. Bott felt it would not stand up very long now. Where had "Thinking" gone? She missed it badly. As she sat shivering on the broken sofa that had for a short while done service as a double bed some bricks fell down somewhere, with a clatter of rubble. Ah, it's beginning, Bott thought almost gleefully. She groped about to repair the damage but it was too dark to do anything but break her nails.

She went into the Dairy & about suppertime, mainly out of habit, and saw the faces change as she walked in. Fear and horror were what she thought she saw on them. She gave a little laugh and heard it come out an old woman's croak. She did it again, letting it rasp out. Everyone was staring at her now; both the Weingartners looked shocked. Bott noticed without surprise that even the biggest fishmen were looking up at her, as if she were two feet taller than any of them. She staggered back to the lair to let them drink their tea in peace.

She sat on in the dark, thinking about her menfolk.

Was Michael even now being seasick? Bott had never been on a ship further than the Isle of Wight. She remembered with a shock that she had the transatlantic voyage to make herself, soon. She also remembered that today she had intended to get her passport and visa.

The visa was a formidable procedure, when at last she did go for it. "This was quick," the official told her severely when she grumbled. "Because you have a sponsor in the States. Count yourself lucky."

It did not seem particularly lucky to Bott. She had never doubted that if Gatzko went she would go too. She had written to his daughter without it ever occurring to her that the daughter might do otherwise than send her her fare at once. She was not interested in the daughter and did not want to think about her. There was another name in all this too, somebody or other called Fieldman. Bott was not interested in him either although he apparently was the one who had come up with the money.

Bott walked home from the Embassy feeling as if she were dragging a chain. Or, no, not a chain, but as if her whole leg were dragging behind her. She had read about it in a book of Hindu legends once. They had a kind of ghost that was half a live body, half a decaying corpse, and the live half walked about with the dead half hanging off it. Bott felt exactly like that. She noticed people recoiling as she came towards them in the street, and grinned at them (with half a mouth, she supposed), knowing why.

All the same it was up to the live half to get the whole on to that ship. She set herself ferociously to pack and get moving. Habit took over as far as packing was concerned but she had never had much talent at catching trains. Also she had lost count of the date long ago. Suddenly in a panic she took a late, slow, crowded train to Southampton that same night. She stood in the corridor and thought she could see the foul miasma that went out from her, the smell of rot. It was filling the whole coach. It was too much to inflict on the other passengers. She must be suffocating them with her presence. She eased her way down the train and sat alone in the guard's van, trembling with cold.

In the event she had to wait three days at Southampton before her ship sailed. She changed some of Gatzko's daughter's dollars with the ship's purser, knowing that this was the one thing she should on no account do because there would be so many expenses over there.

Bott knew nothing about shipboard social conventions, and wanted nothing but to walk the deck alone. She had an idea after a day or two of doing this that the other passengers were coming to regard her as a sort of ship's bogey. But then that was how she regarded herself too.

Bott walked the deck thinking about blackness and forgetting meals. She never really took in the presence of the sea. She liked her bunk, but did not understand that the other woman was her cabin-mate. After the first night the woman petitioned to be moved, saying Bott was a sleepwalker. It was true that Bott walked but even when she was in bed, she never really slept. She dreamt instead, sleeping or waking. Often she would come out of a nightmare with a start to find herself engaged in some perfectly ordinary daytime activity, cleaning her teeth or eating soup.

She did not see the Statue of Liberty, although she was awake, because she was standing at the wrong end of the ship.

"Father!" Mary screamed. "Father! Father!"

She ran across the platform, ran and ran, jumping over baggage, and it was her father, it really was, not changed at all. And she had been quite certain she would fail to know him. She threw herself at him, hiccuping and laughing and crying. He patted her on the back and said, "Wow! This is the most enthusiastic welcome I've ever had."

Mary looked up all a-tremble and a-quiver and saw his bright black eyes and that smile she had dreamt of and thought must belong to some imaginary fairy prince.

"Father, father," she gulped, hugging him tighter. He seemed all clothes. How tiny and thin he must be inside.

"Ah, come on now," he said. "Here's Michael. You ought to meet Michael. He's your brother."

Mary was too chokey with emotion to say anything more. She released her father and hugged the little boy instead. But after a minute he pushed her away saying, "You're all wet."

"And I haven't got a tear-bottle with me," Gatzko said, "so such prodigality is all wasted. Come on! Let's go somewhere, let's do something! I haven't been in this city since I took you to Arizona on the Santa Fe. Let's have a celebration! Let's have a drink!"

He went bounding away across the station swinging his pathetic little pack. Mary stumbled after him, carrying

Michael. She soon realized this was unnecessary when he struggled out of her arms and tore after his father shrieking, "Daddy, wait for me."

Mary caught up with them at the exit where Paul was introducing himself. The men shook hands, looking pleased with each other and with everything. Mary shrunk back, feeling scared and excluded.

"So let's make this a real celebration. And I would start with a drink," her father said, hardly able to stand still for excitement. "Wow! How long is it since I had a drink worthy of the name." He grinned at Mary and Paul and led the way into the street, Michael scampering after. At the crossing he swung on the traffic signal, unheeding of Paul watching. "There's a bar!" he shouted and ran across the road, dodging the cars. Mary waited for the "Walk" signal and looked apologetically at Paul, but he was smiling.

Gatzko was waiting impatiently by the bar entrance, and led the way in. "A Scotch on the rocks for me," he began, obviously enjoying using the American words, "and for you?"

The bartender interrupted. "I'm sorry. I can't let the children in."

"Oh, cokes for them," her father said, not understanding.

"No. I'm sorry. They can't come in here at all, under twenty-one."

"But, hell, I just came from England. I want to celebrate with my daughter. I haven't seen her for six years. She's old enough, isn't she?"

"She doesn't look twenty-one," the bartender said.

"No, I'm eighteen," Mary admitted. Gatzko turned to her and all the sparkle was gone. He looked furious. Mary shrank.

"Why don't you go into the coffee shop next the railroad terminal?" the bartender suggested sympathetically. "That's what I'd do in your place. You can surely get a drink there and the children can have milk."

"What sort of celebration is that!" Gatzko shouted. "Milk in a coffee shop!"

Mary felt herself beginning to cry again. Gatzko stared at her and said in a resigned voice, "Okay. Okay. Come on. We'll all go have milk in the coffee shop."

They trailed out into the street. "Come and have a drink in the apartment," Paul suggested. "There's so much Scotch there I could even spare some for Michael."

"No," Gatzko insisted, "we're going to the coffee shop."

They sat on little, spindly wooden chairs supposed to make the place look like a kitchen and which in fact made it look just like a coffee shop. Mary had happily drunk many cups of coffee in similar surroundings but this time she wished it would all fall down round them.

"The man said they serve drinks here..." Paul said hopefully, reaching for the menu. But Gatzko shouted at the waitress, "Four milks, please." Paul shuddered.

"I hear you were very short of this in England," he said when it came, "even worse than over here."

"Were we? I didn't miss it," Gatzko said.

"Father, if you don't like milk why don't you order something else?"

"If this is what America drinks I want to drink it too. It's proper. I want to do what's proper to the place."

"Did you drink tea in England?"

"Sure I did," he said brightening. "And beer. I drank so much tea and beer I could have swum in it. It was proper there."

All this talk of England! Soon now he must get on to the subject of the woman. Mary sipped her milk nervously and waited, damp all over, hoping she would be able to stick to the agreement she had made with Paul, not to give away what they had done. But they did not talk of England any more for the waitress came with glasses of water and Michael looked at her and said clearly, "I don't like water. It's alive."

She laughed. "You could be right, too," she said and went away.

"I don't like milk either," said Michael and looked at his

father. His father grimaced at him and Michael stood up on the seat and quite carefully pushed over all the glasses of milk and water. Mary squealed and jumped up, wiping her skirt. She looked round, wretched at this new disaster, but saw the father and little boy marching out, the father's arm around Michael's shoulder as if they were accomplices.

Paul apologized, paid and followed smiling.

They sat around drinking until Mary thought they'd go on all night. Both the men seemed really to be enjoying it. They talked and joked of things Mary knew nothing about in loud voices. Michael was asleep next door. They got on to politics, after her father had explained why he left Yugoslavia, and began hotly to discuss communism, and Mary despaired. She fiddled with her glass. Paul knew she hated Scotch and sometimes offered her tequila instead, which she hated worse. At the moment she had Scotch.

At last Paul said he had to go out, with an understanding smile for Mary which made her squirm, and she was left alone with her father. She had an hour before the school bus left for Austin.

"Oh, it's so wonderful to see you again," she began.

"Yes, honey," he agreed. Then he saw Paul's records in a corner. "Hey! Look at these! Let's have some music. I haven't listened to a record in years."

"Why, don't they have them in England?"

"Some people do, I suppose, but I wasn't one of them. You've no conception how I was living in England. Oh wonderful! Louis Armstrong!"

"Well, the thing is," Mary said desperately, knowing that jazz would drive all other thoughts out of her head, "I have to go quite soon to be back on campus—"

"Oh yes. Of course. Well, I'd far rather hear about college life. Is it fun?"

"Oh, great fun," Mary muttered.

"Tell me about it! Tell me about the fun! I want to think

about you having fun." He looked expectantly at her, all eager and sparkling.

"Well, we have social activities—sorority meetings—" There was a silence. Mary could not think of any more that could remotely classify as fun.

"Ah. You're in a sorority."

"Yes. Er ... I play table tennis."

"That's always fun. And you dance a lot, don't you? I imagined you dancing a lot. Do you have lots of boy friends?"

He looked so eager and enthusiastic. Mary felt really guilty that her life seemed so lacking in fun. "Just one boy friend," she said brightly, wondering how to get off this hateful topic. "It's more fun that way."

"Then you can tell me what are the gay night spots in Chicago now. I want to enjoy Chicago. London is so dreary and grim, bleak and depressing, it really is."

"Worse than Chicago?" Mary asked unbelievingly. He looked startled. Oh help, now I've given myself away, she thought.

"What's wrong with Chicago?"

"Oh, father, I've been so unhappy," Mary blurted. "This city—it's always getting at me. You don't know. And it's all my fault, I did something dreadful, I forgot your secret, from all that time ago in Oak Creek Canyon, you remember? There was a secret in the source and in the valley that you taught me when I was little, and I forgot it—oh, I'm so miserable, I'm sorry but I really am. This place, it wants that secret, you see, it wants the life and the water—living water, not that awful lake. But I'm not strong enough to keep it—I haven't a strong enough hold on it. I can't keep it in my mind, my mind just can't seize anything these days—and the city's bound to get it, you see. They're all after it, Paul and my boy friend and everyone I meet. They'll get it, they're certain to, at least until you came I thought they were. Oh, father, thank God you came."

Gatzko listened to her, appalled.

"I missed you so much! I thought I'd never see you again. Sometimes I wondered if you'd ever existed at all, would you believe that! Oh, it seems such a miracle to see you there, you can't imagine, just in time to save me." She looked gooily at him and suddenly threw herself into his arms. "Save me, help me, father! Please, please help me," she hiccuped and burst into tears.

Gatzko felt himself freeze all over.

"Take me away from Chicago. Let's, oh, let's go back to Arizona. Let's go back to Oak Creek Canyon and please, please show me the source again, oh please."

"I don't want to go to Oak Creek Canyon."

"Please, father, oh please! And it can be like it was before, we'll live by the stream and you'll take me up into the mountains, and teach me the secret again, won't you? You must understand. I can't live without the secret. I'm cut off from the source. We must go back—please let us go back, to the secret place."

"Mary! Pull yourself together, girl! We live in Chicago now. We're not going back to Sedona. Understand? There's nothing to go back to."

"There's everything to go back to! Everything! My life is there. That's where things grow and live—not here. I shall die if I stay here."

"You'll do no such thing," Gatzko shouted, disgusted finally. "Don't be adolescent. People don't die for reasons like that. And your life is not in Sedona. Your life in Sedona lasted exactly till age twelve, that's six years ago. I won't have you living in the past. Mooning for your childhood. Snap out of it!"

Mary felt herself pushed roughly away and began to weep hysterically. Gatzko left her and went out, with black depression settling as he remembered that only last week he had been doing exactly this to get away from Bott.

19

"How about the Millionaires' Club?" Paul suggested. "It does quite a good lunch, but it's the atmosphere I go for. Did you ever know it?"

"No, I never qualified as a millionaire."

"Let's both go be millionaires then."

Paul drove up Wabash and gave the car to the parking lot attendant. He led Gatzko to a dark, high door with a sign in gold and maroon, saying in Old Western lettering "THE MILLIONAIRES CLUB".

"This looks great!" Gatzko said, preparing to enjoy himself. "I haven't felt that I owned a dime in six years."

The bar and restaurant were dark and grand with high wooden booths and a distinct gold rush flavour. Big men sat around in ten-gallon hats. Gatzko swaggered in, careful of his cowboy spurs, and stood hands on hips.

"I like it," he said.

Paul nodded. He was showing his membership card to the steward. "It's an advantage being men only."

"Is anyone here a millionaire?"

"I doubt it. They're playing, like us."

The men did not laugh or smile but drank, scowled and argued. Gatzko pulled his dewlaps and took a mouthful of Scotch and thought gleefully how far this was from the George.

Paul ordered new drinks and the menu. Gatzko said, "I would have taken Mary out to lunch but I couldn't face the thought of another coffee shop."

"You can," Paul said, "you can always get beer in a coffee shop, and hard liquor in some of them too."

"I can't bear the atmosphere of a coffee shop. All those clean earnest highschoolers sitting around drinking milk discussing their adolescent emotional problems—ugh!"

"You could have taken her to a restaurant."

Gatzko did not answer. Paul said studying the menu, "I wish I could offer you something really American, like steak or prime rib. You know how things are nowadays. Still, there seems to be corned beef hash. Are you fond of that?"

"I love it! I love it! Corned beef hash! There's a really homely, Western dish. I declare I've been homesick for corned beef hash," said Gatzko ecstatically. When it came it was sizzling and oniony, exactly as Bott always served it, but he had forgotten that. There was a great big pile of it, and he knew he could eat it all.

But in the middle Paul said, "You must be very proud to see how your daughter's grown up."

Gatzko threw down his fork and said, "I am sick and ashamed to see how my daughter's grown up. Not that she has grown up."

"Oh, now, why's that?"

"If I were having lunch with her, as I'd been looking forward to doing all the way across the Atlantic, I wouldn't be eating this and enjoying it, I can tell you. She'd be drying up my gastric juices with her hysterics."

"Oh, you've had hysterics from her, have you?"

"Hysterics, tears, reproaches, oh yes. Everything I hoped I had left behind in London. How come such a sad, dull, humourless girl should be my daughter?"

"Perhaps she takes after her mother."

"Oh no. Oh no."

"But even if what you say is true, which I suppose I must concede, in her own way she's quite an unusual personality. Intriguing. I mean, what is behind all this queer behaviour? I can't help wondering."

"I can, very well," Gatzko said. "She doesn't succeed in intriguing me. I can't stand hysterical women. And do you know what she wants? Me to take her back to that village we lived in before she went to high school! She wants to reconstruct our life of six years ago. It's perverted. She started pouring out some awful stuff about how she must get back to the holy source. God!"

"What source is this?" Paul asked with interest.

"Oak Creek Canyon? Hasn't she told you? Where they shoot movies now? It was holy to the Indians. Oh, it's a terrible place. Obviously I kept her there too long. There was nothing to do but ranch cattle and worship the earth. But how could I know she'd stick that way for good? It depresses me just to think about her."

"All right, we'll forget Mary. Michael seems quite different at least."

Gatzko brightened. "Oh yes. But Michael's been around the world a bit. I was afraid at one point he'd get stuck in London. There was a woman there trying to make us both put roots down. Fortunately she didn't succeed. I expect that's what Mary wants too. To get me back in that poisonous valley, all alone, and have me for herself. Ugh! Yes, let's forget Mary, that's a good idea. I want some apple pie. Do they have any nice pie here? I haven't eaten a good apple pie since I left."

Mary went every day several times to Paul's apartment but it always seemed to be empty. The neighbour downstairs looked after Michael. Her father and Paul were out together the whole time. Her father liked Paul, and was much more interested in him than in Mary. He had scarcely spoken to Mary since she had told him her troubles, that first night. Mary hadn't begun to feel disappointed yet; she just couldn't believe that he wasn't going to help her, wasn't going to rescue her from anything, or explain the secret. So she continued calling and going over.

One morning when she thought there was no one in she had wandered into the other bedroom and found her father asleep.

She stood in the doorway looking lovingly at him and he roused and gave her a look of hate. "Get out," he said. "Don't stand there putting the evil eye on me when I'm trying to sleep." He turned over and even the back of his head looked angry.

Mary felt dumb and desperate. She didn't know where to turn. She telephoned Scott, to Scott's surprise, who immediately came to meet her for lunch. Almost she wanted to tell him the whole story. Over coffee, indeed, he even said, "I know there's something going on, Mary. Now is when you need your friends. Why don't you confide in me?" But she could not quite.

"I want to get out of this city," she said suddenly.

"Oh! Well—all right—I guess I could fix that. I can borrow a car and camp out. I've done it before with Howard. Would you like to? We can go along the lake, or out in the country somewhere."

"Yes, yes, let's do that," Mary said distractedly.

On Saturday, the next day, they drove along the lakeshore and wandered about among fields and rivulets holding hands. All the fields were square and flat and no tree was more than ten feet high. It did not feel like country to Mary, who had seen the towering firs at the head of her canyon. It was all part of Chicago somehow.

They made a camp fire and baked potatoes and Mary cried a bit in Scott's arms and wished he were her father. It was a cool spring night and, Mary discovered when she blew her nose, smelt fresh and flowery. Now she wanted very badly to talk to Scott, but still she could not make herself.

They kissed chastely under the stars and Scott said gloomily, "All ice, as usual." Mary mumbled that she was sorry. They went sadly back to the fire, and it was impossible to say anything now although she felt that she was missing her last chance.

Scott had sleeping bags and they slept in the car, Scott in front and Mary in the back. Mary opened both her windows as far as they would go but could not smell anything of the night air; nothing but the stifling smell of the insides of cars.

On Sunday they drove back to Chicago.

That was the weekend the woman was supposed to arrive, but Paul said he had seen no sign of her.

They all had dinner together. Gatzko was exuberant. He had thought he might get a job on one of the big Chicago newspapers on the strength of his unusual war experience. Mary bowed her head over her plate and listened hopelessly.

On Monday morning after class she went to the apartment, knowing there could not possibly be anyone in. She wandered weakly around and found her father's pyjamas. She carried them out of the dark room, she could not have said why, and laid them out in an armchair in the sun. She went on walking to and fro in front of them, constantly glancing at them as if her father were really sitting there and she were talking to him. She was doing this when she heard a battering and thumping at the door. She stood sweating and after a minute the doorbell rang, hesitantly and then clearly and then insistently, as if the ringer had taken a little while to find out how it worked. On and on it rang until Mary, deafened, managed to get the door open. Someone was leaning on the bell with both hands pushing with all their might.

"Er, hello," said Mary nervously. "Did you want to see Mr. Fieldman? Oh!"

For the person jumped away from the bell and turned to face Mary, and it was the most awful-looking woman Mary had ever seen.

"Is this the right place?" she asked, and her voice was terrible too. "I'm so lost. I'm looking for Gatzko."

It was Mary's turn to jump. "Oh, you must be—" She couldn't remember the Englishwoman's name.

"I'm Bott. I don't know where I am. I've rung about five doorbells already this morning. If this is the wrong place—I've got an address I don't understand. Look." Paul's letter was thrust into Mary's face but Bott's hand was shaking so much that Mary could not take it.

"Yes, of course, we're expecting you! Come in!" Mary said recovering herself. "Nobody's here but me at the moment I'm afraid. I'm Mary Gatzkovic, pleased to meet you."

"Oh, you're the daughter?" Bott came into the room and looked hard at Mary. No resemblance, really. She sighed and looked round and saw Gatzko's pyjamas in the chair. She gasped and dropped her bundles, and her coat tangled round her feet and she lurched over and fell.

"Oh dear! Are you all right?" Mary exclaimed, shocked, and ran to help. The woman was muttering and heaving herself up. She shook her hair out of her face and, unexpectedly, grinned at Mary. "Don't worry. I do this all the time. Don't let me frighten you. I frighten a lot of people, but I only look like an ogress, I don't think I am one really."

Everything she said and did astonished Mary. Her accent, her clothes, her behaviour, they were all equally weird.

"Goodness, you look tired," Mary said suddenly feeling sorry for the wretched creature. "Sit down—er" she hastily gathered up the pyjamas, and couldn't help noticing Bott's eyes on them—"sit down, take off your coat, please, and I'll make you a cup of coffee. You must be feeling dreadful after your journey."

"I was feeling dreadful before that, but a cup of coffee would be nice." She stood awkwardly in the middle of the room, with her hat hanging by one hatpin, staring fiercely wherever she happened to look. Mary steered her to the chair and put the coffee on. Bott's gaze began to focus more often on Mary, and Mary, bumbling around Paul's kitchen, began to feel disconcerted. The woman kept on and on glancing at her and when finally the coffee was ready and she brought it through, gave her a look of outright puzzlement. "Did you say you were Mary Gatzkovic?"

"That's right."

"Then where can I possibly have seen you before?"

"Er, well, did you ever visit the States?"

"Never been out of England in my life. And you don't look like your father in the least, so fair and all. Well, this is very strange. I could have sworn all this had happened before, that I landed on you unexpectedly and you ran around feeding me and being kind to me although of course you were scared of me. Yes, I was walking along a valley somewhere, that's right, and for some reason had nowhere to go, and you took me in. No?"

Mary could only stare.

"Oh, well, strange things are for ever happening, aren't they? Life is quite inexplicable except in God's terms. The only thing to do is to take it all as it comes."

This was beyond Mary. "Did you say you'd met me in a valley?"

"Well, I had walked along the valley, as far as I remember. Yes, I was walking in the mountains. And I came to a tiny village which for some reason I connect you with. Well, never mind, it must have been another girl. If it happened at all. Quite possibly I was just foreseeing you."

She closed her eyes and swayed in the chair, her face grey. Mary rescued the coffee and said anxiously, "Mrs.—er—Bott, are you all right? You don't look well."

"Well!" the woman repeated with something between a croak and a guffaw.

"When did you last sleep?"

Bott's eyes opened again and she looked at Mary. Mary noticed with surprise that she was quite young after all and had baby-blue eyes. "I don't know if I'm awake now," she said, most pathetically Mary thought, "or dreaming or sleeping or something worse. Oh, yes, much worse."

"I booked a room for you," Mary said (in the YWCA—where else?). "I'm going to take you there and put you to bed. I'd like to let you sleep here, but you see, your husband is based here and he doesn't know you're coming to Chicago. So

H

to prevent difficulty perhaps you'd like to come with me? Oh, dear, you look tired to death."

The woman looked sadly at Mary and began to struggle out of the chair. Mary put out her hand to help her and almost yelped at the pain of her grasp. Slowly Bott got on to her feet and said, "I know, I'm always on the point of death. I mean these last ten days or so. It's odd, isn't it? Why don't I ever really die? What am I doing wrong?"

Mary was unable to answer this. She carried Bott's pack downstairs and went out to get a cab on the avenue. When she came back she found Bott still standing where she left her, in the door of the elevator, preventing it shutting. Not knowing what else to do Mary took Bott's hand and led her out on the sidewalk as if she were blind. The cab was waiting on the other side of the street. As they stood hand in hand waiting to cross, Mary saw Gatzko coming towards them down the avenue. He did not look surprised, but his eyes seemed very black.

He walked towards the two women, the eyes of them both drilling into him but they did not know his new resistance. He was not scared of them any more. He did not even care about them any longer. He came up to them and looked at them holding hands.

"I see I've no need to introduce you," he said. "I suppose I should congratulate you, Bott, I hadn't realized your coven was international. Was it you, Mary, who sent us that silver bowl?" He went into the building without letting them answer. Bott turned and watched him go in, gazing miserably after. He shut the elevator and shot up away from her, thinking about Mary's sorority and wondering if they celebrated black masses.

Mary pushed Bott into the cab. "What was that he said about a silver bowl?" she asked.

"Can't explain. It was nasty anyway."

"I guess."

Mary saw her into her room. "I really advise you to try and

sleep," she said, but she knew she would not. She stood at the
window staring into Mary's school, clutching the sill.

"Will you come and see me this evening?" she asked suddenly, pleading.

"Oh!" said Mary, "well, that's terribly nice of you, but it's
rather difficult, because you see I work most evenings—I don't
get off until ten o'clock and then I have to go back to the
campus. Paul will come I expect."

Bott nodded and drooped and her hands fell off the sill.
Mary went on apologizing and asking if she wanted anything
but saw she was not listening. As she went out she saw Bott
standing against the window, sagging, her hands hanging
down empty, all alone in the room with her tiny pack. The
image refused to leave Mary's mind. It stuck there all day, like
a photograph on the wall.

Gatzko and Paul, with just the right amount of drink inside
them, went to Mary's restaurant for dinner. They drank some
more and the lights were low and comfortable and everything
seemed pleasant. Mary was appalled when the cashier gave her
a big grin and told her to serve Table 10 although it wasn't her
station, but in fact the men only teased her affectionately like
any of the other customers. She could almost have forgotten it
was her father.

"She looks nice, like that, in her little cap and apron,"
Gatzko said to Paul, watching her serve out at another table.
"Quite sweet, even. This is obviously the job she's cast for in
life."

"She's always very eager to please. I suppose that's the main
requirement of a waitress," Paul said.

"And it's not so difficult to please when it's merely a question of fetching more ketchup," Gatzko said. "Obviously more
intricate situations are somewhat beyond her."

"Ah come on now—"

"Yes! Yes! Hey, waitress!" He smiled fondly as Mary
scampered over. "Waitress, you'd enjoy to bring me another

lager, wouldn't you? It would give you a kick to run and get one, wouldn't it? And an even bigger kick to bring two?"

"Two lagers, yes sir," Mary said politely and went to pass the order on to the bar messenger. When he brought them Gatzko shouted, "Hey, why doesn't my waitress serve me?"

"She's not old enough to serve alcohol, sir."

"Where's my waitress? I want service from my waitress." The words came out a little thickly, but his voice echoed through the restaurant. Frightened, Mary snatched up a tray and two glasses of water and brought them to her father's table.

"Thank you. You're right, she is eager to please," Gatzko said, gulping water.

"You're welcome," Mary smiled and tried to slip away.

"I'm welcome, am I? That's good. Come here, Waitress Mary. You enjoy doing this, don't you? You're good at it? The customers like you?"

"Er, well, I hope so," Mary stuttered.

"I think you make a lovely waitress. Yes, I really do. I even think it's a pity to deprive the public of you for the sake of a few sorority meetings whose value I question anyway. Correct?"

"You're not going to take me away from college?" Mary gasped.

Paul got up and muttered to her, "Come away, Mary." She followed him to the cash desk. "Don't worry. He's drunk," he said. But Mary was in a state beyond worry, realizing this meant that her father was disappointed in her through and through. She had failed, she had failed him utterly, totally.

20

"Mary, you're wanted on the dorm telephone."

Mary took the receiver and said, "Hello?" A voice asked, "That Mary Gatzkovic?"

"Yes."

"Okay. Here you are, you're connected," the voice said to someone else. There was a clatter of the distant receiver being dropped and she heard another voice, getting louder as it approached the mouthpiece. "Oh damn. I haven't smashed it, have I? Thank you so much. I never can understand these rotten things, even in my own country." There was heavy breathing in Mary's ear and then a shattering "Hello!"

"Hello, is that Mrs. Bott?"

More heavy breathing. "Hello! Bott here! Hello!"

"Yes, all right, this is Mary," she shouted. For all she knew the woman was deaf, after all. "Is something wrong?"

"Mary, I don't know where you are. I don't know how to get to you. How can I come to you?"

"Now? You want to see me now?"

"Yes! Yes! I need to talk to you! I've just had a dream about you. I've got to see you, Mary, I've got to."

"But, Mrs. Bott—"

"Oh, don't bother with the Mrs. I'm no Mrs. Never will be."

"Er—it's rather late, don't you think? And I'm out on the campus."

"How do I get there?"

"Well—oh dear—" The woman sounded desperate, and Mary knew what that felt like. She looked at the time. A quarter to eleven; the El was certainly still running. "I'll come around right away. You're on the third floor, aren't you? Facing out on the side?"

"Gosh. I haven't an earthly."

"Yes, all right, Mrs. Bott. I'm sorry you're feeling bad. I'll see you soon."

She had to cut short the woman's noisy thanks by hanging up. She threw her clothes on again and ran out to the El. It was cold out and her head ached and her feet ached and what she was doing made no sense. She shivered in the train, watching the lights of Chicago come towards her.

The YWCA was locked up, as Mary had expected it would be, by the time she arrived at something past midnight. Mary did not worry at this. She got on to the fire escape of her college building by balancing on the rail of some street diggings and the door lintel. Then she swung across to the other fire escape. The gap was only a few feet. She climbed up looking for Bott's window and identified it at last by seeing a shadow on the wall opposite, a huge long shadow with hair like a bush covered in creeper, marching and turning and throwing its arms about with sudden movements. Mary leant over the iron staircase and called, "Hey! Mrs. Bott!"

The shadow elongated with a wild gesture and the window was thrown noisily up. Bott stuck her head out and called, "Mary? Where are you?"

"Here. I'm climbing up. Wait a bit."

"Gosh!" said Bott, as Mary edged along the facing. "This reminds me of something."

Mary was too busy hauling herself over the sill to ask what. Things were not made easier by Bott seizing her by the collar of her coat and dragging her in. Mary tumbled choking on the floor.

"Yes, really. This all ties up with something. It must. I know I've pre-enacted it. This coming through the window too. What do you suppose it means? Do you believe in meaning?"

"I don't know," panted Mary.

"Well, you ought. You'll never get to the bottom of things—to the bottom of your valley, say—if you don't know what you believe."

Mary stared. "How d'you know about my valley?"

"Why, I dreamt about it of course. Didn't I tell you when I rang up? I expect I was too mazed with having to manage that beastly telephone. Look, I can't talk to you on the floor. Come and sit on the bed."

Mary, who had adopted her favourite supine position, obediently rose.

Bott looked at Mary. "I wonder what caused it? Were you thinking about this valley?"

"I'm always thinking about it," said Mary helplessly.

"I was thinking about a valley too. The Valley of the Shadow of Death. I wondered if that was where I'd got to, you see. I just lay down to meditate a bit and I must have dropped off. Anyway there was this terribly dreamy, heavy atmosphere, really weird, down at the bottom of some deep cleft between mountains. I was looking down into it. There was thick pink vapour rising and everything down there was incredibly lush. Is that right?"

"Was there—did you dream of water, a stream?"

"A stream, was it? I didn't think of a stream. There was something, anyway, issuing out of the ground, all wonderful colours. A spring of light."

"Yes, yes," murmured Mary.

"You love this valley, don't you? A bit more than you ought, maybe?"

Mary muttered.

"I wanted to warn you, in my dream. I had gone down there and that part was nightmare. I couldn't do anything, I couldn't move, and you were up there on the edge of the cliff and I was sure you were going to jump in. You thought there was treasure or something down there and I kept trying to warn you of your mistake but I couldn't make you hear. I got so frantic that I woke myself up."

"But I must get back to the source, Mrs. Bott!" Mary blurted out. "I mean that was only a dream you had. But you can't deny that people in real truth are rooted in something, even if it's only a mass consciousness. And if they lose touch with that then they must wither up. They can't live without water. Can they?"

Bott looked at Mary as if she had said something funny.

"If you were very thirsty, and you found a well, would you plunge into it or draw water out?"

"What are you talking about, Mrs. Bott?" cried Mary, terrified.

"I'm just telling you to watch the underneath parts of your mind." Their positions had reversed somehow. Now Mary felt mad and frantic, but Bott seemed sane and calm. "If you see a mountain reflected, look at the mountain and you'll get both; lean down into the reflection and you won't get either."

"Are you telling me my subconscious is a well?"

"I'm telling you not to want to lose yourself in it. Not your own, nor someone else's, nor any kind of mass consciousness."

Mary gaped.

"This idea of the great motherly world-soul is very tempting, isn't it? A vast amorphous life-force, opening metaphorical arms to embrace you. Aren't I guessing right? Wouldn't it be lovely to be just one little bit of a great living universe? Not to have to think and fight any more? Sink back—rest—let yourself go into it, one little drop in the sea."

Bott saw Mary's eyes widen.

"Yes, you do feel that. I can see you do. But it isn't like that, you know. Nothing so easy, unfortunately. You don't give yourself to the world. You take it up into yourself. Not to possess it, either, as I wanted, but to enshrine it. That's the right end of everything. Believe me, Mary, I'm telling you what I know. You don't jump into the well, you goose, you have it inside you. You can't be a mermaid, but it can be a spring of living water for you."

"Mrs. Bott! How can you know about such things?"

"Because I'm on the brink of the valley myself. I never saw all this before either. But now I'm going down into the darkness, funnily enough, I can see."

There were traces of froth at the corners of her mouth. She stood up and began to pace about.

"You talk about your source, but it was mine too once, when I was your age. But I feel dry now, I can't tell you how dry. If there's any moisture at all it's the moisture of decay. I lived by that water for years and never gave anything back. I tried to wield the life-force as my own power. What a pair we are, aren't we, Mary? You want to sink back into the lifestream of the world. And I wanted to make the world into my lifestream. We're both wrong, of course. But at least you wanted to give, and I only wanted to have. That's why I must go down into the depths, and you must not."

"I—I don't know if I understand," faltered Mary.

"You do really. I can see you do." The woman stopped pacing and looked down on her from an enormous height. "I took that—say water, it's as good a symbol as another—I took that water like tapwater, I used it for myself and never thought about it. Until this year. It was your father who woke me up, or should I say broke me up. I needed breaking up. I never gave anything; now I must give everything. Everything." Her words were becoming more and more sonorous. She loomed over Mary. "For instance I had a nice idea of planting a magic tree before I left London. Yes, a nice idea, a tree to protect me. How's that for selfishness? Still, a great good tree. But life only comes out of death. A seed can't grow till the husk has decayed."

She sounded as if she were reciting.

"The water will never flow again," Bott declaimed, "the seed will never grow, until I have given myself. I should never have come here, Mary. Dragged this stinking corpse around after your father. I should never have tried to hang on to him."

"No! No! You should have come! I'm glad you did!"

H*

"No, I should never have come, and now I must go. Yes, I must, Mary. Down into the abyss."

She stood between Mary and the light bulb, seeming to spread darkness.

"You're not going to die?"

The monstrous figure seemed to grow more monstrous still, raised up before her like one of those giant cacti in Tucson which in twilight often looked so like a man. "Into the abyss," Bott kept saying or else Mary kept remembering, "into the abyss." And Mary suddenly had an image of them wrestling, embracing, on the cliff's edge, though whether in the bedroom she moved to touch Bott she did not know. The idea was more important. She wanted to give herself, surrender herself, submerge herself in the strength and hugeness of Bott who wanted to die. Bott possessed a power of death. And Mary only longed to be in it, to share in it, to die too. To go down into the abyss which was in the woman, to descend into the depths of her. For this, surely, was the secret.

They stared at each other in a strange landscape of stones and cicadas and little unidentifiable sounds from the canyon. Bott thought about the dark chasm of herself and Mary thought about the dark chasm of Bott.

"Mary, what are you doing? Stop it! Stop it, I say! Stop grabbing me!"

"But I'm not grabbing you. I'm the other side of the room from you."

"Are you? You must have got into my dream somehow. Is the light on or off? I can't see it."

"It's on."

"Well, I'm fagged out. Make room for me to lie down, will you?"

Mary slithered off the bed at once, and took up her favourite position on the floor.

"Now don't forget my warning. No more creeping into my nightmares, eh? You don't want to share my old woman's woes."

Mary didn't answer; she felt strangely excited. She was amazed to find suddenly that it was early next morning and she was waking up ordinarily and wanting a glass of water. She felt vaguely and wearily that Bott had let her down. But Bott, looking at the yawning, quite normally alive girl, felt heartily relieved.

21

GATZKO HAD MAYBE not said very much but he was angry for all that, bitterly angry with all concerned, except maybe Paul. Paul had pulled a nasty trick on him, but he might easily have done the same if he were Paul. At least his only motive for facing him with Bott like that seemed to be his own amusement, which Gatzko felt bound to approve. But Mary! And Bott! Conspiring to deceive him, planning to trap him. Filthy bitches.

He woke up suddenly in a rage and shouted.

It was barely light yet. He peered through the drapes and saw greyness and roared, sitting up in bed.

It brought Paul in, shivering. "What's going on?"

"I'm not enjoying life. I want to give a party!"

"Give a party, now?"

"Yes! Now! I want to beat up this dreary city! You have money, don't you? What's money for if not to have parties?" He skipped to the window and hammered on the glass. "Yeow!" he howled.

"It's five a.m., Gatzko! Or is that party time according to you?"

"If it's now, yes. Where are the women?"

"In bed, I guess."

"Come on! Let's go wake them up!"

"Where are you intending to have this party anyway? There's no place you'll get a drink at this hour."

"Then I'll take it with me," Gatzko said, grabbing Paul's bottles of Scotch and tequila, one under each arm.

Paul drove to Austin, wondering how long his curiosity about humanity's eccentricities was going to stand up to this kind of thing, and deciding that Bott must be a tough woman indeed to have lived with him eight months.

As Paul stopped in the cold windy dawn outside the dorm buildings Nicky ran out, fully dressed. "Mr. Fieldman! Thank God you came! We were worrying so much. Is Mary safe?"

"Why? What's wrong? Where is she?"

"She went out around eleven and didn't come back. I was going to call you—I didn't sleep at all—"

"Oh, I know where she is," Gatzko said, suddenly sitting up. He had been slumped against the car door. "She'll be with Bott, having an orgy or a black mass or something. Come on."

Paul drove back to Chicago, to Bott's room. "There they are!" Gatzko yelled, gazing up at the wrong window. "I can see them up there together. Come on down, you two! Come on out of it!"

He ran around the building, rattling the door. He let out another savage shout and a window shot up. Bott's head emerged, looking haggard.

"Come down! And the girl," Gatzko ordered her. "We're having a party."

"But we've only just woken up," Bott said.

"So what? I want to have a party, didn't you hear?"

"All right, all right, we're coming," Bott said hastily.

"We'll go down to the railroad junctions. There's always something happening there, and if it isn't we'll make it happen. Oh, the women at last. Get in, now. We've already been out to the campus this morning."

Paul drove south past Dearborn Station as far as W15th St. "Here! Hey! I know this area!" Gatzko shouted. "It's the Baltimore and Ohio, and Chicago-Rock Island and Pacific. Yes!" He jumped out and careered down to the rails. Paul parked and followed. Gatzko was scampering about the wilderness of lines and trains and shacks as if he did indeed know them. "See, here! They join the Chicago Burlington and Quincy. Yippee!"

He ran among the tracks, jumping over rails. The other three followed nervously. Mary thought she had never been in a place so little to her taste. In all directions was nothing but a landscape of railroad lines and bridges and signals. It was bleak and cold and ugly and Mary hurt her foot stumbling among the sleepers.

"What a place for a party," Paul said.

"Yes, what a place for a party! We'll go down to the sidings. That's where all the down-and-outs have their parties. Hey! Look at that! The Pennsylvania!"

A great train went slowly past. Mary put her hands over her head against the noise and rumbling, feeling as if she might fall to pieces. When it was passed they saw Gatzko running away beckoning to them to follow.

"Come on! Let's go to the sidings!"

He led them along a miserable street between two great gulfs of train lines. Then he disappeared somewhere and they had to search. There was a gate into a goods yard he must have gone through. They stood in a huddle in the empty yard looking hopelessly about and shivering. It was past six, but it was no lighter than it had been at five.

At last Gatzko's head poked out of a shed in the far corner and he waved at them impatiently. "What's the matter with all of you? Aren't you awake yet or something?"

They trooped over and found themselves crowding into a hot, dark shack smelling of trains and old tobacco.

"I was cold," Gatzko explained, hugging his bottles. He pulled out the Scotch and flourished it in Mary's face. "Mary! First suck for you, while the bottle's clean. I'm sure you care about that kind of thing. Oh, yes you will, daughter mine. Think I want to drink alone? This is a party!"

Mary took as small a sip of the foul stuff as she possibly could. She shrank back into her corner hoping her father would forget her, and watched him gradually getting drunk.

She looked at Bott. Bott was sitting on an upturned bucket watching Gatzko as if her surroundings were just what she was used to. (Mary did not know that Bott was indeed used to similar things with Gatzko.)

Bott knew that the end was very near now, and did not care particularly what she was subjected to in the meantime. It was all darkness as far as she was concerned, though something was not quite right, she could still see Gatzko, and as long as she had sight of Gatzko she was still clinging to the edge of the abyss. She blinked slowly hoping the image would vanish, but as he was actually sitting a foot or so away that did not help.

He looked at her suddenly and said, "Christ, Bott, I can smell your bad breath. You'd better have a swig of this. I'd prefer to smell alcohol."

Bott knew he was right. It was the last day on the Atlantic that the foulness had spread inside her as well as out. Meekly she drank from the bottle, but tasted nothing.

Quite suddenly Gatzko jumped up. "Hey, do you know what? I want some breakfast," he announced.

"Have another drink," suggested Paul.

"No, I want bacon and eggs. And coffee. Irish coffee. A breakfast party. Come on! Who's for a breakfast party?"

Swaying a little, he tried to make everyone get up but the women were clumsy and slow. "Oh, come on," he shouted in irritation. "This place stinks." He pushed the door open and Mary nearly fell over in her rush to get out. "Good girl! Mary wants some breakfast. My Mary will come to breakfast with me. Hey?"

Screaming, Mary ran across the goods yard, hearing her father panting after her. He hit the gatepost, fell and swore. Mary looked back and saw Bott running across the yard as though she were just finishing her marathon, her head lolling back and her teeth showing. Mary had the horrors. She screamed and screamed until Paul's calm voice said in her ear, "Save your vocal chords. There's nobody for miles around to hear." She looked about and saw desolate tracts of waste land in all directions.

"I'm too drunk to walk anywhere," Gatzko said. "You'll have to be chauffeur again, Paul."

"Suppose we go home to bed?"

"I want breakfast," Gatzko said petulantly. "A good breakfast. In a nice place. A hotel, a big hotel, lots of hot coffee." Gatzko climbed into the car muttering contentedly and went to sleep on Bott's shoulder. Paul drove to an all-night coffee shop where a sleepy waitress dressed as a squaw was filling the creme jugs from a two-gallon can.

Gatzko woke up and followed the others in playing with Paul's car-cleaning cloth in its plastic bag. "'Do you know what I am?" he asked. "I'm a butterfly in a cocoon." He pulled the plastic bag over his head and smiled at them.

"Father, don't, you'll suffocate!" Mary exclaimed and snatched it off. He grabbed it back, pulled it over his face again and scowled at her.

"Breakfast no. 2 for four, please," Paul ordered without seeing a menu. "There's always a Breakfast no. 2, and it's usually cheaper than Breakfast no. 1," he explained.

The plastic bag had misted over and stuck to Gatzko's face as he breathed in. With a little moan he tore it off and looked miserable. His face was wet.

"Well, if you will play like a baby," Mary scolded.

Gatzko looked as though he were going to cry. His lips hung all loose and red. He looked at Mary and at the bag.

"Ah, Mary, everyone has a bit of baby in them somewhere," Paul reproached her. "Your father just needs his breakfast."

Gatzko looked sullenly at Paul. He stuck his hand under the tablecloth and pulled out a child's whistle, left there by someone. He gaped at it and then suddenly put it in his mouth and blew a loud blast on it. His eyes stared over the top. He looked around to see what effect it had had and then blew again, louder and more shrilly. The waitress jumped. Paul smiled. Mary began to cry. Gatzko blew again, an earsplitting whistle, looking defiantly at everyone. His eyes were very bloodshot. The waitress, obviously thinking he was calling for service, hurried over looking flustered, balancing four plates of pancakes. Bott saw them tottering, an absurd, child's-comic vision of a mound of about twenty pancakes, against a painted wigwam ceiling.

Gatzko gave a great satisfied "Ah!" The whistle, which he had forgotten, fell with a clatter under the table. He folded up one pancake, got it on his fork and pushed it entire into his mouth. He chewed looking like an advertisement for gum drops for several minutes. Then he threw down his fork, looked pathetically up and cried out, "Why aren't I happy?"

Why aren't you happy? Bott thought. Did you expect to be, from eating a pancake? The pursuit of happiness. Was there anything more futile? What does it look like? The Pennsylvania Express? Does it really taste of pancake? Do you corner it with your drinking companions? Do you really look to find it at the rainbow's end one day?

Paul said practically, "Here, Gatzko, have some maple syrup. That might make a difference." He tasted some on his own food and grinned. "Have some imitation maple syrup, I should have said. It's really delicious."

"I'm not happy! I'm not happy!" Gatzko cried, burying his head in his arms. Paul nudged Mary and whispered, "You'd better get as much food inside you as you can. You'll find it'll help."

Bott looked down at Gatzko as if he were far away. Gatzko, dear, she thought, dear Gatzko, I know what it feels like. I'm just like you after all. I expect something gorgeous and wonderful to arrive each day.

What do you want? New life? No, pet, you must die first. You won't find any state, any country, that cultivates it like Devonshire cream. And I'm as bad. What am I waiting for? What are you hoping for?

"Eggs! Oh good good good! And hash brown potatoes!" shouted Gatzko, sitting up delightedly as the next stage of breakfast appeared. It was scrambled eggs made from egg powder, but he didn't realize that. "I want some coffee. This is a real party after all!"

"Aha. I thought solid food might make a difference. Hot cakes are a bit insubstantial," Paul said wisely.

Bott looked round at the dizzy meaninglessness of it all, the ridiculous totems between the strip bulbs, the harassed squaw rushing about organizing four Breakfast no. 2s, Gatzko trying to be happy with his whistle and his eggy breakfast, and saw total chaos descending on the world.

She felt like Samson. She wanted to grasp those glittery looking-glass pillars and pull the whole silly thing down. Her crazy palace of dreams and omens and magic gardens and nights of love and sacred hearths, it was no more real than this foolish place with its mock-wigwam ceiling. All of it was fantasy, folly, existing only in some weird fairyland of the mind. Down it must come, with a crash and a smash and a poof of green smoke.

There they went, great shadows looming and distorted on the wall, her ideas and fond fancies. She recognized them. And she was leading the procession, hands flapping meaninglessly, careering along on—on a unicorn. Oh God, the unicorn. She had forgotten him. And there came the tree-god, and the hero she had never borne, and Botticelli's angels writhing across the ceiling, yes she knew them all, images from her past. The dragon of Logres, yawning at her, her growing things growing and twining horribly—oh, was there no end to it? What a city of mirages she had lived in. Everything she had touched or seen immediately swelled into tremendous, ludicrous proportions, grotesque and outsize like Bott herself.

This was her peculiar gift, the ability to make a fair world hideous and turn a kind man bitter; and as for the power of growing things, why hers was the touch of death, not of life. The touch of death, that was the one thing she had left to exercise. She stood up in her palace of images, tottering and blind, and felt for something to pull. She touched the Navajo rug supposed to be keeping out draughts and thought, this is only pinned up, it'll come away if I tug. Nevertheless she grasped and heaved. Down it must come, down she must come, down into the dark depths below the world.

"Jerusalem Athens Alexandria Vienna London," she mumbled. "Falling towers."

There was an instant when she was still aware of Gatzko glowering at her. Then the towers began to fall.

Mary saw Bott begin to rise and then collapse on the floor, and threw herself at her. Again, as in the YWCA bedroom, they seemed to be wrestling or embracing on a cliff's edge, but this time Mary knew she could do it. Bott was going down into the abyss; and this time nothing could stop Mary following. She clutched Bott. They rolled over on the floor together, while the walls slid and crumbled round them.

Bott was aware of something soft attaching itself to her, winding itself round her, and thought it must be her body trying to return to her. She tried to resist it but it clung the more lovingly, murmuring and cooing. "Go away, nasty thing," said Bott. "Can't you see I want to be alone? I'm dead."

Mary, in the last stages of dissolving, heard and made one last effort, the hardest she had ever made. For an instant there was a hovering and a separateness. She looked down and once again she saw the crack into the timeless, as she had in a reflecting puddle long ago on her rooftop. Mary was not sure whether she was diving into water or falling from the roof into the street or merely about to smack into the puddle. Then with a swift quiver and sudden movement she was over the cliff's edge at last, sailing down through the glow of the red rocks, towards that luminous cleft where infinity came welling up. Further and further she plunged into the depths inside Bott, and Mary and Bott were merged.

Bott's body, with Mary still clinging to it, suddenly arched in a spasm and jacknifed across the coffee shop floor, hitting Paul's legs. Again and again, it jumped like a fish, slapping and banging itself, with Mary still fastened, her limbs intertwined with Bott's. The waitress screamed. Gatzko watched dully. Bott's mouth yawed open and she vomited, rolling with Mary among the chairs. Gatzko came up to Paul and asked if he could borrow his car to drive to Florida. "Sure, sure," said Paul; "look, we must part these women!" He and the waitress managed to drag them apart. Bott looked muzzily at Paul and said, "I feel sick."

But Mary lay on the floor and did not move.

"What's happened? Is Mary all right?"

"Gosh, I'm afraid she may not be. I'm terribly sorry. I didn't mean to, but I think I've swallowed her up."

"You think what?"

"I've swallowed her up."

"What the hell are you talking about! Is she breathing? It looks like a diabetic coma—anyone know if she's diabetic? Hell. We must get her to hospital right away."

"Well, I don't think that'll do much good," Bott said patiently. "You see I've swallowed her up."

"Oh, stop it. Help me carry her out."

Mary was amazingly heavy. Paul and the waitress, panting hard, managed to get her to the parking lot. There they found that both the car and Gatzko were missing. So were the car keys from Paul's overcoat pocket. Gatzko had indeed borrowed the car and was presumably on his way to Florida.

Paul said some bad things and eventually managed to procure an ambulance to take Mary to the casualty department of Cook County Hospital. He took Bott home to his apartment in a cab. Bott, looking dazedly out at the streets, saw nothing but the ruins of her world, and Mary's, piled round her like the debris of a catastrophic blitz.

22

As PAUL WENT in to see Mary he collided with Su coming out. "Why, hello," he said. "How is she?"

Su shook her head. "Just the same! Nobody seems to have any idea what's going on. Well, look at her."

Mary lay as if she were asleep, but her face was not like a sleeping person's, smiling or dribbling or looking peaceful or any of those things that sleepers normally do. She did not look human at all. If there was any expression on her face it was bestial; though it would have to be a pretty stupid beast that looked as Mary did now, so blank, so nothing, so impossible to imagine awake and alive. The very outlines of her flesh seemed to be melting; you couldn't help thinking that her features were running together slightly. Her lips were shut as if they were joined, and appeared to be spreading, so that her mouth covered most of the lower half of her face. It was very red.

Paul looked at her. "It's extraordinary," he said. "Do you know what she reminds me of? One of those really ancient statues of goddesses after it's been corroded and knocked about for centuries, when its nose has gone and all the carving that gave it expression rubbed off, and there's really not much left but a bit of moth-eaten stone."

"Don't! I hope this won't last centuries. It's only a coma."

"Funny things, comas," Paul muttered, "especially when there's no apparent cause. People can lie in comas until they die, you know, though what death would mean in that context I can't quite think."

Su looked at him reproachfully. "Anyway I've asked the

hospital to call me immediately there's any development. Take it easy, now," she said and went out.

Paul listened for Mary's breathing but could hear none. He gave up and went back to his desk and his work.

In the evening he was called collect from Tampa, Florida. "Yes, yes, I'll pay," he said wearily.

"Hello, Paul? Guess where I am?" Gatzko said excitedly.

"The operator just told me. Tampa, Florida."

"Yes, well! Listen, I just saw my first coco palm!"

"Did you now. What a thrill. How about bringing my car back?"

"Paul, you must come too. It's fantastic. I'm going out to the Keys. That's where all the fun is. You must come. How soon can you get here? I don't want to wait around for you."

"Are you mad? I'm not coming to Florida. On the contrary, you're bringing that car back to Chicago rapido-rapido."

"I want to go to Key West! There are thousands of coco palms there, Paul! And you see the sunset all around you, imagine! You've got to come!"

"I don't care for sunsets. And that car is coming back here, see. Listen. Mary's been in a coma three days."

"A coma? Yes, that sounds just her kind of thing. Don't bring her when you come, will you?"

"See here, I'm not coming, you are."

"Has Bott gone?"

"She's going. Her passage is booked. I've persuaded a friend who'll be in New York to see her on to the ship at Hoboken personally. So there's nothing to keep you out of Chicago now."

"Everything went wrong in Chicago. I've had enough. I'm going to the Keys. Did you know it's covered in jungle, southern Florida? Real jungle!"

"Well, I'm not keeping this child in my apartment indefinitely. I don't like kids and I can't look after him. If you go away and play in the jungle I shall send him to England with his mother."

"What kid? What's all this? Who are we talking about?"

"Your little boy. Michael. Did you forget you had a little boy?"

"You're going to send him to England? But you can't! He's on my passport. Bott isn't his mother."

"As far as I'm concerned, she is. I shall simply tell the British Consul that he lost his passport and persuade him to put him on Bott's. I mean it, Gatzko, I shall."

"You're a criminal!"

"I'm not a criminal, or a nurserymaid either. And I'm not going to assume responsibility for him. I'll be sending him to school and paying for him at college before I know what's happened. You only have to come and take him away and he's yours. Otherwise, I mean, it Gatzko, I shall somehow or other get him off with the woman."

Gaazko growled, "You are responsible. You brought us all here in the first place."

Paul thought sadly of all those transatlantic fares. "So I did. But I'm only sponsor for Bott, and that's enough. Christ, Gatzko, what haven't I paid for you already! I won't bring up your child too!"

"I can repay you now, out of Mary's college trust."

"I don't care what you do. Come and fetch him, or else he goes."

There was a silence and then Gatzko said with even more of a growl, "I want to go to Key West."

"Oh, go to Key West then. You could be there tomorrow. And come back fast, you'd still be in time."

Another silence. "I'll find some college kid wanting a bit of pocket money to drive your car back, okay?"

"However long do you intend to stay in Key West? You can't go much further, you know. Unless you take a ship to Mexico."

"Mexico!" said Gatzko thoughtfully, and hung up.

Paul sighed and went into the dining alcove, where Michael, sitting on Bott's knee, was delightedly pulling all Paul's soiled linen out of his laundry bag and throwing it across the room.

"Your husband isn't coming back from Florida," he said to Bott just in case she was listening. "I'm going to try and send Michael with you to England."

It was nearly as hopeless trying to talk to Bott as to Mary. Paul supposed they were suffering from the same illness, if it was illness, probably the result of whatever they had been up to that last night. He had tried to find out from Bott but she simply did not hear when he spoke. Only at the name "Mary" she quickened and looked up. Otherwise she stood or sat about seeing nothing, hearing nothing, but gripping Michael as if he were a babe in arms. Sometimes she made sudden odd movements as if to reach something, and twice Paul found her scrabbling on the carpet like a dog trying to dig. He was afraid Mary had been right: she was mad. Still, she seemed a good enough mother to the kid, except that she didn't appear to mind him throwing Paul's laundry around the floor.

Was Mary mad too? Was Bott semi-comatose? Were the two of them, perhaps, both mad and comatose? What had he let himself get mixed up with?

On the last morning before they were due to leave Bott collared Paul as he was trying to go out. "Do you know what went wrong with Mary? She made an awful mistake. She didn't die at all."

"Hey? hey? hey? what's this?" Paul thought immediately: suicide? murder? a suicide pact?

"Yes! Instinctively she wanted the way of death. She was right there. But then she attached herself to me! Thought I could do it for her! Did nobody ever tell her about the Crucifixion?"

"Why, I guess so," Paul said, wretched. This was the first thing Bott had said in days, and Paul would have preferred not to hear it.

"Well, obviously not so she could get the point anyway. She was still trying to be a pagan. She wanted a mother goddess. But unfortunately there aren't very many mother goddesses going about these days so she fastened on me instead. You see,

I was thoroughly pagan myself not so long ago, and I'm afraid
Mary felt that. I was, you know. I more or less worshipped
trees and the earth, for years and years. It's no good, of course.
You can't worship nature in this age; you can't be a pagan
however much people such as me and Mary would like to.
It was a good old religion, paganism, while it lasted," she
said wistfully.

"What have you done with Mary?" Paul asked sharply.

"That's just it, I don't know what to do with her. She's down
at the bottom of me somewhere. Just a sludge of superstitions.
I wouldn't really say she existed any more. But sometimes
nasty thoughts rise to my mind that I'm sure aren't mine. I
say! Do you remember the old legend that Saracens' bodies
gave off foul fumes when they were killed?"

"Can we keep to the point? Did Mary want to die?"

"Oh, yes, she did. But for the wrong reasons and she did it in
the wrong way. She was thousands of years out of date. She
isn't properly dead even now. Because she sacrificed herself to
me instead of to God. I'm much more dead than she is."

Paul suddenly decided that whatever was at the back of this
raving, he didn't want to know about it.

"If you think you're dead—"

"Can't you see I am?"

And the horrid thing was that she indeed looked deathly
grey and her eyes had a strange faded transparency. She was
gaunt when she arrived, she was emaciated now. "Then stay
dead and stop talking! Save your haunting for England—
you'll be there in a week," Paul shouted and fumbled for his
coat.

"Oh, Bott, look. What's this?" Michael had found Paul's
suspenders.

"I don't know, my pet, but it looks fun," the awful voice
croaked. Paul saw the great corpse-hands untangling his suspenders and pulling them out into a cat's-cradle. Michael
shrieked with laughter and twanged the elastic. Paul did not
wait to protest. He ran for the elevator.

23

"AFTER THE TORCHLIGHT red on sweaty faces," said Bott out of the darkness, "after the agony of stony places, the shouting and the crying," and she remembered the agony all right and the shouting and the crying, was that all hers too? It seemed only too probable.

> "He who was living is now dead
> We who were living are now dying
> With a little patience

"Michael, what are those peculiar lights? Can you see them?" she asked.

"I think we've come to the station."

That had a very final sound to it. "We who were living are now dead," she said.

"We ought to get out."

She had to get down steps and then walk a long way. She didn't want to go anywhere, but it seemed required of her. She staggered on. There was endless bother with a man at the gate until Michael found the tickets in a pocket of her rucksack. Then there was more walking. It was terrible. With each step she had to tear her foot out of the earth.

"Bott, I'm tired," Michael whined. "Where are we going?"

Where indeed. Bott looked round and saw flickers of fire in a brown fog. "Golly, this seems familiar," she said. "Where are we?"

"We're going over a bridge."

It was Waterloo Bridge. "A bridge? Not over a river?"

"Yes, over the river."

"Oh good! Then we must cross it. It's always a good thing

to cross rivers. You never know, it might be the right one."

They came to the other bank and walked along it. Presently a great lumbering thing overtook them and Bott recognized it. "I say! There goes a bus. Let's get on it!" They ran to catch it, and Bott relaxed again until Michael shouted. "I know where we are! We're nearly home! Come on, let's get off!" He dragged her off the bus.

"What's this?" Bott asked, but did not hear the answer. A great black horse had suddenly reared itself up in her path and was champing at her. "No, no," she cried, "I don't know you. I'm nothing to do with you." She pushed forward and the horse gave a dreadful neigh and fell away from her path. But the way seemed uphill and hurt her feet.

"Where are we going? Where are you taking me, Michael? What's this we're walking on?"

"Why, you know this street. It's our street. Nana! Nana!" He ran on ahead. He had seen Mrs. Weingartner come out of her shop. She shouted and whirled him round and carried him in.

"Back so soon! My little man! How was America?"

Bott, unaware of all this, laboured on until she was suddenly faced with the front of the Dairy &. She stopped, amazed. The gates of either heaven or hell would not have surprised her, but the familiar brown shutters of the Dairy & were definitely unexpected.

She seemed to know the way now although Michael was off somewhere. Through here, yes, open air again, and now—and she tripped over something and fell headlong into the lair. She smelt the familiar mildewy smell. Dear, how it brought everything back. She had all but forgotten Gatzko. Now it was right with her again, his presences, his absences, (more common, really), all the times she had lain here just like this. If she opened her eyes she would see the Navajo rug pinned on the wall. She opened her eyes and with a shock saw the offices on the other side of the lair. Disbelievingly she raised herself and looked about. There was no roof or back wall any more. She was lying among rubble of bricks and plaster and the bits of corrugated iron they had patched the place together with. The whole lair was in ruins around her. How could she have expected anything else? Hadn't she pulled it down with her own hands, at that nightmare breakfast carnival?

Moaning and yelping as she broke her fingernails, Bott began to burrow and scrabble down into the stuff. It was proper, entirely, that the ruins of herself should finish up in the ruins of the lair. She crawled under one of the sheets of corrugated iron and crawled on to the door, which had fallen down, beneath it. She heard Mrs. Weingartner calling: "Bott! Bott! Are you there?"

"Not really," answered Bott from under the metal. Her voice boomed and clanged. "Go away. I'm just getting into my grave."

Mrs. Weingartner, perhaps luckily, only understood the words "Go away." She looked placidly at Bott's squirming legs and went back to Michael.

"Where's Daddy?" she asked him.

"It's a secret," Michael said serenely. Mrs. Weingartner gave up and poured him some tea instead.

Bott lay in her grave and felt the ghosts of her old dreams and the fancies surging about outside, rejected. They made little squeaks and rasps on the iron. But she was dead and they could not touch her.

She lay on the broken door waiting for the numbness, the chill to penetrate. If only her brain would go cold quickly; all those dancing memories freeze at last. In particular there was one she most heartily wished at the bottom of a glacier: the remembrance of another night, another cold night, when she had lain out uncomfortably among bricks. There she was, thinking of it again, piling on the heartbreak. She cuffed her own temples in annoyance and barked her knuckles on the corrugated iron. She made a new effort to settle down. She was so tired. Tired of fighting, tired of hoping, tired of dragging herself about.

At last she began to stop being so aware of her aching body and to feel something like peace. Then Mrs. Weingartner came back with Mr. Weingartner.

"Bott, please do come out. You will catch cold sitting there."

Bott pushed away the iron sheet and stared murderously at them.

"There is a bed all ready for you. I've warmed it, you looked so ill. Michael is sleeping now."

"I want to stay here. I want to stay here for ever."

"You are ill, I am quite sure. You must come in."

One of the last customers from the shop came through to see what was going on. "A tramp! Oh, we'll soon get rid of her."

Bott stared murderously at him too and pulled her coat over her head. He grabbed it and started to pull her about but here the Weingartners intervened.

"No, no, be careful, I think she must be very ill."

"Well, I daresay she is but that's the more reason to get her up. You can't have a tramp lying out in your back yard all night," the man protested.

"Leave me alone! Go away!" yelled Bott. "I couldn't move even if I wanted to. And I don't want to."

"Get the police."

"No, no, no, that won't be necessary." Mrs. Weingartner began to explain to the man that Bott was a friend. Bott stopped listening to her muttering. She was exhausted. She hunched herself under her coat and let everything drift away. At last they left her alone. Mr. Weingartner turned going in and looked at the woman lying on the ground. A wisp of thin, old hair fluttered up over her collar. She looked old altogether; the change was dreadful. He left the door unlocked for her to come in when she had finished weeping over the ruins of her home (as he supposed she was doing).

Birdsong was the next thing she heard, an age later.

Annoyed, she tried not to hear, but that wretched bird went

carolling on so loudly she couldn't help listening. "Oh, shut up, you!" she snarled, but it didn't.

Eventually, she dragged herself out with the vague intention of throwing a shoe at it, feeling frowsty and very much as any sleeper might awakened early by birdsong. She stood up and found herself so stiff that she couldn't get down again, having failed to find the guilty bird. Muttering "Bother, bother, bother," she limped over to a stump of wall and sat on it. What should she do now? Trail around in a white gown and go back to bed when the church bells rang?

The bird went on singing and gradually Bott realized she was sitting in clear early sunlight. She had forgotten how beautiful it could be. She blinked and looked about. She felt as if she were in a garden. Yes, she was in a garden, there was green all round her and blades springing up between the cracks of all the bricks. Her seeds must have come up a long way since she last looked at them. Spring, several months late, seemed to have arrived in London.

Bott looked dazedly round and jumped suddenly thinking someone had come out from the Dairy & behind her back. She looked and gasped and stood up, uncertain after all whether someone was not there. "Who is it?" she faltered. She was gazing into a brilliance of light and a leaping, spreading, rising tree. Tree. She was seeing the tree, her tree, and it was all shining with blossom. She could hardly bear to look at it, so great was the intensity of light. She felt vaguely that it was somehow surprising that it should be there at all, that some law of nature had been overthrown. But there it was, bursting out of the earth, taller than her, unquestionably The Tree.

Bott could feel under her feet a power of life flowing through the ground and up into the tree. Slowly she looked up it, through the blossom, and was dazzled, near blinded suddenly, by what seemed like two rays of light coming from the heart of the tree. For a moment she panicked, remembering how Michael had told her it would have two "lights that can see". She fancied the tree could indeed see her, was looking at her. Again she was not sure, she thought it was a man coming towards her. She made a movement and realized it was the sun, divided by the young trunk. She breathed with relief, but it was strange, the impression remained that the tree was somehow also a man.

Bott remembered her old, old bogey of the tree-giant from her childhood. Was this what he had become? Had he come to claim her after all, as she had so often (long ago) dreamt he would?

Yes, he had. Bott knew it now. It would have her—or should she say he would have her. She collapsed on to the ground, feeling weak. She was far too weak to resist. Little by little, over the months with Gatzko, she had been broken down. Her body was like a bunch of old sticks; she found she couldn't get to her feet. The bird sang and the new leaves rustled and Bott could do nothing but crawl towards the tree.

The unicorn was waiting for her under it, so beautiful and so white. "Yes, I know you," she said to it. "I belong to you, after all." She stroked its hide, really surprised that it should be so quiet and tame now when she remembered well what a proper old tyrant it had been all her life before. "No. Wait. That was wrong. You belong to me."

How very odd this is, she thought. My private mythology is all reversed. The Unicorn takes on the qualities of the Ass and a Man comes to claim Bott. Oh, well, just another strange thing to be added to the list. Life is quite inexplicable except in God's terms, she reminded herself of her maxim, which had probably started out as a joke she had picked up.

Yes, it was a long list of strange things. And would this end it? It felt more like a beginning.

She could feel the tree growing.